ADRIAN SLID HIS ~~HAND~~ BENEATH HER BLOUSE

"What's this lacy stuff?" he asked, fingering her teddy.

"Just never you mind, mister," Callie replied, but her mock severity dissolved into shrieks of laughter as Adrian began to tickle her ribs. She began to slide from the sofa and grabbed his shirt.

"Callie!" Adrian cried as he rolled off the couch after her. In a moment they were in a comfortable heap on the rug, with Adrian's lips hovering inches above hers.

"What did your sister mean when she called me the A.B.C. woman?" Callie asked a little breathlessly. "She said you'd called me that."

"I was speculating on our future."

"Oh? Well, if it involves me, surely I have the right to know about it."

He kissed the bridge of her nose and along her cheekbone up to her temple. "I suppose you're right. I said that someday I expected you to be Mrs. A.B.C.—Mrs. Adrian Bradford Coleman. That's all."

ABOUT THE AUTHOR

Since her first Superromance, *Until Forever*, published in 1983, Sally Garrett has attracted a wide following of loyal readers. *Promises to Keep* is the concluding book of Sally's newest series, a trilogy about three cousins from rural Kentucky. Like the women she writes about, Sally loves living far from the city. With her biggest fan, husband Montie, Sally makes her home in beautiful Montana.

Books by Sally Garrett

HARLEQUIN SUPERROMANCE

Don't miss any of our special offers. Write to us at the following address for information on our newest releases.

Harlequin Reader Service
901 Fuhrmann Blvd., P.O. Box 1397, Buffalo, NY 14240
Canadian address: P.O. Box 603,
Fort Erie, Ont. L2A 5X3

Sally Garrett
RAINBOW HILLS SERIES

PROMISES TO KEEP

Harlequin Books

TORONTO • NEW YORK • LONDON
AMSTERDAM • PARIS • SYDNEY • HAMBURG
STOCKHOLM • ATHENS • TOKYO • MILAN

Published May 1988

First printing March 1988

ISBN 0-373-70309-0

Copyright © 1988 by Sally Garrett Dingley. All rights reserved.
Except for use in any review, the reproduction or utilization
of this work in whole or in part in any form by any electronic,
mechanical or other means, now known or hereafter invented,
including xerography, photocopying and recording,
or in any information storage or retrieval system, is forbidden without
the permission of the publisher, Harlequin Enterprises Limited,
225 Duncan Mill Road, Don Mills, Ontario, Canada M3B 3K9.

All the characters in this book have no existence outside the
imagination of the author and have no relation whatsoever to
anyone bearing the same name or names. They are not even
distantly inspired by any individual known or unknown to the
author, and all incidents are pure invention.

® are Trademarks registered in the United States Patent and
Trademark Office and in other countries.

Printed in U.S.A.

CALLIE'S PROLOGUE

CALLIE HARDESTY and her two older cousins worked their way along the creek bank, heading toward their secret meeting place. In the distance to the north they could see a fresh mountain of dirt, rocks and uprooted tree—the piled up overburden of beautiful but worthless earth and forest that had covered a valuable coal deposit. Callie stopped and touched the petals of a blue wildflower, glad that the coal company had not dug up the farm where she lived with her parents and five older brothers.

Callie scrambled to keep up with the other girls. Her pink cotton knit blouse and white shorts accented her summer tan, but her small stature made her look younger than her years.

Eileen Hardesty, the oldest of the three cousins, was in the lead, her brown braids bouncing in the warm August breeze. Red-haired, eleven-year-old Abbie was next in line. Tall and slender, she was the same height as Eileen. Callie, who had turned eight the previous May, brought up the rear. Callie's hair was as black as night. Her fondest wishes that summer had been to grow tall like her cousins, to have her hair lighten from the summer sun as Eileen's had and to be able to do everything her cousins were allowed to do.

Callie touched her hair, envying Abbie her bright copper curls. Callie's hair was straight, and her mother insisted she wear it in a ponytail and out of her face.

Eileen slipped on a wet rock near the water's edge, surprising Callie. Eileen seldom made mistakes. Now about to become a teenager, Eileen had always been the leader in their secret club. Callie knew she could ask questions and Eileen would never make her feel stupid, as her older brothers did when she questioned them.

Callie's mother had often commented that the three girls were more like sisters than cousins, at least when they weren't fighting, and at times Callie wished she could exchange a few of her brothers for Abbie and Eileen.

"Hey, pip-squeak," Abbie said, pointing to an under-developed fern trying to grow in the shade of other ferns. "That's you." Abbie grinned mischievously. "No one will ever mistake you for a grown-up."

Callie took the bait. "I'd rather be short than have hair like a carrot. And with those stupid green eyes of yours, you look like a Christmas tree, 'cepting you don't have any decorations to make you look purty." She pirouetted and ignored the flush of color on Abbie's cheeks. "Remember last year when I won the Miss Muhlenberg contest at the county fair and before that the Little Miss Rainbow Pageant and when I was five the Little Miss White Glove Pageant?"

"Those are stupid contests," Abbie mumbled under her breath. "I wouldn't waste my time." She pushed Callie.

Callie beamed a sugary smile toward Abbie. "Well, Momma said I can be in the Little Imperial Miss Pageant this year, and I'm gonna win. I'm gonna sing two songs and win a trophy taller than I can reach. You could only win a giraffe's look-alike contest," she teased, sticking her tongue out. Then bravely stepping close, she gave Abbie a shove in return.

Abbie took a step backward. "Why you little shrimp, who would choose you for a beauty queen?" Abbie hissed. "They couldn't find you unless they got down on their knees, and then they'd probably squash you— Oh, no!" Abbie suddenly wailed. She lifted her foot and stepped away. "You made me kill it!"

The fern lay in shreds, its stem broken close to the ground.

They stood nose to nose, their faces flushed and their fists clenched. "I did not!" Callie retorted. "You did that all by yourself. You just wait and see. Someday when I'm a famous singer at the Grand Ole Opry, you'll still be jealous, but I'll let you in to hear me anyway. I'll tell them you're my poor adopted cousin, and they'll feel sorry for you."

"Don't you dare call me adopted," Abbie replied. "'Sides, I'd rather be adopted than spoiled like you...and I'd never come to hear you sing. Anyway, when I grow up..." And Abbie launched into another monologue about her own plans for the future, mixed in with remarks about her adopted family, her stepbrothers and why her mother had left her with Aunt Minnie, who had always been the girls' favorite aunt.

Usually Callie could hold her own in any argument with Abbie, but the mention of the way Bernice Hardesty had abandoned Abbie always saddened Callie. She didn't understand how any mother could just give away her little girl. "Poor Abbie," she said, thinking out loud.

"You don't know nothing. You're just a spoiled and pampered little brat!" Abbie yelled, stung by Callie's sympathy.

"I am not!" Callie retorted, her brown eyes snapping. "Just 'cause I'm not as old as you and Eileen doesn't mean I'm a dummy." She thought of the encouraging remarks her mother had said to her when they had discussed the pageant. "My momma says if I know what I want, I can get it. It's that simple," she said, and imagined herself in a long dress, made of some frothy lavender, which was her favorite color. Lost in her daydream, she had stopped listening to her cousins.

Then Eileen's words broke through Callie's imaginary scene. "Momma says you should never put all your eggs in one basket."

Eileen usually made sense, so Callie started listening again. Besides, Callie loved to watch Eileen, especially when she laughed. Her eyes sparkling like amber glass. *She's never sad,* Callie thought. "Finish high school first," Eileen was telling Abbie. "I'm going to go to college. Mrs. Gray says it's never too early to plan for it."

"I know what I want, too. I'm gonna marry Bobby Joe Huff," Callie said, her cherub features lighting up.

"Bobby Joe?" Eileen bent double in laughter. "That skinny little boy with all those freckles?" She covered her mouth with her hand. "Does Bobby Joe know what you have in store for him?"

Callie traced a pattern in the mud with her big toe. "No." The Huff family had moved to Drakesboro a year earlier, and when school had started, the second-grade teacher had arranged her seating chart in alphabetical order. Bobby Joe Huff had been assigned the seat directly behind Callie Hardesty. From the very first day, Bobby Joe had begun to tease and taunt Callie, first by sticking burrs and twigs in Callie's hair instead of doing his math papers and then by stealing some of her take-home papers.

"I gave him a valentine last spring and he didn't tear it up," she said.

"Are you going to give him a few years to grow up?" Abbie asked.

"'Course," Callie replied, wishing they would stop teasing her. "But when he asks me, I'll say yes."

"How are you going to be a singer and marry that ugly Bobby Joe Huff?" Abbie asked, her lips curling into a sneer.

Callie stuck out her tongue at Abbie. "I'll just do both. I'll sing at the Grand Ole Opry on Saturday nights. We're gonna get married and have three little girls and three little boys." She took a deep breath. "And we'll live happily ever after, too. You just wait and see."

"Finish high school first," Eileen warned again, but with the prospect of entering the third grade still ahead of her, Callie could hardly comprehend graduating from high school.

They continued along the creek bank, discussing school and brothers, hair and eye colors, arguing occasionally, but agreeing more often. Once, much to Callie's surprise, Abbie even apologized for teasing Callie about liking Bobby Joe Huff and having straight black hair, and offered to make up. Callie hesitated, suspicious of what might lie behind Abbie's apology.

Abbie glared at Callie. "Well, aren't you going to be a good sport and shake?"

"I guess so," Callie replied, hoping that Abbie wouldn't squeeze her hand so hard.

"Friends and sisters again?" Eileen asked, looking from one to the other.

"I 'spect so," Callie replied.

They arrived at their secret meeting place, a small glen hidden in thick undergrowth in the woods behind Callie's parents' farm.

After a snack, Eileen called the club meeting to order. "The last meeting until next summer of the Rainbow Hills Secret Society of Sisters and Friends will now come to order," she said solemnly. When she called for new business, Abbie opened a paper sack she had been clutching.

Callie leaned forward. Secrets were unbearable, and this one had been building for months, ever since a phone call to Callie's mother had resulted in Callie being asked to take one of the smallest photos from the current year's school pictures over to Aunt Min's house.

"Why?" Callie had asked, her curiosity bubbling over.

"It's a secret," her mother had replied. "Just give it to Aunt Min." Callie had tried to get Aunt Min to reveal her secret several times, but to no avail. Now the waiting was over.

"Here's one for you." Abbie handed a small package wrapped in white tissue paper to Eileen. "And one for you, pip-squeak," she said, handing Callie an identical package. "And one for me."

Callie's hands trembled with excitement as she unwrapped the present. Glancing across the circle, Callie spotted the shiny gold locket and chain lying in the nest of tissue paper in Eileen's hands.

"Oh, it's fabulous," Eileen gasped.

Callie looked at her own locket. It was more beautiful than anything she had ever seen. A script letter *C* had been engraved onto the gold face. "It's . . . it's wonderful."

Abbie leaned toward Callie. "Are they all alike?"

"Almost," Eileen said, studying the three lockets. "But we each have our own initial on the front. See?" She pointed to the fancy script letter *E* on her own locket.

"Do they open?" Callie asked, fiddling with the tiny clasp.

"They should," Abbie replied, pushing on the clasp of Callie's locket. It popped open, and Callie found herself staring at the photo she had delivered to Aunt Min. On the inside left was a tiny counted-cross-stitch image of a rainbow and three small trees on a hillside. On the back side of the center frame, was a photo of Abbie and on the inside back cover, a photo of Eileen. The back of the gold case had been engraved with the words, Sisters and Friends.

Callie was still fiddling with the clasp when the two older girls had theirs around their necks. Abbie turned to her. "Here, let me help you." Abbie fastened the chain around Callie's neck and lifted her black hair out of the way while Eileen adjusted the locket. The gold metal, hanging several inches below her throat, felt cool against Callie's skin.

Callie beamed. "Do I look as pretty as you do?" she asked, searching the faces of her older cousins.

"You sure do," Eileen replied, and Abbie nodded.

"Now let's make our promises," Abbie suggested. "We'll never never take these off...or if we do, we'll never lose them, and we'll always remember what we want to be when we grow up...and we'll stay in touch with each other, always."

Eileen nodded. "We'll never be too proud to ask for help. Now, that's important," she said, shaking her index finger at Abbie and Callie.

"What do you mean?" Callie asked, her dark eyes solemn.

"I'd be willing to help you if you needed me," Abbie said impatiently.

"Oh, that," Callie replied. "I know that. It's like the Golden Rule we learned in Sunday School. Do unto others..."

"Yeah, yeah," Abbie interrupted. "We all know that verse."

"No," Eileen said, and Callie turned to her again. "It's more than that. Momma calls it the other side of the coin in lending a hand to other people. What I mean is we'll never be too proud to *ask* for help."

"The members of the Rainbow Hills Secret Society of Sisters and Friends will never forget each other," Abbie said, "and we'll be best friends forever and ever, even when we're grown-up and living far, far away from here. Our matching lockets will prove it. Now let's promise out loud, or it doesn't mean a thing."

Eileen reached for Callie's hand and then Abbie's hand. "Right you are," she replied.

Clasping hands tightly, they sat cross-legged in a lopsided circle and closed their eyes, repeating their sacred vows to be sisters and friends forever.

Later in the afternoon they followed the creek back to the road and waved as they headed toward their separate homes.

Callie broke into a run, the locket bouncing against her chest. She put her hand over it and pressed it against her skin. The locket was the most precious gift she had ever received, and she was anxious to show it to her mother.

"I'll never lose it," she vowed aloud, then glanced around to make sure no one had heard her. Losing the locket would be like losing a rainbow.

CHAPTER ONE

Twenty Years Later

CALLIE HUFF WORKED HER WAY past the knees of the spectators seated in the open-air grandstand, then down the steps to the ground. Morehead, Kentucky, was in the midst of its annual Harvest and Hardwood Festival. When the announcer made a humorous comment over the public-address system about the attire of one of the contestants in the heavy-mule competition in the arena, she smiled along with the crowd. Begrudgingly, she conceded it was good to get away.

Her parents, along with her uncle and aunt and two of her brothers and their families, had arrived on her doorstep in Harlan, Kentucky, a week earlier, announced that it was high time she took a vacation and offered to pay all the expenses.

Had she ever taken a vacation in her entire life? Only once, when her cousin Abbie had insisted she fly to Montana to be a bridal attendant. That had been the previous October. Now, in mid-September, the memory of that flight to the Northern Rockies had faded, as had so many pleasant memories in her twenty-eight years of life.

But though the memory had faded, it had left behind a strange blend of restlessness and optimism and the conviction that her first move had to be getting out of southeastern Kentucky. She longed to climb a high mountain peak again, as she had done one afternoon at

Abbie's husband's sheep ranch. She wanted to see a distant horizon again, instead of losing her direction stumbling half-blind through fields of kudzu and grapevines.

For too long, she had lived on rent subsidies and food stamps, welfare payments and Medicaid coverage. Her son had begun to ask questions about his missing father. Her daughter lived with a congenital heart condition.

Callie's attention returned to the events in the arena. Four pairs of heavy mules were waiting to compete in a weight-pulling contest. Five men, their bare arms glistening with sweat, surrounded a sled and added cinder blocks to the load, increasing its weight.

Callie leaned against the wooden railing around the field, her interest caught. The team that was to compete first—two magnificent bay mules that were identical except for a deep scar on the left animal's shoulder—was led across the infield. Then a tall, dark-haired man started working feverishly to hitch up the traces. One of the bay mules tossed his head, and the man jumped aside. He wiped his hand on his dusty overalls, leaving behind a streak of red.

Beneath the soiled bill of a black-and-white cap, his mouth tightened, but his other features revealed nothing. Perspiration dampened his dark hair. He pulled a red kerchief from his hip pocket, whipped the cap from his head and wiped his forehead. *What strong features,* Callie thought.

The man pressed the kerchief against his bloody hand for several seconds, then shoved the kerchief back into his pocket and replaced the cap. The sleeves of his camouflage-colored T-shirt had been cut out, and Callie couldn't help but notice his well-developed biceps and powerful shoulders.

He moved comfortably in his loose overalls, as if he wore them often. Definitely a man used to hard physical work, Callie thought. He glanced up. His eyes were dark, but she wasn't sure of their exact color. Then he smiled at her, his features alive with pleasure and excitement.

Callie's smile materialized before she realized she had responded. Embarrassed, she looked away. Surely he couldn't be smiling at her. Looking up, she spotted a man and woman waving from the top of the bleachers. So he wasn't smiling at her. Callie turned again to the arena.

The man was stepping away from the mules. He gave a thumbs-up signal to the teamster he had been helping, and the other man flapped the leather reins against the rumps of the powerful mules.

The team pulled the sled effortlessly, and the crowd cheered. The next team was eliminated. Callie edged her way a few feet down the railing, her eyes following the dark-haired stranger as he worked his way through the teams eliminated earlier to a matched pair of red mules. He guided them to a sled, the links of the chains clinking as they bounced along on the ground. The other man, wearing a blue work shirt with its open tails flapping in the breeze, helped the dark stranger hook up the traces and quickly stepped aside.

The mules and sled were several yards away from Callie. The stranger took up his position near the sled and shouted to the mules, "Manny, Cole, you sweet beauties, show 'em your stuff!" Making a loud kissing sound, he shook the reins, signaling the mules to get a move on. Callie smiled. She had expected profanity. Instead the stranger had spoken to the two sweaty red mules with affection.

Leaning into their collars, their traces taut, the mules strained against the lead. After two unsuccessful attempts they found their footing and pulled the sled the required distance. As the man slowed them to a stop, one of the mules reared. His shoulder thudded against the inside of the railing less than a yard from where Callie stood, sending a tremor through the heavy wood. Frightened, Callie stumbled backward against two men standing behind her.

The dark-haired man spoke to the mules again. Their ears twitching as they listened to the teamster, the animals snorted several times, their sides heaving. The smells of mules and sweaty leather assailed Callie's senses as she watched the man, hypnotized by his words as much as the mules seemed to be. He was directly across the railing from her, waiting for his helper to unhitch the team.

The man turned and looked directly at Callie. His eyes were not dark as she had thought, but a pleasant hazel. He grinned. "Sorry, ma'am, hope you're not hurt."

Callie shook her head.

The errant mule started becoming restless again, and the man lead his team away. Callie followed his movements to the other side of the arena, then lost him in the crowd.

A short time later, after the fourth and final team had made a successful pull, the announcer spoke. "We'll break now for a bite to eat, folks. Remember the final rounds will resume at two this afternoon. Don't forget the draft horse pull at one and . . ."

Callie stopped listening as she walked toward the food stands located partway up the hill near the exhibition building. In the distance, she noticed the rolling hardwood forest had begun to take on the colors of autumn. A light frost had occurred a week earlier but now the temperature was back to a sweltering ninety degrees, with humidity to match.

Her stomach growled as she approached the food stands, and Callie thought that perhaps she would spend a little of Aunt Minnie's money after all. Her aunt had slipped a twenty-dollar bill into Callie's hand the day she had arrived in Harlan and convinced Callie she should go with them on vacation.

Since then, each time Callie had tried to pay for her own meal, one of her brothers had insisted she be gracious and save her money. James and Leander had been taking turns paying for the motel rooms on the trip, and James had paid for two T-shirts for her son. Leander had done the same for a matching blouse and slacks set for Linda. Callie's sister-in-law had insisted on paying for a blouse Callie had found for herself. "I'll just put it on my credit card," she'd said. "Don't worry about it, Callie."

Callie's parents had stayed behind in Harlan with Callie's children, Robbie and Linda, insisting that being with them was as much fun as traveling. As much as Callie was enjoying the week away from her children, for a while the situation had felt embarrassing.

Now, with only two days left in the trip, she knew she could accept their hospitality and still maintain her own integrity.

The aroma of fried onions and steaming hot dogs drifted toward her, and Callie maneuvered her way into the undulating throng of hungry customers at the fourth food stand.

Waiting behind an obese woman in tight jeans, she glanced down at her own clothing. Her red knit top clung to her damp skin. She pulled it away, then smoothed it down over the worn cutoff jeans she wore. Her thongs and bare feet were covered with dust.

The woman ahead of Callie grabbed an armload of hot dogs and left, pushing her way through the crowd. Callie stepped up. A smiling gray-haired man behind the counter took a long drag on a cigarette, exhaled over her head, then laid the cigarette down below the counter out of sight. "What'll it be, honey?"

Callie searched the menu. "Soup beans and corn bread," she said absently.

"Something to drink?"

"No thank you," Callie replied, ignoring the dryness in her throat.

"Special on lemonade," the man coaxed. "The missus made it just this mornin'."

Callie sighed deeply. "Just the beans."

"Then seventy-five cents should do it," the man said, winking at her as he set the Styrofoam bowl of navy beans on the enameled counter.

Callie's mouth watered as she opened her worn blue wallet. It was empty. Callie groaned aloud. "I'm sorry, mister. I . . . I left my money . . ." She recalled the split-second decision she had made that morning to leave the twenty-dollar bill in her suitcase to avoid any temptation to spend it.

The man's expression changed from good humor to irritation. "I'm sorry," Callie mumbled. She stepped backward, anxious to get out of the embarrassing situation. Someone behind her prevented her departure.

"Make it two," a man's voice said, "and we'll have two medium lemonades."

A brown hand laid down a five-dollar bill. Callie stood motionless, mortified at being caught with not even three quarters to her name, and trapped between the impatient man behind her and the hard ledge of the food stand. She couldn't budge. She tried to step back, but the man behind her refused to take the hint as he accepted his change.

Callie's gaze fell on the wounded hand resting on the counter, and her heart leaped. If she turned, she would be looking into the hazel eyes of the man who had worked the red mules.

She tried to ease aside, but the man's other arm appeared near her left shoulder, and he rested his fist against the counter. "One's for you," he said near her ear.

"No, I..." She considered ducking beneath his arm, but the crowd hemmed her in on both sides.

"Take it, please," he insisted.

She balanced the Styrofoam bowl of navy beans in one hand and tried to hold the corn bread and paper cup of lemonade in the other. One corner of the corn bread sank into the weak yellow liquid, and crumbs skittered across the surface. She grimaced and set the corn bread and cup back onto the counter, irritated by the tremor in her fingers.

"Put the corn bread in the beans," he suggested. "I'll carry the drinks. Follow me."

Callie grabbed the steaming bowls of soup beans and turned—only to notice how his smile heightened the tiny crinkles around his eyes. She swallowed and opened her mouth to protest again.

"This way," he said, turning and opening a path through the crowd. He chose a picnic table several yards away in the shade of a giant red oak. Its green leaves contrasted against the autumn foliage of the other trees on the grounds of the college-owned farm where the festival was being held.

The Styrofoam bowls began to collapse, and she quickly set them down.

He removed his soiled cap and laid it on the table. An emblem of a fancy white glove covered the front of the cap.

She read the logo. "Are you a miner?"

"Off and on," he replied, smoothing his damp, dark hair away from his forehead. "Every company has to advertise, and caps seem to be popular." His broad features were chiseled in masculinity, his cheekbones high, his chin firm.

He grinned, sending a pleasant sparkle to his eyes. "Sit down and eat. I'll go wash my hands. Don't leave."

He disappeared into the crowd, leaving her alone with the bowls of beans. Her stomach growled again, and she swallowed her pride.

She was still standing when he returned. Looking up, she realized how much taller than her he was. But at an inch over five feet, Callie was shorter than most adults.

He extended his hand. "Name's Adrian...and you?"

She hesitated. *He's just being neighborly,* she thought as she accepted his hand.

He flinched.

"I'm sorry," she said, quickly releasing his hand. "It must smart like the dickens. Let me see." She took his hand and turned it over. The skin on his middle fingers was torn and swollen. "You should get that tended to before it gets infected."

"It will be fine," he replied. "I heal quickly."

"Then at least put a bandage on it." She opened her wallet again, pulled out a self-adhesive bandage and tore the wrapping off. Without thinking, she covered the wound and patted his hand.

He chuckled. "Are you going to tell me your name is Florence Nightingale?"

She smiled. "Call me Callie."

"Hello, Callie." He grinned. "Let's eat before the beans get cold and the drinks get warm." He sat down, and she did the same. He crumbled the corn bread into the soup beans and ate several spoonfuls. "Needs onions," he murmured.

She took a bite.

"Do you live around here?" he asked.

She shook her head. "Harlan County."

"Bloody Harlan?"

She shrugged, thinking of the reputation the area had gained due to violence during coal strikes over the decades. "Not since I've been living there. And you?"

"Hopkins County. That's in the western part..."

"Yes, I know where it is," she replied, thinking of her birthplace in neighboring Muhlenberg County. She was reluctant to tell this stranger more about herself. "Thank you for...buying me the beans. I left my money in my motel room."

"It's my pleasure to help out a lady in distress." He took a spoonful of beans. "My favorite food. I was raised on them."

She laughed. "Weren't we all?"

"But some folks reject them when they grow up," he said, cocking his head. "I suppose it reminds them of their impoverished childhood." He took another spoonful. "Not me. I love them."

"They're very economical," she agreed. "You can always add more water."

"True," he admitted. "They're cheap, but they're delicious, too. Call me a true bean connoisseur." He grinned. "Now you know my philosophy of life...as it relates to beans." He tossed his empty bowl into a nearby trash barrel. He motioned toward her bowl. She nodded, and he tossed it into the barrel, too. *What a strange man,* she thought, fascinated with his relaxed manner as he sat across from her, his bare arms folded on the table.

She concentrated on her cup of lemonade. Adrian didn't know a thing about her except her name. He was just being hospitable, seeking a break before the competition resumed. Prize money was at stake. Perhaps he needed the winnings in order to buy groceries until his check came after the first of the month. Then she chided herself for thinking that everyone was on public assistance. Someday, she wouldn't be, either.

Hunching her slender shoulders, she lifted the waist-length rope of black hair from her back to let some air circulate. Her hair was held with a single rubber band.

"Are you here alone?" he asked.

She shook her head. "Most of the family came—my brothers and an aunt and uncle.... We're heading back to Harlan tomorrow. And you?"

"Same," he said. "Monday morning it's back to the fields for me. We've got new ground to clear—almost four hundred acres—and we want to get it done before the weather changes, if possible."

She thought of her father's fields of soybeans and his ever-shrinking quota of burley tobacco and wondered why anyone would choose farming over a guaranteed paycheck every other Friday. "Are you a miner or a farmer?"

He smiled. "I've been both."

"Do you compete in mule-pulling contests often?"

He shrugged. "Whenever we can."

"We?"

"My brother and I travel on weekends whenever we can get away," he said. He grinned, his eyes twinkling with mirth as the broad planes of his face shifted. She could imagine him playing high-school football in his youth.

She smiled. "Sounds carefree and fun."

He tossed his head, laughing. "It is. Kentucky and Tennessee are beautiful, especially at this time of year. Why go visiting foreign countries when you can explore your own backyard? Competing at these festivals gives us an excuse."

"You sound as if you have a bit of wanderlust in your blood," she said, grinning in spite of the distance she wanted to maintain.

"Someday I plan to settle down."

"To what?"

He chuckled. "You'll think I'm crazy."

"No, I won't." For a moment she thought he looked skeptical, but it disappeared as quickly as it had come.

"I think a man is entitled to dream," he said. "Why does he have to do the same kind of work all his life?"

Callie looked at him thoughtfully. "My Cousin Abbie says if you don't believe in your dreams, they won't come true."

"Wise cousin," he replied. "I'll try to remember that when my own dreams seem far away."

"And what are your dreams...beyond settling down?" she asked.

"You won't make fun of them?"

"Of course not."

"Someday I want to operate a catfish farm and breed mules." He waited for her reaction, but only a slight frown stirred her features. "I already have two Belgian mares," he continued, "and last month I bought a Mammoth Jack who's a real beauty...but I don't have the room to expand...yet. I own my team of red heavies. That's the pair who tried to run you over. Cole is young and has an unruly streak.''

She suppressed a laugh, and it came out as a giggle. "I thought everyone in this state wanted to breed Thoroughbreds or Tennessee Walkers or American Standards." She shrugged. "So much for my knowledge of horses. Daddy has four old draft horses he keeps because he doesn't have the heart to sell them to the slaughterhouse. He used them with his tobacco, but the quotas are so restrictive now, he finally bought a small tractor. He can do a little logging when it suits him, and he started growing soybeans when he bought my uncle's place next to ours."

She admired his captivating smile. When she realized she was studying his mouth, her gaze shifted to his eyes. His demeanor sang with the joy of living. He seemed to have found happiness, in spite of being poor. But maybe he did have some money. How could she tell? And what did it matter? Had she become so controlled by money, or the lack of it, that she measured all of life's experiences by it?

Shifting uncomfortably on the wooden bench, she took a sip of lemonade and glanced up again. Was he staring at her breasts? She took a deep breath and immediately regretted the act.

"That's a beautiful locket you're wearing," Adrian said. "It must have sentimental value."

She fingered the gold oval locket resting a few inches above the red-and-white binding of her tank top. "An aunt gave them to the three of us—me and my cousins—when we were children. I don't wear it often. I'd hate to lose it. Someday I'm going to give it to—" She clamped her lips tightly shut. "I prattle too much. My daddy always said I did. Listen, thanks again for the beans." She rose from the bench.

"Much obliged," he replied, one corner of his handsome mouth quirking up slightly in a restrained grin.

The awkward moment hung between them.

"Do you have time to see some of the exhibits?" he asked.

Callie hesitated. "Don't you have to get back to the competition?" She glanced at the digital watch on her wrist.

"I can spare fifteen minutes if you can." He grinned and came around to her side of the picnic table. "Harlan and Hopkins Counties are on opposite sides of the state. We may never see each other again."

She studied him pensively. "Fifteen minutes it is," she agreed, finding his request irresistible.

They set off across the grounds and strolled through a large display building filled with commercial exhibitors. Most of the exhibits pertained to logging. They moved on to a smaller building devoted to mountain crafts and quilts.

They paused by a table displaying wreaths made of grapevines, and Callie touched them lightly, turning them over to see how they were made. "You do nice work," she said to the woman behind the table.

Adrian's hand dropped to her bare shoulder, and she flinched. It was the first time he had touched her, other than their handshake, and her initial reaction was to pull away.

"Do you like them?" he asked, his breath warm near her ear.

She nodded. "I've tried to make them from the kudzu vines, but I couldn't get them to wind around properly. I gave up."

"A person must never give up too easily," he said. His hand dropped from her shoulder, and he pointed to a tiny wreath no bigger than a saucer. "How much?"

Money exchanged hands before Callie could protest, and she found herself in the awkward position of being presented with a gift.

"It looked like it belonged to you," he said. "It's small, and you're not very big yourself. Besides, the red ribbon matches your top. Take it, please, for my sake. I don't handle rejection well."

The expression in his hazel eyes was unfathomable. A wave of emotion swept through Callie, and for an instant she felt on the verge of tears. "Okay," she murmured, swallowing the lump in her throat, "but I have to find my family now." The words tumbled from her lips. "Thank you... and thank you for the beans and... and goodbye." She whirled away and ran out of the building.

ADRIAN COLEMAN WATCHED Callie disappear into the milling throng of festival patrons.

He had first noticed her when she had worked her way down the grandstand steps. He'd paid for that distraction with an injured hand. He touched the tape still on his finger. When she'd left the grandstand area, he'd followed her through the crowds. Why he'd felt an absolute necessity to speak to her, he didn't know, but he'd learned years earlier that his instincts were usually right.

He was the only unmarried member in his large family, and at reunions and holiday gatherings, the subject of when was he going to get married usually reared its head. Years earlier he had been involved with a woman, Lucinda Louise Oldham. Cindy Lou and he had gone through high school together and Murray State University, but after graduation he'd taken a position in his family's coal company. Cindy Lou had continued her education at an out-of-state school and was now a professor of English at a university in Tennessee.

His family operated several surface coal mines in the state. He had gone into the business directly from college, then took a break by joining the military. After a four-year stint in the air force, he had returned to the company, only to begin separating himself from the business after a few years. He had purchased forty acres of woodland and had built a log house. That had been six years earlier. Those forty acres had become his sanctuary, his own Walden Pond. It was a good spot for thinking, and after reaching his thirty-fourth birthday in mid-July, Adrian had finally dealt with the realization that his career had been preordained by his birth into the Coleman family. Someday soon he planned to break free completely and find his own destiny.

He spotted Callie's dark head bobbing through the crowd, and he felt an unexpected tightness in his chest. He took a step, then two. He didn't even know her last name. How could he get in touch with her again? She had said she lived in Harlan. The county or the county seat? Or was it Hazard? Perhaps Hyden. The towns were all in the same general area. He had to talk to her again.

"Callie!" he called. Several people turned to stare at him. His height gave him an advantage. When he reached the doorway he spotted Callie again, but now she was surrounded by people. A thin dark-haired man hugged her and laughed. Inwardly Adrian withdrew. Perhaps he had jumped to conclusions. After all, she hadn't said whether she was single or not. He should have asked.

Callie and her family worked their way toward the parking area, swept along by the crowd. In the distance the announcer called for the resumption of the mule-pulling competition.

Prizes were at stake. He didn't need the money, but he had a spot on his mantel for the trophy and certainly didn't want to see it go to his brother, Jarrett. They had a one-hundred-dollar bet riding on the outcome of this weekend.

Jarrett had never joined the rest of the Coleman men in the family mining business. These weekend trips to competitions organized by the Kentucky Draft Horse and Mule Association gave them an opportunity during the summer and fall months to renew the deep friendship that had started in their early childhood and which for a while had included their younger brother LaMar.

Adrian glanced at his watch. Ten minutes to get the team ready. He hoped his brother hadn't gotten side-tracked, too. He had to choose now between the myste-rious young woman with the hauntingly beautiful brown eyes whose company he had enjoyed for less than an hour and the competition that had brought him here. But he and Jarrett worked as a team, helping each other with the equipment and the animals. He certainly wouldn't want Jarrett to lose because of him.

Callie's dark head disappeared behind the huge Paul Bunyan sign at the entrance gate. With heavy regret, Adrian Coleman headed toward the arena.

CHAPTER TWO

CALLIE GLANCED at the farm-implement calendar she had thumbtacked to the green wall of her living room in Harlan. Tomorrow she would be moving.

After carefully studying the freedom her brothers and their families had, after seeing all the money exchanging hands at the festival and after coming to grips with how hopeless her own life would be if she didn't take charge of herself, she had finally made her decision. Why had it taken so long? Why hadn't she listened to her cousins, to her parents? She had discussed her feeling with her case worker and learned of a state-wide program of adult education geared especially for women in her situation. Why hadn't she heard of the program before? Perhaps she had failed to listen.

Her friend, Debbie Holland, who had recently obtained a good-paying job at an automotive plant near Bowling Green, had written her a letter, detailing her excitement about buying her first house. Debbie had been on welfare for longer than Callie yet she had found a way out.

It wouldn't be easy. She would have to take risks, but why not? She had talked it over with her parents, and they had suggested she and her children live with them. So she would return to her childhood home and go back to school, pick up where she had left off and get a college education. She would take charge of her destiny and provide a decent and comfortable life-style for her children. If not she, then who?

She surveyed the cardboard boxes filled with her belongings—some toys, kitchen utensils she had picked up at roadside rummage sales, plastic dishes that had cracked in spite of the promise on the package, a box of paperbacks without covers and some hardbacks—discards from the local library.

Two boxes needing special handling had been set aside. The larger box contained her materials for making wreaths she sold at summer arts and crafts fairs to earn spending money—vines and willow cane, nuts and pods, leaves and dried flowers and other treasures she had collected from the hardwood forest behind their cabin during the years she and Bobby Joe had lived up Kudzu Hollow. They had been sorted carefully into plastic bags she had saved from the produce department of the grocery store in town.

The other box held two mountain dulcimers, simple stringed instruments given to her in her youth, along with some sheet music and materials for a third instrument. Aunt Belle had given her a three-string dulcimer made by Callie's maternal grandfather and Belle's father. Leander Campbell had carved his name and the date 1900 inside. Callie could still recall the moment she had shone a flashlight through the heart-shaped sound hole in the instrument's face and discovered the embellishment.

Aunt Belle had also given her own four-string dulcimer to Callie when Callie had graduated from grade school. She had promised Callie a brand-new instrument from a shop in Berea, Kentucky, when she graduated from high school, but that promise had never been fulfilled. Aunt Belle had passed away the same winter

Callie had become pregnant, and both their lives had stopped.

Callie shook her head. No, that was wrong, she thought. Her life had merely been put on hold. Now it was about to gain momentum again.

She dropped to her knees and glanced inside the box, smiling as she touched the pieces of wood that would someday be her own handmade instrument. Belle's widower, L.T., who now lived up a wooded hollow near Jackson, had given her a piece of black walnut for the back, sides, peg end and fret board. Her father had sent her a sizeable piece of wormy chestnut for the face. The pieces of wood were still in the condition received, with only the faint tracing of soft gray graphite marking the possible outlines.

Without the proper tools and someone to consult and give her encouragement, Callie had been hesitant to begin construction. Now the pieces of wood represented one more project that had been shelved for a while. A wrinkled piece of paper contained some pointers she had been given one Saturday when she and Bobby Joe had packed up their infant son and driven to Pine Mountain near the Cumberland Gap to spend the afternoon at a dulcimer festival.

She shook her head sadly. Such a long time ago. Her loose black hair fell into the box, and she pushed it away from her face, tucking it behind her ears as she reached for the four-string instrument.

Returning to her chair, she laid the dulcimer across her knees and began to strum and pluck the strings. *It's out of tune and I'm getting rusty,* she thought. She began to sing verses from several ballads she knew, adjusting the pegs occasionally. Her voice was clear and melodious.

"You've got perfect pitch," her seventh-grade music teacher had said.

Callie launched into the fun song called "Turnip Greens," humming the verses extolling the virtues of eating corn bread, buttermilk and good turnip greens. She smiled as she mouthed the words of the last verse about mountain girls. "Well, the reason for their beauty is plainly to be seen—for the precious little honeys have been raised on turnip greens."

"Now that's a song Adrian would appreciate," she murmured, recalling the pleasant hour she had spent with the handsome dark-haired man with the friendly hazel eyes, who had bought her beans and a miniature wreath. She had wrapped the wreath in tissue paper and tucked it away in her suitcase alongside the case that held her oval locket. Someday she would have the right place to hang the wreath.

Callie plucked the strings of the dulcimer for several more minutes, then put it carefully into the box. She walked back to her worn overstuffed chair and dropped into it. Tucking her feet beneath her, she pondered the months ahead. For the first time since Bobby Joe had left them, she felt the time was right for a significant change.

She had tried before. After Linda had started school, she had managed to get a job waiting on tables in a local café. Within a couple of days Linda had become ill again, and Callie had lost the job because of "excess absenteeism." She'd found and lost several more waitressing jobs after that until finally her welfare worker had encouraged her to stay at home to be a full-time mother. "Your children need you," the woman had said. "Some women would envy you being able to stay home with your kids. Count your blessings, Callie honey."

Callie rubbed the side of her neck. Perhaps she had taken the path of least resistance, but she had always accepted full responsibility for her plight. Eileen and Abbie had sent her money more than once. Each time Callie had mailed the money orders back uncashed. Her family had given her assistance, usually cash or clothing, the gifts thinly disguised as birthday or Christmas presents. Callie had accepted them, but beneath her appreciation she'd resented that she was in no position to refuse the gifts.

But when her parents had asked her to move back home, for the first time in years she'd felt no resentment, just excitement.

"We rattle like two peas in a dry old pod," her father Finis had said. "So you just come home. You and the kids will make this house lively again."

Her mother, Ellen, agreed. "You can't do a good job at your schoolin' if'n you're worried about the kids. I can watch over them, even if Linda gets sick again. Cousin Abbie is right, honey. You can't just sit around collecting them benefit checks forever, now can you?"

"Pack up all this stuff, honey, and come home with us—right now," her father said.

"You can sell your furniture," her brother James added. "We have enough room in the two vans for what's left."

"I need a few weeks to make arrangements," she'd insisted, and her parents had given her exactly two weeks from that day when she'd returned from the festival in Morehead.

Thoughts of the festival brought back the image of Adrian again. *What an intriguing man,* she thought. *Not a care in the world. Handsome, too.* She smiled, conjuring up his face. *Breeding red mules and farming catfish.*

Now, how's that for getting away from the pressures of life?

She chuckled aloud. *What would my life have been if I'd met someone like Adrian instead of Bobby Joe?* She visualized Adrian's smiling mouth and for a moment wondered how his kiss might feel. *Silly,* she thought, suppressing the sensual response that had come from nowhere. Passion was a pleasure she had pushed aside long ago. Besides, the odds against her ever seeing Adrian again were astronomical.

She closed her eyes and stretched her legs, recalling her teen years. No one had forced her to explore her budding sexuality that winter before her seventeenth birthday. Bobby Joe had been pressuring her for two years and she had resisted. But that lonely year had awakened many emotions in her.

First, her cousin Eileen wrote to tell Callie about the newly found love of her life. Eileen was in college in Knoxville and had met a fabulous young man. Her letters were filled with detailed descriptions of Duncan Mills and his family's business in Idaho. Then the letter came revealing their secret engagement.

Meanwhile, her other cousin, Abbie, had changed from a lanky redheaded girl into a tall shapely auburn-haired woman. She applied for and won a scholarship to the University of Utah and spent the summer at a weaving workshop in Seattle, a city too distant for Callie to even dream about. Abbie was as passionately in love with weaving as Eileen was with Duncan.

Callie found herself at loose ends. Her closest girl friend's family had moved away. Then Bobby Joe started dating another girl.

"I'm tired of waiting, Callie Ann," he said, his strawberry-blond hair curling over his forehead. "A guy can

only stand so much teasing and I've stood about all I'm
going to. I thought we'd get married someday, but did
you ever buy a pair of shoes without trying them on?
Why, we might not be compatible at all."

She promised him she would be more responsive if he
promised to drop the other girl. Once again they dated
every Friday and Saturday night. Then at Christmas,
when his parents took a trip to Louisville, he stayed behind.

Callie went with him to his empty house that first afternoon, and when his kisses changed to hard urgent
thrusts of his tongue and his hands found their way beneath her sweater and inside her jeans, she succumbed to
her budding desires. They tumbled into his parents' bed,
and she gave up her virginity, regaling in the brief ecstasy that followed.

She missed her next menstrual period, but he told her
not to worry, they were safe.

Bobby Joe had saved his earnings from his part-time
job at a grocery store and bought a pickup. After the
holidays, their trysts shifted to the sleeping bags he always carried in the back of his truck.

Her period in late February failed to come, but she
discounted the possibility of pregnancy, ecstatic because
she and Bobby Joe had just become secretly engaged.
Then her belly began to swell. She finished the spring
term wearing oversize stretchy T-shirts.

Her mother confronted her one Saturday morning in
June, and a week later she and her mother sat together in
the physician's office in Greenville.

"No test is necessary, Mrs. Hardesty," the doctor said.
"I have no doubt after talking to Callie and examining
her. Your daughter will be a momma come October."

When they informed Callie's father, the normally even-tempered man exploded, then called Robert and Emaline Huff and demanded their son take responsibility. They agreed, and the wedding took place quietly in early August. Robert Huff found Bobby Joe a job in a coal mine in eastern Kentucky where Bobby Joe's uncle worked. They had moved the week before the fall school term was to begin. *Shipped off into exile was more like it,* Callie thought.

She'd given birth to Robbie with only her resentful, panicky young husband in attendance. They had been unable to get to the hospital in town due to a freak October snowstorm.

For a few years, they had managed. They lived in a dilapidated cabin up Kudzu Hollow, two miles from the underground mine where Bobby Joe worked. He took up the habit of buying a six-pack of beer each night on his way home.

Friday would come and Callie would ask how much he had made.

"A man's pay is his own business," he would reply. "Yours is to take care of the house and kids."

House? Did he consider the dilapidated cabin they lived in a house?

"That dog-hole operator is shadier than this kudzu vine," he said one evening. "The state mine inspector was sniffing around last week. I wouldn't be surprised if he shuts us down. So don't you go gettin' any fancy ideas about moving into town," he warned.

Then Linda was born with a congenital heart problem and a cleft palate, and a month after her birth, the dog-hole mine had closed, fulfilling Bobby Joe's prediction.

Out of work and out of hope, Bobby Joe walked out of their lives, leaving Callie to manage as best she could.

And she did manage until the cupboards were bare and the weather turned cold. Then she walked into town, Linda balanced on her hip and Robbie tagging along at her side. A man working at a gas station pointed her toward a shelter for homeless families. There the manager fed them, gave them a night's lodging, then gave Callie directions to the county welfare office.

The woman who processed Callie's application went over the details three times before she seemed satisfied that Callie wasn't withholding information.

"You're a pretty little thing," the woman said, her smile filled with skepticism. "Surely some boyfriend comes by and helps you sometimes?"

Callie squinted back at the middle-aged woman. "It was a boyfriend who got me into this mess. All I'm askin' for is a decent place to bring up my kids. Don't they deserve that? And I don't want to be hungry no more, nor my kids. And when they get sick, I want to be able to bring them to the clinic and get them the medicine they need. Is that askin' too much?"

The woman snorted and reexamined the forms. "What about your parents? Can't they help you? Why don't you go live with them? I could arrange for a bus ticket to Central City. Harlan County would be more than willing to..."

"To ship me out, so that Muhlenberg County can pick up the tab 'stead of Harlan County. No, thank you, ma'am, but my parents have enough to worry about."

"You young girls are all alike," the woman said, annoyed now. "You have your fun and expect the county to support you when the inevitable happens. Do you know how many girls have come to me this month asking for assistance?"

"I can't speak for others," Callie replied, her slender back rigid. "I'm only askin' for myself and my kids. They gotta eat, ma'am. They're hungry." Her gaze dropped to her clenched fists lying in her lap. "Do you want me to beg? Is that what it takes to get help? My baby's sick."

"Take him to the doctor," the woman said.

"My baby's a little girl, and I don't have the money," Callie replied. "They want cash up front. My little boy is two years old and weighs twenty-two pounds. I'm not exactly fat, as you can plainly see. The cabin we lived in has no heat. I 'spose I could go chop wood, but I don't have an ax. I could go pick up coal, but the damper on the stove don't work right. I'm afraid to use it. The cabin's a firetrap. All last winter I was afraid it would burn down."

"They're predicting a mild winter this year," the woman murmured.

Callie blinked away the threatening tears. "I moved the kids to the shelter in town, but the woman in charge says we can't stay. She says they're crowded and need more space and there's families worse off than us."

"Okay," the woman said. "I'll check out your information and let you know next week." She tossed Callie's forms into a wire basket with several others.

"But my kids are hungry now," Callie persisted. "My baby's just a year old. Robbie don't even have a pair of shoes that fit him, and it's cold at night. I can't take him out because he don't...doesn't have a jacket...not even a little coat to keep him warm."

The woman shook her head in disgust. "You welfare mothers are all alike. No wonder those bleeding hearts think you're all so deprived...." She stopped when she saw the tears running down Callie's cheeks.

Callie wiped them away with the back of her hands. "Please," she murmured. "It won't be forever."

The woman gave in.

Callie and her children had lived in the apartment the welfare office found for them for nine years. Her parents had given her a small color television set for Christmas the next year, and Callie had used it to learn to speak what she perceived to be proper English. Only occasionally, did she catch herself slipping back into the colloquial speech patterns of the area.

Now Callie shook the painful memories away, left the chair and peeked out at the darkness from her second-story apartment window. What good did it do to rehash the past? That degrading interview had gotten her the apartment she had wanted, an emergency box of groceries from a food bank at the Baptist church down the street, and a promise to process the application as a rush.

Now she was about to return to the home where she had been born and to a second chance at life.

CALLIE AND THE CHILDREN moved into her parents' home, and within a week Robbie had found a friend in his classroom. After the second week, Linda brought two towheaded girls home from school. Life settled into a comfortable routine.

When Callie applied for benefits at the county seat, she was told they would have to send to Harlan County for her records. Since she was living with her parents for now, her situation was marked nonemergency.

"I heard about a program called Second Chance," Callie told the welfare worker. "Do you have one here in Muhlenberg County?"

The interviewer smiled. "We sure do. It meets right here in Greenville four days a week. We've had some real success stories coming from that program. Interested?"

"Definitely," Callie replied, accepting a brochure. Within the hour, she had enrolled in the classes.

When the classes started, Callie found that most of the women were closer to her mother's age than to hers, but Callie threw herself into the classes and group discussions. Always, though, she was careful to not discuss her past. It was the future that mattered now.

The program offered career counseling in the spring, but for now the main aims of the program were to instill self-esteem and to prepare the women for earning their General Equivalency Diplomas—or G.E.D.'s, as the women called them. To Callie's surprise, only one enrollee was a high-school graduate, the others were all taking classes with Callie. Project Second Chance appeared to be just what she'd been looking for.

CHAPTER THREE

IN LATE NOVEMBER, after a long day in Greenville, Callie parked her old Chevy pickup near the porch of her parents' place and climbed out. The weather had turned warm again, and her parents were sitting on the front porch. Callie glanced toward her mother, then her father as she climbed the steps. "Hi."

Her father grunted and pushed himself from his rocker, then stomped down the steps and around the corner of the white frame house toward the tobacco shed in the rear.

"What's the matter with Daddy?" Callie asked.

Ellen Hardesty sighed deeply and brushed a strand of gray hair from her temple. "He's kinda upset."

"What happened?" Callie asked, dropping into her father's rocker and giving it a push.

"The bank in Central City turned him down last month for a crop loan," Ellen murmured. "He tried again a few days ago, and they just called him...to say they were sorry but the answer was still no. Said the land was depleted." She turned to Callie. "What do those young men at the bank know about farming? They grow up in Louisville and get themselves a degree in business and then act like they was instant experts. They may know Thoroughbreds but they don't know beans about—" she chuckled "—about growing beans and tobacco."

Callie frowned. "Why is he borrowing? You said he carried on so when he had to borrow to buy Uncle Harry's place that you didn't think he'd ever set foot inside a bank door again except maybe to make a deposit."

"The crops didn't bring in as much as usual this year," Ellen said. "We used to manage to make ends meet, but each year lately the meetin' gets harder to manage. Thank the Lord this place is clear of a mortgage. I don't think we could've managed, otherwise."

Callie pushed the rocker with her toe. "Did he try the bank in Greenville?"

"Sure did," her mother replied. "They said they was cutting back on their crop loans."

"What's he going to do?" Callie asked.

"I don't know, but he's got an appointment on Monday to see a banker in Madisonville. Mr. Dickens recommended him, said he was a fine man and helped him out when he needed it most."

"Mr. Dickens?" Callie frowned. "But the Dickens sold their place to the White Glove Mining Company."

Ellen shrugged. "Maybe the coal people offered them a better deal. The earth can only take so much tampering with. Then it rebels. We haven't had the money to fertilize like we should've. Your daddy knows that, but the Hardestys have farmed this land since before the Civil War—cleared the timber, broke ground for cotton, even had a few slaves.... But that was a long time ago. The world has changed a lot, thank goodness, and mostly for the better, I reckon." She heaved another deep sigh. "Last year's crop of soybeans was way down from the previous years. But it was dry. We needed water."

Ellen Hardesty gave her rocker another push and stared across the yard to the highway, her gaze following three loaded white coal trucks rumbling toward the east.

"Maybe the banker fellow is right and this land is a'wearing out, just like your daddy and momma. Maybe there are worse things than coal mining...like starving."

"Are those trucks coming from the White Glove mine over yonder where the Dickens used to live?" Callie asked, her gaze following the trucks until they disappeared around a gentle curve in the road.

Ellen nodded and pushed the rocker again. "Them Colemans have it made, I reckon. They got money, land, good health, fancy houses...and they have a passel of boys to carry on the Coleman name. What more could a body ask for?"

"Do you know the Coleman family?" Callie asked.

"Not really," Ellen replied, "but I spent half a day in a hospital room with the old woman once."

Callie laughed. "You did? When?"

Ellen tipped her head back against the wooden slats of the rocker. "Well, the doc was expectin' problems when I was carrying Riley... Let's see now, Riley's thirty-four, isn't he? Yes, that's right. So thirty-four years ago your daddy took me over to the hospital in Madisonville just in case I had...difficulties, you know. Mrs. Coleman had had a boy herself a few days before and was going home the day I came into the room. I don't even remember what they named the little fellow, but he was sure cute. Had this full head of black hair, and Riley was as bald as a pullet egg and almost as small. Her baby weighed in at eight and a half pounds, while little Riley was less than five. He was early, you know. I had him during the night, so I only had the morning to visit with her."

Ellen pushed her rocker, and Callie kept silent. Her mother always became quiet when she talked about the son who had been sickly most of his childhood. Even now Callie knew her mother worried about Riley living in Taos, New Mexico, and trying to make a name for himself as a potter.

"Well, we visited for the morning until her husband could come for her," her mother continued. "We had a lot in common, y'see. We'd each had our fourth boy, 'cepting she had a girl, too, and you didn't come until later. I never saw her again, but I did see her picture in the paper a few times. I remember reading she went on to have another boy, just like I did. The Colemans get in the newspaper a lot more than the Hardestys do."

"Was she nice?" Callie asked.

"I recollect she was. 'Course she married into the Colemans, actually, so you can't tell about those men by her."

Callie rested her head against the rocker and smiled, lost in thoughts of the past.

"What's making you so happy, baby?" her mother asked.

"Just recalling a pleasant memory," Callie murmured. "Once upon a time I met a man in Morehead who worked for White Glove. I wonder which mine he worked at? Don't they have mines all over the state?"

"I'd imagine," her mother said.

Callie turned her head and looked at her mother. "How did the Colemans get so rich?"

"Their great-granddad bought up a lot of rights to the coal around here."

Two more loaded white trucks rumbled toward the east.

"I was talking to Sophie Dickens just last week in the grocery store," Ellen said, frowning after the disappearing coal trucks. "They bought a little place in Drakesboro, near where the old Baptist church used to be before they built that fancy new building closer to Central City. The Dickens paid cash for the new place, but she says Josh sure misses working the fields. She says he tries not to think about it but it keeps gnawing at him. He just never thought they'd want his land along with the underground rights to the coal.''

"They can't get to the coal without stripping the land," Callie said. "If no one forced him to sell, he should stop blaming White Glove."

"Sophie says the men from White Glove are nice people and gave them a fair price. She just hated to see the place disappear: house, barn, the old oak trees—all gone."

"Did you ever consider selling to them?"

Ellen shook her head. "Not until recently. Your daddy's begun to mull over the possibility. Great-grandpa Hardesty passed on the mineral rights when he passed on the land, and no one's sold them since. Even your cousin Abbie still owns the rights on that acreage she owns down the road."

"Abbie owns land here?" Callie asked, putting her foot to the floor to stop the rocker. "I didn't know that."

"Abbie's daddy willed it to her right after she was born," Ellen explained. "He must've known the odds of his being around to see her growed were against his favor. When Uncle Harry sold his land to your daddy, she leased it to us but didn't want to git rid of it completely. Said in a letter she liked the tie to Kentucky."

Callie rested her head against the hard maple of the rocker. "I owe Abbie a favor, Momma."

"And what might that be, daughter?"

"She paid for my airline ticket to her wedding."

Her mother nodded. "She said you didn't have to pay her back. Consider it a gift. I'm sure that's what she'd prefer."

Callie shook her head. "She refuses money, but I still intend to pay her back, only I'm not sure how." She smiled. "I'd sure like to see her and her baby. Goodness, little Anna is three months old already. It's hard to imagine Abbie with a baby. You should have gone to the wedding, Momma."

"We're hardly rich enough to go flying around the country," Ellen replied, her gaze following a crimson leaf as it fluttered down from the huge white oak tree in the front yard. "What's her husband like?"

Callie smiled, recalling the two dances she'd had with Dane Grasten at the wedding. "A handsome blond giant. Stern but warm, strong but sensitive…and very much in love with Abbie."

"Sounds like a contradiction," Ellen said.

"Perhaps he is, but I liked that about him. Abbie is very lucky to have found him."

"And this new husband of cousin Eileen?"

Callie made a face at a convoy of coal trucks rumbling past. "I just met him once at the reception. He asked me to dance, and we chatted about Kentucky. I never suspected anything was going on between Eileen and him. You know how prim Eileen can be at times, always concerned about what people might say. Maybe she's changed since meeting Dan Page. Did you see him on national TV when Arizona had the earthquake?"

Ellen shook her head. "Can't say that I did."

"I saw him twice," Callie continued. "Very photogenic. And now he's a potato farmer, and Eileen is expecting twins again in a few months and, gracious, haven't Abbie and Eileen found happiness in unexpected ways?''

Ellen chuckled. "You Rainbow Hills cousins go your own way, that's for sure."

Callie grimaced. "I should have taken a different route."

"If them companies keep stripping this land, there won't be no Rainbow Hills for my grandchildren to come home to," Ellen said. "I love these hills at this time of year. With all the fall colors, they really do remind me of a rainbow."

"I always thought they got their name from the springtime," Callie said, "when the wildflowers are in bloom and the creeks are flowing high and the dogwoods are in full blossom. Then the hills turn green, the birds in the meadows sing and everyone goes to church in their Easter outfits—that's what I always like best."

Ellen laughed. "And you three girls just added to it in your little frilly dresses. Abbie with her red hair, Eileen with her brown braids, and then you with hair as black as the stuff they're toting away in them coal trucks." Ellen reached over and patted Callie's small hand. "Your time is coming, honey. I feel it…here." She touched her chest. "You'll find happiness. Maybe it's right under your pretty little nose."

They were quiet for a few minutes, with only the creaking of the rockers against the slabs of the porch to break the silence.

Ellen stopped rocking. "What time is it?"

Callie glanced at her watch. "Ten after five. Can I help you with supper? We'll be eating late if we don't get started."

"It won't be necessary," Ellen replied. "Your Aunt Min and Uncle Harry are driving in from Lexington.

They should be here any minute now. They're taking us out to Catfish Gap. You know how those men love their fried catfish, and that place lets them eat all they can. I don't know how that restaurant stays in business. They must own their very own private catfish farm.''

Callie smiled. ''I met a man once who wanted to own a catfish farm. There really are such businesses. This fellow is just crazy enough to have one some day.''

''Around these parts? What was his name?'' Ellen asked.

Callie shrugged. ''He was the man in Morehead. We never had time to learn much about each other—except he loves beans and corn bread... and catfish farms and red mules, too. He helped me out when I was hardpressed.''

Callie closed her eyes and savored the sweet memory that had strangely become more pronounced as time went by. Sometimes at the least likely moments, she would get the strongest feeling that if she opened her eyes, she would find him right beside her. She stopped rocking. ''Well, I'm glad Aunt Min is coming. I haven't seen her for a long time. Besides, I promised Abbie I'd try to find out more about her momma and daddy. Aunt Min must know a lot more than she's ever told Abbie. Maybe Aunt Min could write to Abbie's momma.''

''Don't count on that,'' Ellen said.

''Why not?''

''Aunt Min never learned to write much more than her name.''

''She used to get letters from Abbie's momma all the time,'' Callie said. ''She used to read them to Abbie when she was little, only Abbie's momma's handwriting was so terrible Aunt Min couldn't make out the words. Abbie told us all about it.''

"Honey, that wasn't the problem," Ellen said. "Aunt Min can't read, neither. She was ashamed to let Abbie know. She told me once she finally stopped telling Abbie about the letters."

"What?" Callie rose from the rocker. "But Abbie thought her momma stopped writing. What a terrible deception! How could Aunt Min have done such a thing?"

"Your Aunt Min and Abbie's momma, Bernice, have been a'fussing at each other for years. They're sisters, you know."

"Sisters!"

"Well, actually half sisters."

"But why haven't they got along?"

"They had words...about Phillip Hardesty, old P.A. And the scars run deep," Ellen replied, rocking several times. "When Minnie took Abbie into her house and heart that just made the wounds deeper and the story more complicated, honey." Ellen grimaced. "Bernice's handwriting was terrible, but not illegible. Min didn't want Abbie to be embarrassed about having an adopted momma who couldn't read, and she didn't want Bernice hanging around, either, so she hid the letters when they came to break the chain between Bernice and Abbie, and Abbie just assumed that her momma had stopped writing. I tried to talk Min out of it once, but you know how hardheaded she can be. I told her it would come back to haunt her someday."

"That's terrible!" Callie exclaimed. "What could Bernice have done to Aunt Min that was so unforgivable?"

"Just never you mind. I've said too much already."

"But Aunt Min gave us those lockets and was always doing special things for us. Why would she do such a selfish thing when she's so nice?"

"Bernice took advantage of her, and Min knows it."

"But how?" Callie asked.

"Just never you mind," Ellen replied. "It's water under the bridge now. Min loved Abbie as if she were her own, and maybe she should have been. Who's to say? Anyway, not knowing how to read or write can do things to a person, Callie. Don't be judgmental. Min's paid for her sins over and over. She just can't bring herself to admit what she's done to Abbie."

"But—"

Before Callie could continue, a late-model sedan drove into the yard and parked. A tall gray-haired man got out of the driver's side and strolled around the vehicle, then assisted a large rawboned, redheaded woman from the car. "What's wrong with her?" Callie whispered, staring at her aunt Minnie's swollen ankles. "She wasn't that bad at the wedding."

"A lot can happen in a year's time," Ellen replied, shaking her head. "Min's in her seventies. She's worked hard until these last few years. I'm worried about her. Her heart's been acting up."

They waited while Minnie worked her way up the steps to the porch, her husband, Harry, at her elbow.

Minnie held out her arms. "Callie, honey, it's good to see you back home where you belong."

Callie found herself engulfed in a soft embrace. How many times had she been squeezed against Aunt Minnie's large bosom? she wondered. The older woman planted a warm kiss on each of Callie's cheeks before releasing her.

"Where's my brother?" Harry asked.

"Admiring his tobacco drying in the shed," Ellen replied. "He hopes to take it to Russellville week after next. He heard they was paying a few cents more than the local auctioneers."

"Guess I'll go find him," Harry said, and headed toward the tobacco shed, seeking his brother.

Callie looked up to see her son pedaling down the road, her daughter balanced precariously on the handlebars of the bicycle. Robbie turned into the driveway and braked to a stop a few feet from the porch, then lifted Linda to the ground. Linda was as small for her age as Robbie was tall for his.

Linda had inherited Bobby Joe's strawberry-blond hair and blue eyes. Robbie's hair was a rich chestnut brown, his eyes dark like Callie's.

The children were hugged again and again by a tearful Aunt Minnie, until the men returned.

Harry touched her arm. "Catfish Gap will be plumb out of food if you keep this hugging up much longer, Min. I didn't drive all this way for nothing. You kids get washed up, and we'll get the heck down the road."

Callie smiled, listening to her relatives. It was truly good to be home again.

CALLIE GLANCED AFFECTIONATELY at the people gathered around the table at Catfish Gap. With two of her brothers and their families present, there were sixteen seated at the long table, enjoying deep-fried catfish filets rolled in cornmeal batter and hush puppies, with all the usual trimmings and side dishes for which the restaurant was famous.

Callie's father turned to his brother. "Harry, why did you and Min drive out all this way? Did they close down all the catfish houses in Lexington?"

Harry looked fondly at his wife before replying. "We want to come home. We don't belong in the city."

Minnie nodded. "We never should have left."

"We don't regret selling to you one iota, Finis," Harry added, "but we want to move back into the country. We've been talking to a real-estate fellow in Greenville. Tomorrow we're just gonna relax, maybe sit on the porch and jaw a bit, but come Sunday after church, we're gonna check out the addresses of a few places he gave us, and if we see anything that looks promisin' we'll go with him and see the inside and get the particulars. We just want an acre or so, with a small house that won't tax Min with the housekeeping. The doc says she needs to take it easy. And I want to garden again, this time just for fun and eatin' instead of for profit."

Callie, who was sitting next to her aunt, touched the woman's arm. "Aunt Min, do you have anything planned for tomorrow?"

"I want to look over some quilt patterns in your ma's magazines," Minnie replied. "That's all, but you know how your ma and me get when we start talking quilts."

Callie chuckled. "That's for sure, but since you're staying with us anyway, could we talk privately tomorrow morning?"

"Why sure, honey," Minnie replied. "What's troubling you?"

Callie stared down at the pieces of catfish still on her plate. It was not her favorite fish. "It's about Abbie. She's asked me if I'd talk to you...about her mother and father."

"Her momma? Why, I haven't heard from Bernice in years, honey," Minnie said. "I sent Abbie some old photos of her daddy. His name was Phillip Andrew, but he went by P.A. most of his life. He was a fine looking man. He and Harry were first cousins. What else does Abbie want to know?''

Callie glanced at the children interspersed among the adults around the table. ''The kids are getting restless. Could we talk about it tomorrow?''

Minnie nodded. ''Why don't we get up real early and drive to Greenville for breakfast, just the two of us?''

Callie hesitated. ''My truck is almost out of gas, but maybe I can borrow Daddy's pickup.''

''No, no,'' Minnie replied. ''If you'll drive our car, I'll treat for breakfast. My legs don't let me drive anymore. I can't hit the brake. You can be my chauffeur, honey. I 'spect you're still a little tight on funds.'' She patted Callie's hand. ''We're all proud of you for going back to school. Education is very important. Look where it got my Abbie and Cousin Eileen. Some of us didn't get a chance to go to school for long, so you take advantage of that program you're in. What's it called?''

''Second Chance,'' Callie replied.

Minnie nodded. ''Well, some of us never got our second chance. You count your blessings, honey.''

Callie studied the older woman's rosy features. ''I think I've found a way to repay my debt to Abbie. It won't be easy or fast, but she could never do it herself. Can you help me?''

Minnie frowned. ''I'd do anything for Abbie. You know that.''

The family members began to rise from their chairs, gathering their purses and jackets. Harry Hardesty motioned to the waitress and took the check. The others protested to no avail. Callie's oldest brother, James, left the tip, though, and Leander added to the amount. Laughing and joking, the party worked its way through the crowded restaurant toward the exit.

Callie, sandwiched between Minnie and Leander, failed to notice the tall dark-haired man rise from his seat across the room and call out her name. Before he could call again, a blond woman yanked at his arm and pulled him back into his chair.

"ADRIAN, HONEY, I asked you a question," Cindy Oldham said.

Adrian Coleman's attention lingered on the woman whom he had spotted only when she had turned to leave the crowded restaurant. Callie? Impossible. Then again, twice lately he could have sworn he had seen her walking down the sidewalk of Greenville's main street. Both times he had been en route from his home near Madisonville to the Dickens surface mine near Drakesboro.

But hadn't Callie said she lived in Hazard or Harlan? The irritating tugging on his arm continued until he tore his gaze away from the door. "I'll think about it," he mumbled, his gaze swinging back to the group of people now outside. He brushed Cindy's hand away. "I'll be right back." He left his chair and strode to the exit.

The family group from the restaurant was milling around a pair of vans and a car. The woman he had thought was Callie was wearing a quilted lavender car coat. Her rope of black hair hung down to her hips. A slender young girl with reddish-blond hair held her hand.

"Callie." As he mouthed her name from the steps, another car pulled between him and the woman. Two couples got out, laughing and joking. Adrian took the steps two at a time, but the distance between him and the cars seemed endless. He sidestepped the two couples in time to see the first car back out of its space, brake, then accelerate. For an instant, he thought he recognized the large red-haired older woman sitting on the passenger side of the sedan. Hadn't she been with Callie in More-head?

"Callie!" he shouted. One of the vans drove away. The driver of the second van turned and gave Adrian a men-acing stare before climbing inside and slamming the door. The glow of the van's taillights disappeared into the darkness.

Two of the vehicles had definitely carried Muhlenberg County license plates. It was her. He was posi-tive…almost. *Damn it,* he thought. He didn't even know for sure which car she was in, but he thought the first one. Had she moved into the area?

He turned back toward the restaurant. If the woman had been Callie, perhaps he would spot her again in Greenville. By damn, he would stop the truck, regard-less where he happened to be, and confront her. If she turned out to be a stranger, he'd swallow his pride and apologize, but if she was in fact pretty Callie from Morehead, so help her he would kiss her on the spot and demand to know why she had put him through pure hell fretting about where she lived and wondering why she hadn't given him her full name or told him when could he see her again.

He tossed his dark head back and laughed aloud. He had truly taken leave of his senses. All he knew about Callie was that she didn't seem to have much money and she ate beans to get by. Still, he wanted to shout to the heavens that he had found her again.

A couple leaving the restaurant looked his way, and his dark features turned somber as his mood shifted again. Now he could handle anything, even Cindy's suggestive remark that they go to his home and catch up on old times. The only thing he wanted to catch up with now was Callie with the pretty brown eyes and bewitching smile.

He wanted to brush away the disillusionment he had sensed in her manner and the suspicion he had seen in her eyes. He wanted to wine and dine her on something fancier than bean soup, to shower her with gifts, to get to know her . . . and to have her want him someday as much as he wanted her this very moment.

He studied the stars overhead, wondering what had happened to him. He had felt no inclination toward matrimony during his adult life. Now he wanted to propose to a lovely stranger. It made no sense, yet he knew it was as right and proper as tomorrow's sunrise.

CHAPTER FOUR

MINNIE HARDESTY slid her bulk onto the bench and pushed the table toward Callie. "They make these booths smaller than they used to," she said.

Callie gave the table a helpful tug. The drive to Greenville had been pleasant, filled with reminiscing about the carefree summers of Callie's youth. Now, as the waitress filled their mugs and slid the menus in front of them, Callie searched for the right way to open a discussion of Abbie's parents.

"Get anything you want, honey," Minnie said. Then she told the waitress, "I'll take sausage gravy and biscuits and a side order of grits. And if your fried apples are fresh this morning, some of them."

"The same for me," Callie added. The waitress left them to enjoy the coffee.

"Now what could be bothering you that involves Abbie?" Minnie asked, pouring cream into her coffee and stirring.

"Perhaps we should wait until after we eat," Callie hedged.

Minnie shook her head, then tucked a strand of graying red hair back into the bun on the back of her head. "We might as well hang it out to dry."

Callie met the steady green gaze of her aunt. "It's about her mother...and the letters."

Minnie's complexion paled for an instant before flushing. "The letters?"

Callie nodded. "Aunt Minnie, I just can't understand why you'd do such a thing, especially to Abbie."

Minnie stared into her cup but didn't say a word.

"Abbie asked me to look up some records for her at the courthouse," Callie explained. "Since it's right across the street from here and I've been coming to Greenville for classes anyway, I got the idea to make Abbie's little girl, Anna, a scrapbook of her heritage."

Callie's brown eyes sparkled. "I found the marriage licenses of the Hardestys for generations at the court-house. At the library, I learned to read the census micro-film, the indexes and other records—and goodness gracious, within a few days I'd tracked the Hardesty family back to 1760 in Virginia. But I'm completely lost on Bernice's family. I was looking for Smith, but it was Dickens and Reed and Murdock I should have been re-searching."

"Where did you hear those names, Callie?"

"Momma told me. Since I've been home again I've found out Momma knows almost everything about our families."

Minnie smiled and patted Callie's hand. "And how did you get so good at finding things in books and such, child?"

"A very nice man in the library here in Greenville showed me where to look for information. He said I had a knack for research. Gracious, Aunt Min, half my re-search was on my own family, so I'm not only doing something for Abbie, but for my own kids. They'll know all about who they are! Searching through the microfilm makes you think you're going blind at times, but there's so much there. Relatives, friends and neighbors—even old family stories. Did you know that Great-grandpa Riley lived with Great-grandma Calandra's family and worked as a farm laborer for three years before they got married?''

Minnie smiled. "There are no secrets, are there?"

Callie chuckled. "Not for long. I always wished my name was Calandra instead of just plain Callie."

"Callie's easier to spell, honey," Minnie said. "Thank the Lord for small favors."

Callie grinned. "Did you know that Grandpa was born just six months after his folks married?"

"How do you know that?" Minnie asked, frowning.

"Grandpa Hardesty's marriage license gave his birth date and when I found his parents' marriage license, I compared the dates. I'm not the only Callie in the family to get pregnant before she got married."

Minnie patted Callie's hand and gave it a squeeze. "You've got more company than you think, honey, that's for sure, but it don't do no good to hang it out for airing now. Sweep it under the rug, why don't you?"

"I know," Callie replied, "but it sure eases my conscience."

The waitress arrived with their meals, but Callie left her fork on the table. "I've been thinking that what I'm doing for Abbie and Annie won't be complete until I put Abbie in touch with her natural mother—if she's still alive. I can't do that without your help. Why, Aunt Min? Why did you break the bond between Abbie and her momma?"

Minnie's green eyes filled with moisture.

"Was it because of...growing up together?" Callie asked. "If you were half sisters, I'd think that would bring you closer."

"I...I can't tell you."

"Why not?" Callie persisted. "It's because of Phillip Andrew Hardesty, isn't it? Good old P.A., who everyone in the family brags about being such a fine upstanding man?"

"Don't you go bad-mouthing P.A.," Minnie said, wagging her finger at Callie. "He *was* a fine man, handsome, too. There's no arguing that."

Callie leaned forward. "Then what did he do that drove two sisters apart?"

"The man's dead, Callie. Leave him be and leave me be."

"I can't," Callie insisted. "I want to help Abbie, and Abbie's mother, as well. Too many people have been hurt here. You must have had a good reason to do what you did. Tell me, please."

Minnie fingered the bill the waitress had dropped on the table. "Let me look through some boxes."

"Do you still have the letters?"

"I . . . think so, but they're packed away," Minnie replied. "I've always been . . . so ashamed that . . . Never mind. Let's talk about all this later. You caught me off guard, to say the least, Callie, but maybe I would feel a might better to clear this from my conscience." She chuckled. "All us Hardestys have a heavy dose of conscience, even if we've just married into it. It rubs off, just like pride. Sometimes I even have a hankering to see my sister." She reached for her purse. "Well, if'n you're done, why don't we leave? We can talk on the way back."

Callie gathered her jacket and purse. "I'll meet you outside after I've been to the ladies' room."

A few minutes later as Callie was heading toward the exit, a man reached out from one of the booths and grabbed her wrist. Frightened, she glanced quickly from the masculine hand, up the sleeve of a beige corduroy sport jacket and into a pair of hazel eyes—eyes that had been in her thoughts many times since September.

"Callie?"

"Adrian?" Her eyes widened.

He pulled her down onto the bench beside him. Embarrassed, she glanced at the thinner good-looking man sitting across from Adrian, recognizing the other half of the team of handlers from Morehead. Her attention shot back to Adrian's somber face.

"Don't you live in Hazard?" he asked.

"Harlan." The thrill of meeting him again shifted to uncertainty. She tried to pry his fingers loose, but he tightened his grip. "You're not from here, either," she added.

"Hopkins County," he reminded her. "I work in Madisonville, but I live near the county line." His dark features softened. "What are you doing here?"

She stopped trying to pry his fingers loose, and he eased his grip. Warmth crept up her arm. "I had breakfast...with my aunt." Her gaze slipped from his eyes and his thick black lashes, moving to the faint shadow of his beard below his strong cheekbone. He'd shaved that morning, she thought, inhaling a lingering trace of spicy fragrance. Her attention shifted to his mouth.

He gave her a subtle smile, and she reciprocated. "And you?" she asked, aware that they were now simply holding hands.

"Breakfast with my brother. Jarrett, this is Callie." He nodded to the other man in the booth, who acknowledged Callie with an arch of his brow. "Have I imagined you here in Greenville?" Adrian asked. "I'd swear I've seen you more than once."

She nodded. "I've been coming to Greenville." She tried to unscramble her thoughts. "The mules...how are they?"

"In retirement until next summer. Competition is over for now. Still adding water to your beans?"

"The only way to survive sometimes." Her voice faded as they studied each other, oblivious to their surroundings.

A shadow fell across them, and they glanced up to find Aunt Minnie standing beside the booth.

"Callie, honey, are you all right?" Minnie asked. "Who is this man? Is he bothering you?"

"No," Callie murmured. "Adrian, this is my Aunt Minnie."

Adrian squinted up at the woman. "From?"

"Lexington," Minnie replied, her fists on her ample hips as she scrutinized Adrian for several seconds.

"And this is my brother, Jarrett," Adrian said. "We're from Hopkins County, just out for breakfast. I never expected to see your...niece here." Adrian paused, a smile moving across his features. "I've been wondering about her."

"And I've...been...curious about him," Callie murmured, feeling a wave of heat rush up her cheeks.

"Honey, we'd better get back," Minnie said, frowning down at Adrian. "Your folks are expecting us."

Callie's hand slid from his. "I really must go." She inched out of the booth and got to her feet. "See y'all," she murmured, nodding to both men.

"Yes, ma'am, you can count on that," Adrian murmured, lounging against the corner of the booth, his long arm resting on the back of the bench, as he watched her leave. He propped his dark head on his fist, his thoughts drifting back over the months.

"Who is she?" Jarrett Coleman asked.

Adrian turned reluctantly away from the door and back to his brother. "It's as simple as *A*, *B*, *C*. That might well be the future Mrs. Adrian Bradford Coleman, though she doesn't know it yet."

Jarrett laughed aloud and took a long swig of coffee. "And what is her name?"

"I think of her as little Callie Bean." Adrian straightened in his seat and gave his undivided attention to the uneaten blueberry pancakes on his plate.

"Bean. Bean?" Jarrett asked. "I don't recall any Beans living around here."

"Damn!" Adrian exclaimed. "Her name isn't Bean, it's...damn it, I don't know her name."

"And her aunt?" Jarrett asked.

Adrian smiled sheepishly. "Minnie. Know any Minnie Ample-Hips around here?"

"Best be careful, Adrian. It looks to me as if you've got to impress that aunt before you have any hope of getting to her niece. How did you meet her?"

"Well, do you remember that festival in Morehead?" Adrian asked, then explained how he had met Callie.

"So she's the reason I had to hitch the teams by myself," Jarrett remarked. "What's Cindy Lou going to say? Have you told her? She'll be disappointed, to say the least."

"She and I parted company long ago," Adrian said.

"I thought she spent the weekend with you a few weeks ago."

"She used the guest room," Adrian said. "Sometimes a man has to stand on his principles."

Jarrett chuckled. "I've been out of the courtship race for some time now. Isn't a man suppose to be smart enough to—"

"To be sure he's in pursuit of the right woman?" Adrian finished. "Cindy Lou isn't the right woman."

"How can you be so sure this woman is?"

Adrian grinned. "Instinct. Want to be my best man?"

Jarrett reached for the check. "My pleasure. I was beginning to worry that you'd never settle down. The rest of us Colemans have finished having kids, and you know how Momma loves the grandbabies. It's time you took up the standard and kept them coming."

"Don't rush me," Adrian replied. "Before the babies start coming, I'd better find out the bride-to-be's last name."

"I THINK IT'S REAL NICE that you've met some feller, but be careful," Minnie Hardesty said, as Callie drove them back to the farm. "You don't want a repeat of Bobby Joe."

Callie smiled. "Adrian and I are just acquaintances. He's good to talk to. He's a simple man, with simple plans for the future. He wants to raise mules and catfish."

Minnie huffed. "He didn't look like a mule skinner to me. That fancy jacket with the leather patches didn't come from a cut-rate clothing store. It looked more like something a banker or a lawyer might wear. Maybe you don't know him as well as you think you do."

Callie frowned. "I never said I *knew* him. Maybe he bought the jacket in a used-clothing store like Second Editions in Central City. I think it's nice to see a man get dressed up once in a while." Her mouth softened into a faint grin. "I think he's rather charming...good-looking, too." She flicked on the left-turn signal and waited for the oncoming traffic to clear. Two empty white coal trucks rumbled past, stirring up dust from the pavement. "I hate those trucks, don't you?" she asked. "Why do they have to work on Saturdays?"

Minnie nodded. "Money."

Callie turned into the entrance to her parents' farm. "It would take a lot to make a romance for Adrian and me, Aunt Min. First we'd have to date, become friends and . . . well, it's against all odds. I'll send you a wedding announcement if it happens, but don't hold your breath." She parked and turned off the engine. "I've been thinking."

"About this man?"

Callie smiled. "A little," she admitted, "but other things, too. Just how well can you read?"

Minnie's mouth dropped open, then clamped shut. "Why?"

"Did you ever want to learn to read?"

"What makes you think I can't read?" Minnie asked.

"Momma said so," Callie replied gently.

Minnie frowned. "Your momma shouldn't of told, but I reckon the cat's out of the bag now. 'Course, I wanted to learn to read, but . . . the few times I tried, I just couldn't get the hang of it," Minnie said. "I was too old to go back to school by the time I realized how much I'd missed."

"A person's never too old to go to school, Aunt Min," Callie said. "Look at me. I'm no kid and I'm going."

"That's different," Minnie said. "I'm proud of you, but what's right for you ain't necessarily right for me. Harry tried to teach me, but he got impatient and I got angry . . . probably because I was embarrassed. No grown woman wants to admit she ain't smart enough to read."

Callie gave her aunt's hand a squeeze. "If you're going to move back here, we can work together. You can help me track down Abbie's momma, and I'll teach you to read.'' She stared at the huge oak tree in the yard. "I don't know what I would have done in Harlan if I hadn't known how to read.''

She smiled at her aunt. "When I do the research on the family, you can practice your reading by checking to see if I've put it down right. Why, the Second Chance program is starting a literacy class next spring. You can sign up, and between Second Chance and me, we'll make a reader out of you yet. It's never too late to learn.''

Minnie shook her head slowly. "Are you sure you can work that kind of miracle? I'm a tough old bird, honey. Maybe it's too late to change me.''

"It's never too late, Aunt Min," Callie assured her.

"I could maybe read the Bible, couldn't I?" Minnie asked. "All those years of teaching Bible study, I always had Harry with me to read the scriptures and the lessons.''

Callie nodded. "And think of all those quilt magazines Momma has. You could read them for yourself and learn so many new ways to make a quilt, you'd probably get a headache just absorbing them all.''

Minnie stared out the car window. "I'd sure like that. I've always been curious about some of the writings in them craft magazines. I quit working at the loom years ago when I got stuck trying to figure out the diagrams. I taught Abbie all I knew about weaving, but that wasn't much, I reckon, compared to what she knows now. I'm so proud of that girl it makes me downright tearful at times. And I sure want to see that baby of hers someday. Do you think she'll ever come home?''

"If we give her reason enough," Callie replied.

"Even when she finds out about the letters?''

"Maybe making peace and amends can be part of my promise, too," she replied, kissing her aunt's full cheek.

Minnie stared out the windshield. "Bernice can read."

On Monday morning Callie drove to Greenville for her Second Chance classes, but she had trouble keeping her mind on her work. Her thoughts kept turning to Adrian. *Why didn't I ask him his last name?*

During the lunch break, several of the women went to the restaurant near the courthouse, and Callie went, too. Her stomach did a somersault each time the door opened, but Adrian never appeared. Disappointed, she left with the other women and returned to the center, leaving her bowl of soup barely touched.

Callie received a preliminary test score in math and was pleased to see she had missed only one problem. The G.E.D. tests were scheduled for the week before Christmas, and she'd been worried about them. Now she was confident she'd be able to give herself a Christmas present—becoming an official high-school graduate after a twelve-year delay.

Filled with newly found confidence, she took the counselor's suggestion and sent for the registration packets from Western Kentucky University in Bowling Green and Murray State University in Murray. Then she examined the universities' catalogs, which were available in the center's library.

If Callie had a problem, it was that every subject listed interested her. The catalogs opened up a world of endless possibilities. After many hours of deliberation, she settled on business administration, envisioning a solid core of job opportunities at the end of her studies.

But could she afford university, even with a grant? She had to think about Robbie and Linda. Would qualifying for a grant cost her the monthly assistance check she had become dependent on? Unsure if she could take such a risk, she headed home to her children and parents.

"WHERE'S GRANDPA?" Robbie asked, as the family gathered for supper.

"Shush," Callie whispered.

Ellen Hardesty pursed her lips. "He called and said he'd be a little late." She pushed a bowl of creamed carrots toward Robbie, ignoring the face he made. "Now eat, young man. You're as thin as a cornstalk." She smiled. "Almost as tall, too."

Robbie grinned and took a spoonful.

Callie had a harder time eating her supper. That morning, dressed in his only suit, her father had driven to Madisonville to see a banker about the loan he needed.

"Did he get it?" Callie asked at last as they finished eating.

"We'll discuss it when he gets home," Ellen said. Abruptly, she rose and began to remove the serving bowls from the table.

The children were in bed when the lights of Finis Hardesty's truck turned into the driveway. Callie glanced at the clock above the mantle. Half past ten. She followed her mother into the kitchen, got her father's favorite mug down and set it on the table while her mother brewed a fresh pot of coffee on the stove.

When her father entered the kitchen, Callie could smell the whiskey. *He's not a drinking man,* she thought, glancing toward her mother. He steadied himself against the doorjamb before concentrating on walking to the table and finally dropping into a slat-backed chair.

Ellen poured the hot black coffee into his cup. "I was thinkin' about worryin'," she said, sliding into the chair next to his and touching his hand.

"I met old man Dickens, and we had a few shots of Jack Daniels at his brother's place in Greenville," Finis said, his words slightly slurred. "I followed him home. I drove real careful."

"Did you get the loan?" Callie asked.

Finis shook his head. "That Jarrett Coleman is a man without a heart," he said, his shoulders sagging. "No heart at all. The whole damned family is that way. Josh Dickens told me that behind that great image, those Coleman men are known throughout western Kentucky as the Heartless Colemans."

He squinted at his wife. "He turned me down flat. Said the land was worn out, asked me about the mineral rights and wanted to know who owned 'em. I told him it was none of his damned business, but that the coal beneath this land had been in Hardesty hands since before the Civil War. He asked me if I'd considered selling, and I told him I'd given it some thought but hadn't made up my head. Then I left. He had the gall to apologize for turning me down. Said he was real sorry. Said if he thought of some way to help, he'd give me a call. Likely as not, he forgot all about poor old man Hardesty as soon as I left."

"Oh, no," Ellen groaned. "What'll we do now? The tobacco paid for the taxes, but we still owe for part of the fertilizer, and the soybeans didn't bring as much as we'd hoped and..."

"Don't tell me about farming, woman," Finis said. "It's a losing proposition, no matter how you figure it. Maybe Harry and Shelby were the smart ones in the family. Maybe it's time we got out completely! Sell to the coal companies and let them have it all—house, barn, timber... but hell, they'd just tear it all down. All they want is the coal. Don't matter what it takes to get to it. Why, Dickens told me they had his house gone in less than an hour. He watched 'em from the highway. Didn't tell the missus, 'cause she would have just bawled. That house was more than a hundred years old, and in less than sixty minutes it was gone... gone!'' He brought his fist down on the table, splashing his coffee onto the yellow-checked plastic tablecloth.

"You should've used more fertilizer last year," Ellen murmured.

"I can't use what I can't buy, woman," Finis said. "I can't buy if'n I ain't got the money, and I can't get the money if I can't find a bank. Damn it, even the Farm Credit Service man said they're tightening up. When everyone who has the money tightens his purse strings, what's a farmer to do?"

Callie smiled encouragingly. "Maybe you can find a new career, maybe in Cincinnati or Kansas City or—Listen, I've sent for information about colleges in Murray and Bowling Green. If I can get a grant, I'll be moving. You can sell this place, and we can start over together in a new town. Don't you see? We could all have a second chance."

Her parents stared at her as if she had lost her senses.

"Our family has lived here for too long to move now, Callie," Finis said.

"Why?" she asked. "Didn't your great-great-grandfather's family take the plunge themselves one time? Didn't they take a greater risk than we would be taking? This was wilderness then."

Finis laughed. "That's for sure, honey. The first Hardesty settled on this land in 1782 when this whole state was still a county of Virginia. After fighting in the War of Independence he come to Harrodsburg in 1780. Harrodsburg got too crowded, so he headed west and brung his woman, and they had a fine crop of younguns, even though the corn and cotton didn't grow so well. When he had a run-in with a disagreeable Indian and was kilt, his brother stepped in and married his widder, and they had some more Hardestys. Damn, I wish I could have lived in those days." He shook his gray head sorrowfully.

"Oh, Daddy," Callie said, laughing softly, "you say that every time you tell that story, but I'll bet you're glad you have that truck instead of a team and wagon, and paved roads take out a few bumps, now don't they?"

"But they weren't bothered by all them coal trucks, neither. Them dang things are like a bunch of ants, running every which way," Finis retorted. He took another gulp of coffee. "'Course, the crops are a might easier to grow. Too bad we still can't make any money on them. Shoot, maybe we should move."

Ellen held up her hand. "It don't seem right talkin' about moving away when Harry and Minnie are movin' back next month."

"You're right," Finis said, tipping his chair back to peer at his wife. "What kind of job could I work at in a city, anyway? Factory work ain't as plentiful as it used to be. I don't know a thing about runnin' one of them computers like everyone uses nowadays." He laughed cynically.

"You could retire," Ellen suggested.

"A man shouldn't retire at sixty years, woman," he replied. "A man retires when he's too old to earn his keep. I ain't that old yet, not by a long shot. And you'd be obliged to remember that, ya hear now?"

"Of course," Ellen murmured.

"Maybe we could borrow some money from that rich rancher feller your cousin married," Finis said, turning to Callie. "You can't run a big ranch like his without money. Didn't you say it was thousands and thousands of acres?"

"You wouldn't dare!" Callie exclaimed. "Don't you dare talk to Abbie, or Eileen, either. Do you want their husbands to think we're just poor dirt farmers back here? I know for a fact that Eileen almost lost her potato farm, and even if her husband did sell that book, that doesn't mean they have lots of money. Everybody has his own problems to solve, and we'll solve ours."

"Easy, honey," Finis said, "don't get all riled up. I was just speculating on what's available." He yawned. "Geez, I'm sorry I came home smelling like a still. Thank the Lord I made it home safely, and thanks to your momma here for this strong coffee. I think it's diluting that Jack Daniels, 'cause I'm beginning to think straight."

Callie covered a yawn. "We won't find the answers tonight, that's for sure." She kissed her parents and bid them good-night.

After checking on her children, she went to her room and undressed. She slipped into a flannel gown and let it drop down over her slender body, smoothing it with her palms. As her hands slid over her breasts and past her tiny waist, she smiled. Perhaps poverty had its good points at that, she thought, recalling the meals she had skipped so that her children had something to eat.

The dark lashes of Adrian's eyes opened in her mind's eye. She remembered how his gaze had lingered on her breasts that autumn day in Morehead. True, he had commented on her locket, but surely he had noticed more than the necklace.

She slid beneath the blankets and laid her cheek against the back of her hand, wondering if Adrian had had the same reaction to their clasped hands in the restaurant as she had had. Did he think of her occasionally?

She smiled, letting her thoughts dwell on Adrian. No woman ever got pregnant from fantasizing about a stranger, she thought, and fantasy was all she had time for now.

CHAPTER FIVE

ADRIAN COLEMAN WATCHED the affectionate play of his brother's children as Jarrett's wife, Carol, coaxed them off to bed.

He accepted a kiss on each cheek from the girls and waved to his nephew from the comfortable chair near the fireplace. Christmas was just weeks away and already the house had been decorated for the holiday season. Carol came to Adrian's chair and kissed his cheek. She went to her husband and gave him a lingering kiss on his mouth, said good-night and left the two brothers alone.

"Drink?" Jarrett asked.

"Sure," Adrian replied. "Whatever you're having." The melancholia of the season had begun to make him moody, especially when he was alone in his home. The log house he had built contained too many rooms for a single man.

He accepted the glass of straight bourbon Jarrett offered and absently pushed the ice cube around in the glass with his fingertip while he waited for his brother to speak. When he didn't, Adrian looked up. "You said you wanted to talk business. What's on your mind?"

Jarrett dropped into an overstuffed leather chair that matched the one Adrian sat in. "It's about a man who came to me a few days ago for a crop loan. I had to turn him down."

"You do that all the time, don't you?" Adrian asked. "Bankers are in the business for profit. Farmers are having a tough time of it, so it's only natural some won't make it."

"I know," Jarrett said, "but this situation is different." He described the man, the depleted condition of his land, his past credit history. "Actually he has very little history of borrowing. I asked him about it. He made no bones about having an aversion to loans. He's a proud man, suspicious of bankers and lawyers and probably coal operators."

"Smart man," Adrian murmured. "You and I are trustworthy, but I'm not sure about anyone else." The sparkle in his eyes reflected his teasing jest.

"I'm serious," Jarrett replied. "He's a man of the soil, and he's gotten out of step with the modern world. He's trapped now in a bind of his own making. I suspect he's skimped on fertilizer and not rotated his crops like he should have, maybe because of financial problems. I'm not sure why or how long he's been negligent, but now he's paying the price."

Adrian shrugged and took another sip of his drink. "Smooth whiskey," he said. "Where did you get it?"

Jarrett named the brand. "I bought it in Mannington," he said, referring to a town in the county to the south where liquor could be purchased legally.

"Would you sell me a bottle?" Adrian asked. "My supply is low and I can't get away for a few weeks."

Jarrett laughed. "Want to see me arrested for bootlegging? Dry counties like Hopkins and Muhlenberg are like the churches that have tobacco patches in their backyards but insist their members not smoke. We grow and sell all the raw materials, but the good citizens of the county insist we should abstain from the vice." He motioned toward the wet bar. "Take a bottle when you go and pick up the tab the next time we eat out."

"Which brings us back to the tobacco farmer in need of cash," Adrian said. "How do I fit into your farmer's plight?"

Jarrett grinned. "He still owns the coal beneath his property."

Adrian straightened in his chair. "You're kidding. I thought all the remaining leases were bought up decades ago."

Jarrett chuckled. "Well, this family has been in the area for decades, centuries, come to think of it. The rights to the coal have been passed down from father to son for generations. Now Finis Hardesty owns what's left. He's hung on to his coal the same way he's hung on to his land, free and clear. Damn, the man is sitting on a bucket of money and doesn't seem to know it, or just chooses to ignore it."

"How many acres does he have?" Adrian asked.

"Five hundred or more," Jarrett replied. "He bought out his two brothers several years ago. We talked about so many things I can't remember just what he said, but this next part will surprise you." He paused, grinning at Adrian.

Adrian rose from his chair and set his empty glass on the wet bar. He reached for his suede jacket. "Either tell me now, or let's forget it. I've got a heavy schedule tomorrow."

"It's next door to your Dickens operation."

Adrian paused, one arm in the jacket. "Now you are kidding."

Jarrett joined Adrian near the door. "I thought you might want to visit him. But be forewarned. He hates the surface mining going on all around him. He thinks coal companies are ruining the county. But he's a beaten man. I think he's ready to sell. Treat him fairly and you might not only end up with land to add to your Dickens site, you might bail out the owner at the same time." He handed Adrian his business card with the man's name and address on the back.

"Thanks," Adrian said, accepting the card. "Why didn't you talk to Dad about this? Why me?"

"You have more tact than Dad," Jarrett said. "If I were you, I'd call on Finis Hardesty in person. He'd probably hang up if you phoned him. In person, you can turn on the charm." Jarrett squinted. "The man is in his early sixties, I'd guess, so if he has a family, they're surely grown and left home by now. Maybe that's one reason for his plight. No cheap labor. Let me know how it works out. This fellow needs you. You may be his last resort."

EARLY SATURDAY MORNING Adrian dressed in rust-colored corduroy jeans and an ivory flannel shirt, grabbed the navy blue flight jacket left from his brief stint in Germany with the air force and headed out the door.

Might as well get it taken care of before the man gets an offer from some other operator, he thought. *If the land is destined to be stripped, White Glove can do it better than any of the others.*

Often because the timber standing on the land was not worth harvesting, it was bulldozed away, exposing the soil to erosion until giant cranes peeled away the overburden of earth, exposing the coal. He felt that nothing was as grotesque as the mountains of overburden strip-mining created, and he knew that even with the reclamation required by federal and state laws, the land would never look the same.

That was one of the reasons he had decided to leave the business completely, selling his shares back to the family corporation, or even to an outsider if necessary. He had discussed his plans with his father, who had extracted a promise from him to stay at least one more year. But that promised year didn't preclude him from shopping for the right place to build another log house and to start his own business.

He smiled as he sailed out the door. His family had teasingly nicknamed him Catfish Coleman. Perhaps that was a better name than Mule, he thought. Obstinate mules and curious catfish, the two interests that would shape his future, maybe they represented facets of his personality, he mused. His sister-in-law Carol had once said as much, and she was a smart woman. Carol had also said his brothers Gavin and Nate could easily take over his responsibilities at White Glove. Doubtless she was right. Adrian grinned. It was nice not being needed sometimes.

Adrian double-checked the address of his destination as he drove through Greenville. He resisted the urge to stop for breakfast at the restaurant where he had last seen Callie. Business before pleasure, he thought, smiling as a vision of Callie materialized. He knew little about her, but if he were given the chance, that would certainly change. The next time he ran into her, he was not going to let her escape.

About halfway between Greenville and the small town of Drakesboro, Adrian began applying the brake and trying to read the names on the mailboxes. He drove past the entrance to the Dickens mine. In the distance he saw the spire of a church. Adrian returned his attention to the mailboxes. He'd thought he knew the area thoroughly, but apparently he'd overlooked a parcel of land right under his nose.

The area had been named Rainbow Hills by some early settlers. The land's beauty was one more reason Adrian had thought the hills of overburden from the Dickens mine looked progressively more grotesque as the land was reshaped to expose the six-foot-thick platter of number-nine coal. The newest mine in the White Glove portfolio, the Dickens mine had also become one of their most profitable ventures, primarily because the coal was just sixty feet beneath the surface.

He spotted a gray metal mailbox standing askew on a weathered post. "H-A-R-D... This must be it," he murmured.

He turned into the driveway, scanning the house as he rolled to a stop near the front porch. The large, two-story frame dwelling was in need of a fresh coat of paint.

Climbing from his truck, he made his way up to the porch, carefully missing the loose board on the second step. He rang the doorbell and waited. When no one responded, he rang again, then turned around to survey the fields. Perhaps he should have phoned after all. The man had probably taken his wife to the city for shopping. The only vehicle around was an old dilapidated Chevy truck he had spotted as he drove into the yard.

Adrian rang the bell once more, leaning on the button, irritated that he had wasted most of the morning. He'd count to ten, and if no one answered, he'd walk the property to get an idea of what kind of offer to make. Not knowing the acreage made giving a realistic quote impossible. *Damn,* he thought, kicking at the head of a nail that had worked its way out of a board.

THE DOORBELL REVERBERATED through the quiet house a second time. Callie had begun sorting the letters Aunt Minnie had given her into chronological order before starting to read them.

With the children and her parents gone to a tobacco auction in Russellville, she was relishing her privacy and resented the interruption.

The bell rang again. *How rude to lean on a person's doorbell. Can't they take the hint and just leave?*

"Oh, pooh," she murmured. "Might as well get rid of them as quick as I can." She eased up from the floor, shoving the purple plaid tails of her flannel shirt back into her jeans as she stepped over the piles of letters. Still surprised at the number of letters her aunt had kept secret from Abbie Grasten, she was now eager to get started on the project.

She took a few steps, rubbing her thighs to aid the circulation. One foot tingled, and she stomped on it as she hurried down the stairs.

Through the lace curtains of the window, she saw the blurred image of a man, his back turned to her. *Probably looking for work,* she thought. Three unemployed men had knocked on the Hardesty door earlier in the week, willing to do whatever labor needed done. Her father had turned them all away.

She eased the door open, leaving the screen latched. The man was quite tall, his shoulders broad beneath a navy jacket that came just below his waist. His hips were trim, yet in proportion to his height, which was well over six feet. His black hair reminded her of Adrian's. The man had obviously not heard her open the door. His irritation was evident in the way he jammed both fists into the pockets of his jacket. He kicked at something on the porch with the toe of his work boot.

"Sorry, mister, we're not hiring," she said. "Things are tight right now. Maybe if you came back when we're working the tobacco beds or setting out the transplants, my daddy might have something. Won't pay much, though."

The man turned around. "Oh, God," Callie gasped. Of all the people who could have knocked on her parents' door, the teamster from Hopkins County had to be the least likely. Her heart thudded against her ribs.

His shocked expression equaled hers as he stepped closer to the screen. "Callie?"

"Wh-what are you doing here?" she asked.

He frowned. "I could ask the same of you." He removed his hands from his jacket. He held a white business card. "I came to talk to a Mr. Finis Hardesty. Maybe I have the wrong address."

"That's my father," she replied, her voice weak and breathless as she fought to regain her composure.

His eyes narrowed. "Then your name is Callie Hardesty?"

She shook her head. "Yes . . . no . . . I mean not now."

"You're married?" His scowl deepened.

She stiffened. "What difference does it make?"

"A hell of a lot of difference," he insisted, his face flushing. "Now just what is your name? Do you know how long I've been trying to find out your last name?"

"It's Huff. H-U-F-F. I'd prefer Hardesty, but for the sake of the children, I've decided to keep Huff . . . for now."

"Children?" His perplexed expression deepened. "You have children?"

She raised her brows. "And what's so unbelievable about a woman having children?"

He scratched his temple, then shrugged. "Nothing, I guess. How many?"

"Two. An eleven-year-old son named Robbie and a daughter, Linda. Linda is nine."

"Good Lord," he said, taking a deep breath. "I never would have guessed it."

Callie tried to suppress a smile.

"Callie, you're the last person I expected to see when I came here. Now let's get this straight. Your name is Callie Huff. You have two children. Let me guess. You're divorced. Right?"

She frowned. "You don't know that."

"A widow wouldn't be thinking about reclaiming her maiden name." His hazel eyes glinted as he broke into a smile. "You must have been a child bride."

"Almost," she admitted, glancing away from his steady gaze. "Now that you know so much about me, why don't you introduce yourself. Adrian who?"

"Coleman," he replied. "Adrian Coleman. I'm thirty-four years old, and I've never been married."

"Not even once?" she asked, then wished she hadn't.

"Not once," he replied, grinning boyishly. "What else do you want to know?"

Her smile broadened. "I already know you raise mules and compete in pulling contests...and someday you want to grow catfish, although why in the world you'd want to do that is beyond me. They stink, don't they? Imagine all that fishy smell. What would you do with them?"

"I'd sell them, of course. At least I'd sell what I didn't eat myself." He grinned. "It would be a business."

She laughed. "I think we're back where we were when we met the first time. Now please tell me why you're here."

"How about unlocking the screen and inviting me in first?" he suggested.

She unlatched the hook from the eyelet screwed into the jamb. "How about a cup of coffee? I've been working upstairs and could use a break myself."

He followed her through the living room, which was filled with slightly worn and very comfortable-looking furniture, into a sparkling white kitchen. The woodwork was painted a lime-green enamel. She followed his gaze around the traditional kitchen until it fixed on the coal cookstove that had served several generations of Hardesty women.

"Momma prefers it," she explained. "Frankly, I'd rather use an electric range." She shrugged. "I've cooked on wood and coal stoves, and thanks, but no thanks to that life-style.... Say, what do you use in your coffee?"

"A little sugar," he said, sliding into a chair across from her at the table near a bay window.

Callie tried to ignore him, but each movement he made drew her attention. She gave up the charade and set her cup down. "Why did you want to see my father? Do you know each other?"

"No, but my brother gave me his name," Adrian said.

"Your brother?"

"Yes, Jarrett said ..."

She stiffened in her chair and gripped the edge of the table. "Jarrett who?"

"Jarrett Coleman, of course. You met him at the restaurant in Greenville. He's a lending officer at Hopkins National Bank and Trust."

"Coleman." Her eyes narrowed.

"Yes, the White Glove Mining Company is interested in ..."

She shot from her chair. "You're one of *those* Colemans?"

He stood up. "What's wrong with being a Coleman? I've always been rather proud of my family."

"I'll just bet you have," she replied. "Hauling the county away in your silly white trucks. It makes a mockery of the land. It's all in the name of progress, I suppose you're going to tell me, but in the process you Colemans get richer!"

"Well, yes, but..." He ran his fingers through his hair. "Damn it, why am I defending my family's reputation to you? My business is with your father." He came around the table. "Why are you here? Do you live here?"

She stiffened, her fists on her hips. "It's none of your business, but I'm going to school."

He laughed. "There's no college around here."

Her jaw tightened. "What school did you graduate from?"

"Murray State."

Her confidence wilted.

"And you?" he asked. "Are you just home for the weekend? Where are you enrolled? What major?"

"My major is survival, and I'm attending...the Second Chance program in Greenville." She studied her shoe. "I'm trying to get my G.E.D."

"From high school?" His hands grasped her shoulders, pulling her closer.

"Some of us never had the chance to finish what others take for granted," she said, trying to pull free.

"Why didn't you graduate from high school?" he asked, tucking an index finger beneath her chin and tipping her face upward.

She refused to look at him.

"You got pregnant." The softness and warmth of his voice brought her gaze back to his.

She shifted uncomfortably, and his hands tightened.

"It's what you're doing now that counts, Callie, not a mistake made years ago."

She shook her head. "You don't understand. Those years near Harlan...they were a nightmare—except for my kids, of course. My husband wasn't...he was frustrated, too. Our marriage was a shotgun wedding, and we were too young and he wasn't...we were both trapped.... I had very little to be happy about...but...but..."

"What's important is that you're back in school...and that I've found you again." He smiled. "That's the most important part of all this. I've found you again." His hands slid from her shoulders to cup her head, his thumbs massaging her ear lobes.

Her fingers touched the front of his shirt. "Why is that so important?" she whispered.

"Because now I can do what I've been wanting to do since I saw you walking down the steps of those bleachers in Morehead."

"And what's that?"

"Kiss you." His head dipped as his lips brushed lightly against hers. Then he pulled away slightly and gazed down at her wide brown eyes. "Oh, Callie." His arms wrapped around her, bringing her against his body as his mouth sought hers again.

Lost in his embrace, Callie gave herself to him, the years of abstinence forgotten as his lips caressed hers. He offered her a potent drink after an eternal drought, and she wanted to quench her thirst. The kiss held no trace of innocence.

A shudder or reality raced through her, and she slowly pulled away. Passion was something she had learned to live without. For her, security had become a tiny lifeline to a more stable future, and she had learned the painful truth that security had to come from within, not from the promises of some man who wanted her.

"I'm sorry," he said, releasing her. "We've just met again, and here I am making a pass at you. I'm sorry, Callie."

She smoothed her hair and brushed at her shirt. "It's okay. I didn't exactly refuse, now did I?" She smiled. "You're a rather overpowering man, Adrian. I accept your apology."

His eyes sparkled. "Thank you, ma'am. Say, do you go to church?" he asked.

She nodded. "At Ebenezer's down the road. Why?"

"Tell your family I'd like them to be my guests tomorrow after the service. We'll go to Catfish Gap." He grinned. "I know your daddy likes catfish."

"How do you know that?" she asked.

"I spotted you there with your family. I called to you, but you didn't hear me and got away before I could get to you. It was the night before we met in the restaurant." He frowned. "How many are there in your family? There was a sizable group that night. I'll see about borrowing my brother Nate's van. It can hold a dozen or so. Is that big enough?"

"If we keep it to me, my children, my parents and maybe my aunt and uncle."

"The formidable Aunt Min?"

She nodded. "They're driving down from Lexington, and we're all going to church together. Want to join us?"

"Not this time. How many would that be for dinner?"

"Seven. Is that too many?"

"Of course not," he replied. "After all, I'm one of those rich Colemans, am I not?"

"That might make a difference," she warned.

"Give your daddy my card," Adrian said. "Tell him this is business, but is that any cause to decline a free catfish dinner?"

She squinted up at him. "What kind of business? Do you want to buy the place and dig it up like you're doing at the Dickenses'?"

"Let's keep the business until tomorrow afternoon, Callie. Pleasure before business... at least on Sunday. Fair enough?" He brushed her cheek lightly with the side of his thumb.

The touch drew her closer. "Okay," she murmured.

He kissed her lightly. "I'd like to stay but..."

"This being Saturday, business probably comes first."

"Yeah, something like that."

"I have work to do, too," she said. "But I'm glad you stopped by."

Adrian reached for his jacket. "Not half as glad as I am." His brow furrowed. "Two children?"

She hesitated. "Yes, two children. Is there something wrong with having two children?"

"No, it's fine. It just takes some getting used to. I'll have to modify my plans a little."

"What plans?" she asked. "For dinner tomorrow?"

He shook his head. "No, Callie, for our future."

CHAPTER SIX

CALLIE WATCHED HIM GO, resisting an urge to race down the porch steps after him. Adrian Coleman had swept through her morning like a tornado, leaving her carefully planned life in a shambles.

How could she justify his gallant invitation to Sunday dinner to her family? Her parents would be prejudiced. Aunt Min had met him and seemed to distrust him. And how could she explain Adrian to her children?

She made her way back up the stairs to her aunt's letters. Kneeling on the bare oak floor, she started sorting them again—into years, then months, but her thoughts clung to the embrace in the kitchen, keeping the heat of his kiss vividly alive. She paused from her work, and her fingers followed the path of his lips on hers.

She put the stacks of letters in chronological order on her dresser. *I'll read them later,* she thought. *If I try to do it now, I won't remember a single word.* Pulling an old wooden rocker over to the window, she sat down to meditate his parting words. *Our future.* They were still strangers, yet he had linked their futures. She sighed. Confident though he might be, he was wrong—arrogant in his assumptions and ignorant of her goals.

She would be attending college once she qualified for financial aid. She planned to find an apartment close to campus so transportation would be no problem. The Chevy truck, which was the same one Bobby Joe had bought twelve years earlier, was on its last leg. Each time she turned the key in the ignition she was surprised it started.

And Adrian was obviously a dreamer. This nonsense about raising catfish was pure fantasy. He was a partner in one of the largest coal companies in the state. He wasn't going to just walk away from such a lucrative career.

"Momma, what's the matter?"

Callie started, hearing the unexpected voice, and turned.

Linda stood by the arm of the rocker, her blue eyes reflecting her concern. "We just got back from the auction. It was great, and we ate at this place where you can pick your own food . . . and take as much as you want." She giggled. "Robbie ate a whole plate of shrimp, just shrimp, and the waitress didn't even get mad. Can you imagine?"

Callie smiled. "That's great, honey."

"I called you three times. You never answered. Are you okay?"

"I'm fine."

"Can I sit on your lap?" Linda asked.

"Of course." Callie patted her blue jeans.

Linda smiled and crawled onto Callie's lap, her thin legs dangling down. "I'm getting too old to sit like this, eh?" Her soft voice sounded muffled against Callie's breast.

Callie hugged her daughter for a few seconds. "Maybe when your legs start dragging on the rockers, sweetheart, but there's always room for a hug or two." She nuzzled her daughter's soft curly hair, marveling at its color. Not quite a match for Bobby Joe's, too light to be like Abbie's auburn curls, not as red as Aunt Min's, perhaps it was more like a new-burnished copper penny shining through a layer of voile—muted but with a promise of brilliance. "I hope you're happy about moving here. Robbie, too."

"I like it anywhere!" Linda said. "Robbie hated it until he met another boy with the same last name as us. His name is Huff, too, can you imagine?"

Callie frowned. One of her concerns about moving back had been the possibility of running into the Huff family, but her mother had assured her Robert and Emaline Huff had moved away the summer after Linda's birth. "What's the boy's name?" she asked.

"Everyone calls him G.W. His real name is Gideon, and he hates it!"

"Where does G.W. live?" Callie asked.

Linda shrugged. "I don't know."

Could Bobby Joe have possibly moved back to Drakesboro? Callie wondered. Surely not, but he did have a brother and sister who had been a few years ahead of them in school. "Do you know his parents' names?"

Linda shook her head. "Now tell me," she said, taking a long strand of Callie's hair and curling it around her slender index finger. "Why didn't you hear me call for you?"

Callie pushed the rocker. "I had a gentleman caller while you were gone, and I was thinking about him."

"Was he the man in the white truck?" Linda asked. "We saw him turn onto the road as we came home, but he went the opposite way. Grandpa didn't have any idea who he was. What did he want?"

"To take us all to dinner tomorrow after church."

Linda straightened and stared wide-eyed at Callie. "But why? Do you know him? Why did he come to see you?"

Callie smiled. "Actually he came to see your grandpa, but he was looking for me, too."

"Was he happy when he found you?"

"I think so," Callie replied. "But I don't think he knew quite what to make of it all."

"Do you?"

Callie cocked her head to one side. "No."

ADRIAN PARKED the copper-colored van borrowed from his brother Nate several yards from the Hardesty front porch, fighting the doubts that had plagued him since extending his impulsive invitation the previous day. He had been grasping for straws to see Callie again.

The misgivings were swept away when he heard the screen door bang and spotted Callie Huff coming down the steps. He slammed the van door and walked to meet her, his hands deep in his jacket pockets.

"Good afternoon," she said, her voice soft with a drawl.

He grinned. "Did the other members of the family accept my invitation, or is it just you and me?"

"My aunt and uncle declined, but the others agreed, mostly out of curiosity," Callie said. "Aunt Min is inside. She's not feeling so good, but she wants to meet you again anyway."

"I was hoping she had forgotten our previous meeting," he admitted.

"Not at all. She found you quite memorable."

He wanted to take Callie's hand, but decided to let her make the first overture.

She turned. "Come inside and I'll make the introductions."

He followed her, admiring her soft gray woolen shirtwaist dress that swung with her movements. The black patent-leather pumps she wore boosted her height a few inches, but she was still a head shorter than he.

"Callie, I—" He stopped. For the life of him, he couldn't think of a single word that made sense. She stopped, too, and glanced up at him, shading her eyes from the bright winter sun overhead.

"Nothing. Let's get this over with. Frankly, I never expected to meet your family this way. I still can't believe we've met again, much less that we're going to dinner."

"It's hardly a date," she said.

"That can come later."

"You don't know me."

"That, too, can come later," he promised.

"I have plans."

"So have I."

"Mine are firm." She stared at the neckline of his rust-colored knit pullover and the button-down oxford-cloth collar showing inside his jacket.

"Mine are flexible," he countered. "But for now, let's go to dinner. First things first."

His boyish grin made her heart thud against her ribs. She sensed his good-natured smile hid a persistent and determined nature. She shifted from one foot to the other. Money, wealth—that was what made them different. He could afford to dream because he had solid financial security. His dreams were wishful fantasies to give him a diversion; in reality he collected more income in a month than she could expect in a year...when she finally got a good-paying job.

How could a person like Adrian ever understand her driving need for assurance that the rent would be paid and that there would be food on the table?

"Come inside and I'll introduce you," she said again. "Daddy is very curious about you." She hurried up the steps, leaving him to follow her into the house.

After introducing her parents, her children and her uncle, she turned to Aunt Minnie. "You two remember each other?"

Adrian smiled and extended his hand to the older woman, who remained seated. She patted the sofa cushion beside her, and he sat down, as if he had all the time in the world to devote to her.

Chalk one up for gentlemanly manners, Callie thought, as she watched Adrian charm her aunt.

After chatting with Minnie for a few minutes, Adrian took his leave of her and went out to the truck with Callie and the rest of her family.

Callie encouraged her father to sit in the front of the van with Adrian. She sat next to Robbie in the rear. When they arrived at the restaurant, she maneuvered a seat between Linda and Robbie, but to her chagrin, found herself seated directly across from Adrian. Each time she glanced up, he would catch her eye. Intent on avoiding this direct eye contact, Callie concentrated on her plate and ate more catfish than she had ever consumed before. Each bite reminded her of him.

Adrian was discussing the generalities of surface mining with her parents, giving them the same undivided attention he had given Aunt Minnie. She waited to see how he would react to the children, but he was able to discuss sports and fishing with Robbie, and he told Linda about his numerous nieces. Callie searched for his faults and, other than ignoring her except for an occasional glance, she could find none.

As they approached the Hardesty mailbox on the return trip, Adrian turned to Finis. "If you're not busy, sir,

I'd like to take you over to the Dickens site and show you around.''

"Sounds interesting," Finis replied. "Everyone want to go?" he asked, tossing the words over his shoulder.

"I promised G.W. we'd go trapping along Rainbow Creek," Robbie said.

"And I have to read a book for school tomorrow," Linda said, "but I could skip it. Maybe the teacher won't call me."

"In that case, you'd better get busy and start reading," Callie replied. "I'd like to see it, but I need to change my shoes. These pumps aren't made for walking."

"Min and I are going to put my sampler quilt top on the frame," Ellen said, as they traipsed single file into the house.

"I'll wait here," Adrian said, jamming his fists into his pockets again, and waited just inside the door.

Several minutes later, Finis reappeared wearing his comfortable bib overalls and a denim jacket. Callie joined them in jeans and well-worn canvas shoes, tugging the waistband of a red sweatshirt down over her slender hips. Her oval locket hung from her throat.

Adrian listened to her father, but he had eyes only for Callie. He suspected Callie's opinions carried more influence with her father than either would admit. Perhaps, if they had the opportunity to go down into the pit and stand on the exposed seam and if he explained in detail what was involved in extracting the coal, they would be willing to listen to his proposal.

"There's room for three in the front," Adrian said casually, as they approached the van again.

On the short drive to the site, Adrian glanced toward the older man who was staring ahead, his expression unreadable. "Have either of you ever been to a surface-mining operation before?" he asked. They both shook their heads.

They stopped at a padlocked gate, near a sign warning of blasting and trespassing. Adrian unlocked the gate and drove through.

"Need it closed?" Finis asked, opening the door and stepping onto the ground.

"Just latch it, and thanks," Adrian replied.

They drove past mountains of rock and debris, along a winding dirt road, and past a series of rounded cone-shaped piles of dirt. "That's the topsoil," Adrian explained. "We've been trying to save it separately for the reclamation. Time will tell if it's worth the extra effort." When neither of them commented, he continued. "We have ten years to complete the project. It takes from three to five years to get out the coal and five more to let the replanted vegetation get a good start. The government inspects us constantly."

"It's hideous," Callie said.

"I'm afraid so... at this stage," Adrian admitted.

"Will it ever look as pretty as it did before?"

Adrian took a deep breath and exhaled. "Not in ten years. The trees take a long time to grow. But we've stopped the erosion."

"A few kudzu vines could do that much," Callie murmured.

Adrian chuckled. "You're probably right, but I'd prefer grasses and shrubs for now and trees later. Actually, we're reclaiming the land continually. After we've removed the coal, we gradually fill the hole and dig on a new spot. It's not as though the entire site is dug up at once. That way the early reclamation is years ahead of the last site."

"Does a farmer ever get his land back?" Callie asked.

"Not really," Adrian replied. "Some have tried, but the soil isn't what it was when it was farmed. Maybe some day. Some people want us to level their hills so they can farm more land, but the government insists we return the hills to hills and the gullies to gullies, though I wouldn't want you to think your land would ever be back the way it was. We'll talk about that later . . . this evening if you have time."

Finis nodded. "Farming has been in my blood for generations, but times change. I'll listen to what you have to say. Just don't you jump to any quick conclusions. Me and Ellen will have to chew this one over a bit."

Adrian nodded as the van bounced over some ruts in the road. He drove around a curve and past a row of empty yellow ore-transport vehicles.

"Big," Finis said.

"They carry 120 tons of coal at a time," Adrian explained. "The coal goes to the tipples where it's washed and sorted and graded. Most of this is number nine. The tipples are over there." He pointed to the south. "You can't see them from here. The trucks haul most of it to Paradise."

"My uncle used to live near where Paradise used to be," Finis said. "That was before the power plant went in, you see. It still pains him to talk about what happened to his land."

"I know," Adrian said, "but the nation needs electricity, and we're sitting on coal. Wherever we dig, we find it. Maybe the best solution is to move the people to fresh land and dig it up once and for all. I don't know what's right anymore."

His knuckles whitened as his grip on the steering wheel tightened. "The coal is here, and the landowners might as well share in the profits. I could never cheat the people out of what's rightfully theirs. Coal operators don't have a good reputation, but when my grandfather had a chance to expand the company by buying out a smaller operator, he vowed he would run a different kind of company. He always resented being lumped with the others.'' Adrian stared thoughtfully at the equipment.

"Eventually, the coal will be removed, one way or another," he continued. "White Glove's management—that's us, the Coleman family—we care about the land and the people here. We reclaim the land. It's our policy. We pay union wages. That's our policy, too. I couldn't be part of the company if it didn't operate fairly. I know there are operators who bend the rules, but not White Glove."

"Bobby Joe worked for a dog-hole operator north of Harlan," Callie murmured.

"Bobby Joe?" Adrian asked.

"He's...he's my children's father. He made three dollars an hour for risking his life underground."

Adrian frowned at her bowed head. "Surface mining is much safer, but it has its hazards. I was the governmental safety and health representative for a while. I know."

"Must've been a terrible life, working in a mine," Callie said, thinking out loud. "No wonder Bobby Joe ran off."

"Ran off?" Adrian asked. "Your husband just abandoned you?"

Finis patted Callie's hand. "Enough about that boy. Most of my sons have worked in the mines. James and Everett worked at Rainbow Number Two until it closed down. Leander and Farley were at Number One. Now they all have other jobs. Thank the Lord those mines closed down. It was the best thing that ever happened, for my boys' sake. I worked underground for six months for Evergreen Coal when I first got married to Callie's ma. I hated each and every day I had to ride that car into the ground."

"I don't think I could last that long," Callie said.

"I may not be rich," Finis replied, "but when I plow the fields and look up into the sky and see the sun, I thank the Lord because I have things money can't buy— freedom, fresh air and sunlight."

"So all your sons are out of the business now?" Adrian asked.

"I got another boy, but he's always been puny. Maybe Riley's the lucky one. He lives out west in New Mexico. He's trying to make a name for himself in pottery. Can you imagine?"

"Is Callie your only daughter?"

"Callie here is my baby, and my only little girl, though I reckon she's not a little girl anymore."

"That's enough, Daddy," Callie said. "I'm sure Adrian doesn't want to hear any more about our family."

"Let's go into the pit," Adrian said.

They drove down an incline and onto a flat surface, where Adrian parked the van. "Why don't we get out and walk around?"

"Is it safe?" Callie asked, as he helped her down.

He chuckled. "You're standing on a platter of coal that's probably fifteen miles in diameter and from six to nine feet thick. Yes, it's safe."

"Purely amazing," Finis said after walking the distance of the pit and picking up several chunks of shiny black coal.

Adrian explained the operation, pointing out the giant drag lines whose buckets loomed overhead waiting to remove the overburden after the next series of blasts, and the huge backhoes used to break up the seam of coal and load it onto the transports.

"Can we see one of those big haulers up close?" Finis asked.

"Sure. Get back in and we'll drive there."

At the parking area, Finis examined the vehicles from one end to the other.

"Where does the driver sit?" Callie asked. Instead of answering her question, Adrian grabbed her around the waist and lifted her to the second step of a metal ladder leading up the front of the transport.

"Climb up and see for yourself," he said. "Open the door and go inside."

She followed his directions and worked her way along the platform to the door of the cab. Soon she was sitting in the seat, her hands on the controls, pretending to work the levers. "Where's the brake?" she asked. She leaned over, searching for the petal she was sure was beneath her. The door opened and Adrian joined her. Suddenly the compartment felt very small indeed.

CHAPTER SEVEN

CALLIE JERKED UPRIGHT, startled by his closeness. She heard a tinkling sound as something hit the metal floor. "Oh, no," she exclaimed, clasping her breast. "I've broken the chain on my locket! Where did it go?"

"Stay put," Adrian said, laying a hand on her thigh. "I'll find it." She pulled her legs up onto the seat while he crawled beneath her in search of the locket. Finally he stood up again.

"Did you find it?" she asked, unable to stop the tears forming.

He shook his head. "It must have bounced and fallen through the heater vent. I think I can see it but I'm not sure. Callie, I'm sorry. I can't get to it without the proper tools. I promise I'll get here early tomorrow, and before anyone starts up this hauler, I'll get your locket out. I promise."

"It's an omen," she whispered. "Aunt Min always said we should never lose our lockets. You don't understand. I was eight years old when she gave me that locket. How could I have been so careless?" She blinked several times, and a tear trickled down her cheek.

He wiped it away. "Don't cry, honey. I'll get it back to you." He clasped her face between his palms, using his thumbs to wipe the moisture from her cheeks. "You're being sentimental, and I do understand. I'll get your locket. Everything will be fine. You'll see." He gazed at her shimmering eyes. "You're a lovely woman." He drew her closer.

His features blurred as his mouth claimed hers. She sought his comfort, responding to the fire ignited by his kiss. Her hands slid up his arms, feeling his heavily muscled biceps through his clothing. She caught the tip of his tongue with hers, dancing with it until his plunged into her mouth, sending shards of desire through her.

His ragged breathing matched hers as he pulled her closer, her head resting beneath his chin. He stroked her torso, his hand exploring her body through her fleecy sweatshirt. One hand slid beneath the edge and touched the soft material of a silky undergarment. Holding her in his arms, he gazed out the window of the cab, trying to still his heart. Never had he been touched so deeply by a woman. As sure as the sun would rise the next day, he knew that someday they would find happiness together.

Crazy, he thought. *Can I love a stranger?* Yet in his heart he knew she had never been a stranger.

A movement caught his eye, and he glanced down toward the ground. Finis Hardesty was standing several paces from the transport, staring up at them.

"Callie, honey, your dad is waiting," he whispered.

She jerked from his arms, her face flushed. "Did he see us?" she asked, wiping her eyes.

"Probably."

Embarrassed, she slid off the seat opposite from where Adrian stood and into the narrow space between the seat and the cab wall and dropped to her knees.

"What are you doing now?" he asked.

"I want to see where it is," she said, pressing her face against the slats of the vent by the floor and peering into the darkness of the compartment. Her hair fell forward. Adrian said something above her, and she turned to hear him. When she turned again, she couldn't move. Blindly, she tugged at her hair. "Adrian, help!"

"What the devil?"

"My hair," she cried. "It's caught on something. I can't move my head. Help me."

He leaned across the seat and balanced on his stomach, his long legs sticking out the door, his buttocks in the air and his broad shoulders squeezed between the seat and the wall.

Footsteps sounded on the metal ladder. Upside down, Adrian looked under the seat and out the doorway to find a pair of faded overalled legs firmly planted near the door.

"What in tarnation is going on here?" Finis asked.

Adrian felt the man grab one of his boots. "Hold on to my feet, sir. Callie's hair is caught, and I'm trying to free it." He searched with his fingers, attempting to find where her hair had snagged, but trying to see through the mass of black hair lying on the floor was impossible, and every time Callie shifted her position, more hair fell through the cracks in the floor.

"Damn it, Callie, hold still. You're making it worse." He worked feverishly for several minutes, knowing he was hurting her even while he tried to free her.

He got to his feet and reached into his pants pocket. "I'm sorry, folks, but the only way to get her free is to cut it."

"No!" She groaned. "Please don't cut my hair. You can't." She tried to pull away.

Adrian leaned over the seat again. He gathered up a portion, coiled it around his fist and then handed it to her. "Can you hold this out of the way?" He began to slice at her hair.

"Please don't cut any more than you have to," she pleaded.

"I won't." But as he worked to free her, more and more of her luxurious dark hair fell to the floor.

"You're free," he said at last, panting as he regained his footing, and carefully pulled her from beneath the seat. As soon as she was standing under her own power, he turned her around. "Oh, God, Callie, I'm so sorry!"

"Oh, baby," her father said, "your hair is all hacked up."

Callie's hand went to her head. Adrian touched her shoulder, but she jerked away.

"I'm sorry," Adrian said. "I'll get you a haircut. A perm, too, if you want. Please, Callie, say something."

"Let's get down from this darn hauler," she said, swinging onto the ladder. "I have classes tomorrow, a field trip to...Murray State to meet with...I'll...maybe if I can braid it...or...or...I'll manage. Let's go home."

All three were now back on the ground. The two men looked at each other uncomfortably. His mouth tight with regret, Adrian led them back to the van.

As they drove into the Hardesty place and parked, he grabbed Callie's arm. "Callie, wait. Give me another chance. Mr. Hardesty, I'd like to come back tonight, about eight o'clock, and talk to you about your property. But first I know a woman who works out of her home. She's a genius with women's hair."

Finis opened the van door. "A woman sometimes thinks different about hair than a man does. My Callie's hair hain't been cut since she was four years old. She's taken great pride in it. Seems sometimes that it's the only thing Bobby Joe didn't take away from her." He patted Callie's hand. "But I reckon the damage is done now.

If'n you can make it pretty again and it's okay with Callie, I can wait on talking about my coal."

Finis climbed from the van. "I been just tinkering with the idea of selling. Don't you forget that. I might still decide to just hang on and grow one more year's harvest."

He slammed the door shut and, strolling around to Adrian's side, waited until Adrian rolled down the window before continuing. "A man's entitled to a mistake or two, I reckon," Finis drawled. "I'll give you a listen, but you'd better make it simple and no tricks. I have my opinions about coal operators."

Adrian grinned. "My brother advised me of that. I'll treat you fairly, sir. I can assure you."

"If'n you're not here by eight, I'm going to bed. It's been a trying day." Finis turned to Callie. "Do you still want to go with this man?"

Callie sighed deeply. "I'll be okay, Daddy."

Adrian spun the van around, and soon they were through the city of Greenville and headed toward the next county.

"Where are we going?" Callie asked, still fingering the empty space where once her hair had been.

Adrian glanced at her. "To my sister's home."

"She's a beauty operator?"

"Contrary to what you might assume, some of the Colemans have gone their own way. Emma was the first. She's not a rich lady of leisure. My father wanted to groom her to be the first woman executive in White Glove, but after getting her degree in business administration, she decided she wanted to be a cosmetologist, so she went back to school. She's a damned good one, too. She owned and managed three shops for a while, but sold them all. Now she's at home raising her family and running her business out of a converted family room. She's six years older than me. Gavin's the oldest. He's forty-two. Then there's Emma, then Nate, who's thirty-eight, then Jarrett, the family banker—he's thirty-six."

"No lawyers? I'm surprised that wasn't your assignment."

"That's not fair, when you don't even know us. I'm fifth in line and planning to be another stray, like Emma. There was one more of us, my little brother, LaMar. He died of bone cancer when he was twelve."

He paused. When Callie gave him a weak smile, he continued. "You'll like Emma. She's got Mom's down-home sense of humor." He glanced toward Callie again. "You'd never know she had money."

A sign near a crossroad read, Hair Care By Appointment Only. They turned onto the narrow asphalt road and traveled a quarter of a mile before turning into a driveway leading to a sprawling brick-and-stone house.

"Doesn't look like poverty row to me," Callie remarked.

"Don't be prejudiced."

"Who's prejudiced? It's beautiful. I'll bet it's even air-conditioned."

"Right. Have you lived in an air-conditioned home yourself?"

"Sure," Callie said, thinking of the cabin near Harlan in which she could see the forest through the cracks and where she had spent hours stuffing rags between the logs to replace the chinking that continually fell out.

She followed him to the entrance. A tall slender black-haired woman with wings of premature gray at her temples opened the door. Callie's skepticism eased when she saw the jeans the woman wore, but her chinchilla-gray cashmere sweater spoke of elegance. Her feet were bare, and they sank into the deep pile of the smoky-blue carpeting.

"Why, Adrian, what a nice surprise," the woman exclaimed, kissing him lightly on his cheek. "We haven't seen you in ages. Come on in. We were just beginning to decorate the tree. You can help." She turned to Callie. "And this is . . . ?"

"Emma Jordan, meet Callie Huff . . . a friend."

The two women shook hands.

"Come in, please," Emma said. "Coffee? Hot chocolate?" she asked, closing the door behind them. "Oh, Callie! What happened to your beautiful hair?"

"That's why we're here . . . and hot chocolate sounds great," Adrian said. "Okay with you, Callie?"

Callie nodded but didn't speak, her attention drawn past the flagstone entryway to the spacious living room decorated in shades of pale yellow and blues to complement the floor covering. A gray-haired man and four teenage children were engrossed in unraveling several strings of Christmas lights. A tree stood nearby, its tip brushing the ceiling. Adrian waved.

"Come help us, Uncle Adrian," one of the girls called. "We can't reach the top and you can."

"In a while," he called back. "First we have business with your mother."

"Come into the kitchen where we can talk," Emma suggested. She peered down at Callie, arching a brow as she smiled. "I called Jarrett yesterday. He told me about having breakfast with you. Could this be the A.B.C. woman?"

Adrian cleared his throat. "Might be," he admitted, "but that's not why we're here." He turned Callie around. "It's my fault. Can you fix it?"

Emma removed the rubber band from Callie's hair and fluffed it a few times. She walked around Callie, pursing her lips as she moved. "A shorter style will certainly be easier to care for."

Emma prepared the hot chocolate, then said, "Come with me. You can tell me what happened while I work."

In the other room Emma had Callie sit in a chair and evaluated her hair. Callie closed her eyes, taking in the sounds of the people in the other room, remembering the richness of the furnishings, the spaciousness of the entire house. She was definitely out of her element. The sudden loss of her hair still angered her. "How come you still work fixing hair when you're rich enough to have a fancy house like this?"

Adrian nudged her, but she was too angry to be silent. "If I had money, I'd never work again. I'd do what I wanted to."

Emma chuckled. "And what would you want to do?"

Callie squeezed her eyes as the scissors snipped across her back. She imagined the three feet of hair falling to the floor. "I'd become an apprentice in a shop that makes mountain dulcimers. I'd convince that useless kudzu vine that it would make beautiful wall hangings. I'd take voice lessons and learn to read music, and I'd have time to write songs."

She stiffened in the chair. "That's my daydreaming druthers. Instead, I'm going to school and plan to get a good-paying job somewhere far far away from Kentucky. A person can get smothered if he lives here too long. The trees, the hills…you can never get above them. You can't see the horizon. Sometimes I feel like I'm never going to be able to draw another breath."

Emma laid her hand on Callie's shoulder. "Each of us must find our own place to bloom, Callie. For me, I love working with hair. I did as a child. I fixed all my girl friends' hair when we were teenagers. I keep my shop here because I love my work. It's that simple. I don't have to do it. My husband is a lawyer and brings in good money. I work because I love it.''

Callie frowned. "Sorry," she mumbled. "I wasn't being very polite. Losing my hair makes me..." She sighed deeply. "It's water under the bridge now."

Emma patted her shoulder. "I think you'll be pleasantly surprised when you see the results." She touched the side of Callie's neck with her finger. "I'm going to bring it up to within a few inches of here. Now, while I work, tell me how this happened."

When Adrian explained how he had rescued Callie, the snipping of the shears stopped. Emma chuckled. "Any more rescues like that and you'll lose her for sure."

"He can't lose what he doesn't have," Callie mumbled, but her words were drowned beneath the rush of warm water as the chair tipped and Callie found herself in the midst of a shampoo and rinse. Gradually, some of the tension left her.

At last, when Emma was satisfied with her work, she turned the chair around. "What do you think?" she asked, pointing to Callie's reflection in the wide mirror on the wall.

Callie couldn't believe her own eyes. Her hair fell to her shoulders, forming a dark cloud around her face, and Emma had coaxed out a hint of a wave that Callie had long since forgotten she had. She shook her head, and a section of silky hair cascaded over one eye.

"You have very beautiful hair," Emma said. "It will be even prettier now that it's free to move."

"Sexy," Adrian murmured.

Sexy? Callie thought, running her fingers through the breezy cut and fluffing it.

Emma spun the chair around, and Callie found herself face-to-face with Adrian. His smile was casual but the sensuality in his hazel eyes was undeniable.

Callie glanced away. "I look ... older," she said.

"Women don't get older, dear, they mature," Emma said. "What do you think, Adrian?"

"I ... think ... she's ..." His dark complexion turned ruddy.

Emma laughed. "You? At a loss for words? That's a change." She showed Callie the techniques she had used with the brushes and the dryer, put them back into their boxes and laid them in Callie's lap. "You'll get the hang of it with a little practice."

"Oh, no," Callie said, putting the appliances back on the work counter. "I have no money ... I ... didn't bring my purse."

Adrian pulled his wallet from his hip pocket. "I'll pay for them."

Emma shook her head. "Put your money away, Adrian. I'm giving them to Callie."

They spent a half hour with the family—or Adrian did. Feeling shy and embarrassed over her rudeness to Emma, Callie stayed on the periphery, waiting patiently until Adrian had placed a star on the top of the tree. "I should get back," she said at last. "I have two kids to check, and, Adrian, don't you have a meeting with my father at eight?"

A mile away from Emma's house, Callie glanced at Adrian. "I misjudged your sister. She's very nice. Her family acts just like mine does when we're all together." She cleared her throat. "They don't act rich at all."

Adrian shrugged. "And what do rich people act like?"

"I dunno.... I guess I expected them to sit around with their knees together and tea cups balanced on their laps and their little fingers pointed up in the air, but they acted very ordinary, and ... well ... I liked them."

He grinned. "And I'm sure they liked you. They didn't know a thing about you, so they didn't have a chance to become prejudiced. They simply accepted you the way you were."

Callie sank into the corner of the van, mulling over his remarks. Things were moving too fast. Should she clear the air, make him understand that she had her own plans, that she wanted his friendship but nothing more? But had he offered her anything more? Perhaps she was reading too much into his actions.

A touch of hands, a brief kiss, a dinner with her family—all these could be innocent overtures of friendship, nothing more, unless he expected... There was absolutely no way she was getting involved with him, she vowed, and began to rehearse her speech as they drove.

When they reached the main highway, to Callie's surprise, Adrian turned north instead of east.

"I need to return my brother's van," he explained.

"Okay," Callie agreed.

Exchanging the van for Adrian's car only took a minute.

"Are we going home now?" Callie asked.

"One more stop," he replied. "It's on the way."

Several miles later, he made a left turn into a wooded drive.

She stiffened. "Who lives here?"

"I do."

Callie slid toward the door of the cab. "Listen, Adrian, you've got this all wrong. You've been nice to my family and taken us to dinner, but if you think I've forgiven you for what you've done to my hair, you're sadly mistaken and..."

He held up his hand. "I just wanted to let the dog out. He's been inside all day."

"I'll bet you don't even have a dog," she replied. "This is just an excuse to get me inside."

He killed the engine and draped his wrist over the steering wheel. "What makes you so sure I want to get you inside? Are you speaking from past experiences?"

"How dare you!"

"Then why make such a big issue of it?" he asked. "I never brought up the subject. You're the one who's apparently been thinking about it."

Frowning heavily, she stared out the windshield. Through the darkness, she could just make out the faint lines of a log house. "This is where you live?" she asked.

He opened the door and got out. In the distance, a deep bark could be heard.

"And you really have a dog?" she asked, feeling sheepish.

"His name is Klaus. He's a German shorthaired pointer."

She edged across the seat and out his door. "Why do you keep him inside? Dogs should be free to run and exercise." She slid to the ground before he could help her and closed the door, casting them in darkness again.

"I put him in his doghouse when I was repairing the back fence of his run this morning. I thought I was going to be late getting to your place and simply forgot to let him out again, so he's still in his house. Would you like to meet him?" He held out his hand.

"I'm sorry. I jumped to conclusions again," she murmured as his fingers wrapped around hers.

"Accepted." He led her to the house and, unlocking the front door, ushered her inside and right through the house and out the back door, flipping on a yard light as they exited.

When they arrived at the dog run, he reached over the fence and unlatched and opened the door to a doghouse that was almost as large as the tiny cabin she had once lived in. A mottled white-and-liver nose appeared, twitching and sniffing the air.

"Come, Klaus," Adrian coaxed, and the animal bounded into freedom. His head and neck were solid liver-red, his body the same mottled white-and-liver as his muzzle, except for the saddle of liver on his back and buttocks.

Callie laughed, and the dog turned to her. Curious, he sniffed the air. She extended her hand to the wire fence. Lean and conditioned, the dog trotted over. His stub of a tail began to wag when she scratched his head.

She laughed again. "He's as ugly as the blue heelers I saw out in Montana."

Adrian came to her side. "No one calls a man's dog ugly. It's like insulting a mother's child, only worse. I'll have you know, his daddy was a field champion and his momma a champion on the show bench."

Callie turned to him. "Oh, I'm sorry, I didn't mean he was really ugly—" she giggled "—just unusual." She scratched the dog's head again. "But he's friendly. Do you let him out of the run sometimes?"

"When I'm here. We hunted grouse last weekend."

"Why don't you let him out now?" she suggested.

"Klaus will be your friend for life, I'm sure. He loves to run at night, and I don't let him do it much. Just for you, he can have his freedom for a few minutes," he said, unlatching the gate.

Klaus raced out, disappearing into the woods in a flash. They followed his trail several yards into the trees. Thick timber and undergrowth shut out most of the light from the yard.

Callie stopped. "It's dark here."

"Scared?"

"I don't like to be alone when it's dark," she murmured, hugging herself.

"You're not alone," he said, his voice husky behind her as he touched her shoulders. He wrapped his arms around her, easing her against his chest.

She leaned back against him and felt her hair stir as he kissed the top of her head. For a moment, they stood motionless, surrounded by the night sounds of the forest. Then she touched the back of his hand where it rested on her arm, and he nuzzled the side of her neck. She tilted her head, waiting. When his lips touched her skin, a quiver of excitement raced through her.

She turned in his arms. "Adrian?" Her hands slid up his jacket to his chin, her fingers tracing the line to his jaw and up to the tip of his earlobe. Her heart pounded against her ribs as she tilted her head to see his face in the shadows. "Adrian, I don't understand all this. It's too sudden. I didn't want it...but...kiss me, just once...please."

His mouth brushed against hers, nibbling, caressing, until hers opened, encouraging him closer, closer.

"Oh, Adrian," she murmured, stretching to close the distance between their mouths again. His kiss grew hard, demanding, frightening her with its intensity. Just as quickly, his hunger changed to tenderness, and her apprehension burst into desire. Her lips opened again, coaxing his entry, accepting his passionate response to her simple request.

As his hands slid beneath her sweatshirt, she regretted her choice of undergarment and her unsexy sweatshirt. If only his hands could touch her naked skin. His hand slid up her slender body and stopped when his fingertips touched the lace across her back.

Lifting his lips from hers, he frowned. "What is that damn thing you're wearing?"

She kissed him lightly and smiled. "It's a teddy."

"A teddy? What ever happened to panties and bras?"

She laughed. "The teddy takes their place."

"Even the bra?"

"I don't always...wear one."

"And now?"

"No."

"Why not?"

"I...there's not much of...me...to have to hold in place," she murmured. "Bobby Joe used to make fun of me and..." She stopped, angry for mentioning her husband's name.

Adrian's arms loosened, but he continued to hold her, pressing her head against his chest. "Catch your breath, Callie."

Klaus crashed through the woods on his return from disturbing the night life. Adrian and Callie stepped apart.

"Is he always so quiet?" Callie asked, relieved at the distraction.

Adrian chuckled. "Klutzy Klaus would be a better name than his official Klaus Von something-or-other. He flunked his first set of obedience classes. Now that he's two years old, we're going to try again. He's got a nose for game, so there's some hope for him, but graceful and light-footed, he's not. Maybe that's why the breeder sold him to me at a discount. I don't care. Klaus and I have plans."

Klaus watched his master intently, and when Adrian pointed to the gate of the dog run, he trotted obediently through the opening, laid down in a corner, curled up with his nose tucked beneath one paw and closed his eyes.

Adrian locked the gate and glanced at his watch. "I think I'd better call your father and reschedule our appointment. It's almost eight o'clock."

"You'd better take me home," she said. "The children go to bed at eight. I should be there with them."

He stopped her with a light touch to her arm. "Not yet. We need to talk."

"No."

He shook his head. "We're strangers, and we need to take care of that. I want to find out more about you, how you feel about things, your past, your hopes and plans for the future... whatever you're willing to share with me."

"It's a dull story."

"I doubt that. Let's go inside. I'll show you my little log cabin, and we'll have a drink ... wine, coffee—whatever."

Inside, he phoned her house and spoke to her mother. After a minute, he extended the receiver toward Callie. "The kids want to talk to you."

She spoke to Linda and Robbie, gave them some last-minute instructions, then said good-night.

As she hung up, Adrian took a bottle of chilled red wine from the refrigerator and held it up. She nodded, but her steady gaze swept over the glossily finished knotty-pine cabinets, the rust-and-beige tile floor beneath her worn canvas shoes, the china visible behind the glass doors of the upper cabinets, the food processor and the automatic coffee maker on the unscarred counter.

He filled two stemmed glasses and offered her one. "I'll show you around," he said, switching on recessed lighting in the living area.

Callie scanned the stone fireplace covering most of one end of the room and the large windows, which she was sure would present a breathtaking view of the grassy yard and the woodlands beyond. A built-in pine bookcase, which covered the entire wall opposite the fireplace, was filled with books and trophies. The highly polished oak floor was bare except for a large oval braided rug that covered the area in front of the fireplace. Comfortable overstuffed furniture was arranged around the room. Several loose pillows were scattered on the sofa.

I'll bet sticky-fingered kids never touch this place, she thought. In one corner, the louvered doors of a tall cabinet hung open, revealing a television screen, a video-cassette recorder, compact-disc player and stereo components. "This is your idea of a little log cabin?"

He shrugged. "I don't like to feel closed in." He waved his hand toward the open kitchen area. "Anyone who comes to the door can see my dirty dishes. It makes for tidy housekeeping."

She took two sips of wine and surveyed the area again. "I suppose you're going to tell me you clean this place yourself?"

"Would you disapprove if I admitted a cleaning woman comes in every Friday?"

She shrugged. "Not if you can afford it."

He set his glass down on the counter. "Money means a lot to you, doesn't it?"

"It's important…especially when you don't have it."

He frowned. "I'll show you the rest of the house." The first room they came to was empty. "I don't know what to do with it," he explained.

She peered inside. "My cousin Abbie would put her loom here, but I think it would make a marvelous workroom for crafts or sewing. I've always wanted to learn basket weaving, but I've never had the money or space. Someday I'm going to make my very own dulcimer, too."

"Do you play them?" he asked, motioning her inside.

"A little, when I have time," she said, walking across the room and peering out the window into the night. "I can't see a thing, but the woods are out there, aren't they? The view must be beautiful. I used to like to walk in the woods. I'd collect vines and dried pods and flowers, and I'd make wreaths and wall plaques. I did it to make some extra money." She stiffened and turned toward the door. "Make it into a den."

She walked into the hallway, taking another sip of wine from her glass. He followed her, shutting the door behind him.

"Down here are the bedrooms," he said. "Three of them. The master bedroom has its own bath, and here's the other one." He opened a door leading into a bathroom larger than her bedroom at her parents' house.

She scanned the wide hallway to the linen cabinets at one end and back to the man standing beside her. "It's a lovely house, Adrian, but you know that already. It's very large for a man alone." She met his gaze directly, knowing the wine was loosening her tongue. "Why haven't you ever married?"

CHAPTER EIGHT

HE FROWNED. "Is it pertinent?"

"Surely you've been in love a few times," she said.

"I have, but not enough to warrant marriage."

"Were they affairs?"

His mouth quirked at one corner. "One was, the other two were merely close encounters."

"Sexual encounters?"

"Yes."

"Recently?"

He hesitated. "I think I know what you're getting at, Callie. You want to know if I fool around a lot. The answer is no. I had an affair with a young woman named Cindy Lou. I thought it was love for a while, but it turned cold when she made unacceptable demands on me. She said if I really loved her I'd get out of the coal-mining business. I don't like that kind of manipulation. Then again, maybe my decision to break it off proves it wasn't love after all. For the rest, I don't believe in casual sex. It's too risky, and if I don't feel something more than a physical need, I can wait. I have stronger morals than that. I'm a healthy, normal man, but I'm under control."

Abruptly he stomped back to the kitchen and emptied the contents of his glass down his throat. She knew as she followed him that her questions had angered him. He poured himself another glass of wine, and before she could decline, he refilled hers, too.

"And you, *Mrs.* Huff," he asked, "have you been in love many times? Are you a liberated woman? Do you come prepared with something in your purse in case the opportunity presents itself?"

Callie flushed. "My sexual habits are my business, but since we're laying our cards on the table, I'll tell you. I've been in love once, and it turned very sour. Since then, I've dated occasionally, but I don't fool around. I've been with one man in my entire life, and that was enough...."

Her voice faltered. "He made me promises...but he broke them all. He...he left us alone with empty cupboards and forty dollars when he couldn't handle the pressures. He wasn't mature enough for marriage and family. Neither was I, but at least I tried."

The words came tumbling out as the wall Callie had carefully built around her rage and disillusionment crumbled under the influence of the wine. "He got me pregnant again just three months after Robbie was born. He blamed me and knocked me around. I'd cower in the corner praying he'd leave."

"Callie, don't..."

"I started to cramp one Saturday afternoon, and he walked out on me," she continued, wiping the stream of tears from her cheeks. "I was just four months along and I miscarried alone in a godforsaken ramshackle cabin not much bigger than that fancy doghouse of yours. My baby was only seven months old himself, and I tried to take care of him while I waited for someone to come. Finally Bobby Joe came back and found us."

Adrian reached out, but she brushed his hand away.

"Bobby Joe took me to a clinic. He kept apologizing for leaving us alone and made all kinds of promises. He started bringing me cheap jewelry. God, how I hated it, as if that trashy plastic could make up for what he had done. Do you know what he said when we had our first fight?''

She squinted up at him through her tears. ''He said, and I quote because I'll never forget the words, 'It ain't a baby if'n it's only four months along.' He said we didn't need another mouth to feed anyway.'' She nodded her head sagely. ''You would've thought I'd learn, but a few months later I was pregnant again. I was a fool, a stupid fool for putting up with it. I was eighteen years old and pregnant for the third time.'' She closed her eyes and stepped away from him, pressing her back against the cabin wall.

''I never told anyone about that second pregnancy. I didn't tell my parents much about those two years. They'd write and ask how we were, and I'd write back 'we're fine.' I didn't want them to be ashamed of me, and I was afraid of what Daddy might do to Bobby Joe if he found out how bad things were. I couldn't tell my cousins because...because...I felt so humiliated.'' She stared at his sweater. ''Eileen, Abbie and I promised to help each other when asked...but how could I ask for help without telling them what a mess I'd made of my life?''

''They would have come to your aid,'' he said softly. ''True friends don't judge. Didn't they suspect? Didn't they ask?''

She nodded. ''But I lied.''

''You did their friendship an injustice, Callie. Didn't anyone come to visit you?''

She shook her head. ''Not the first few years. They all said they were leaving the 'honeymooners' alone, and we never had a phone, so all they knew was what I wrote in my letters. I didn't write very often. Never more than one page."

Adrian's heart pounded, his stomach knotting in anger over the hardships she had endured. He wanted to take her in his arms and shelter her from all the pain, but her rigid stance told him she would reject any offer of comfort.

"You didn't have to carry the load alone."

"Don't feel sorry for me," she cautioned him. "You wanted to know, and I'm telling you. Bobby Joe left one night when the power company cut off the electricity. I was cooking on a coal stove, so he got his belly filled, but after supper he got mad when there was no television to watch. That's what made him snap." She laughed, her voice on the edge of hysteria. "He shoved his clothes into a tote, tossed two twenty-dollar bills on the table, and walked out of our lives. He left that old Chevy truck behind, and I thought he was being kind, but I was wrong. The gas tank was empty and one of the tires was flat."

"When did all this happen?" he asked.

"Nine years ago, when Robbie was two and Linda was just past a year," she said, her voice steadier. "Linda was born with a congenital heart defect, an opening between the left and right ventricles. And her mouth was . . . messed up. Bobby Joe always hated sickness. He wouldn't have a thing to do with her. She had a heart operation when she was a month old and corrective surgery on her palate and lips a few months later."

"Weren't your parents with you during the surgery?" he asked.

She shook her head. "I wanted everything to be all right. I didn't tell my parents I was pregnant again. I was embarrassed. I wanted them to see a pretty little girl when they came."

"Oh, Callie, she's a beautiful little girl."

She looked up at him. "I think so, but sweet Jesus, she looks just like him, same hair and eyes, even her thin little face is his. He was working at a dog-hole mine with no benefits when she was born, so we got stuck with the hospital bills. He resented that, but by the time she needed the first operation, the mine had been shut down and the county picked up the entire bill. If you ever wonder where some of your tax dollars go, just look at my little girl."

"I have no quarrel with that, and I'd gladly pay it again if it becomes necessary. You have two wonderful children. I like them. Callie, you've told me enough."

She shook her head. "He thought it was my fault that Linda had been born that way. All he ever paid on her delivery was fifteen dollars. Once he joked that they could always repossess her. He wanted me to give her up for adoption—Robbie, too. We had more than one fight over that subject. I love my children. I could never give them up."

"No one expects you to."

She wiped her face again. "So you see, while you were having your affairs, I was trying to survive on bologna and peanut butter. You were taking your women out to fancy restaurants, and I was home cooking grits and beans because they're cheap. Isn't that something to ponder?"

"Did you get a divorce right away?" he asked.

"How can a woman on welfare afford an attorney?"

He frowned. "You're still married to the bastard?"

Her chin lifted, accenting the delicate bone structure of her face. "I've managed to save 115 dollars. I've squirreled it away, and when it gets to be two hundred, I'm going to Greenville to try to convince some lawyer to help me. He deserted me so long ago that getting a divorce should be easy. Do you know any attorneys who work cheap and would take my case?''

He didn't reply.

''I'm not surprised.''

He took the glass from her hand and went to the sink, rinsed both glasses and set them on the counter, then returned the wine bottle to the refrigerator. He rested with his hips against the counter, his arms crossed on his chest and his head bowed as he studied the tile floor. He tried to think of a solution to all the heartaches she had shared with him, the unresolved problems that had stolen her dreams.

He wanted desperately to help, but he had already been burned by her strong sense of pride. Pretty little Callie had turned out to be a very complex woman with an even more complicated past.

She came into the kitchen area. ''What's the matter? Have you changed your mind? Do you find me less interesting now that you know so much about me?''

He pinched the skin on the bridge of his nose, his heavy frown bringing his dark brows closer. Still he didn't speak.

''Maybe you've never fooled around with a married woman.''

Her words stabbed at his heart.

''Well, don't worry. Bobby Joe won't be coming back.'' She took a deep trembling breath. ''And most people today don't care about adultery anymore—not when the couple's been separated almost ten years. Why don't you take me home?''

His silence continued.

She reached for her jacket. ''I knew it would be a mistake ever to tell anyone about what happened. I should forget it myself. I can't do anything to change it. Well, now you know more than anyone except Bobby Joe and me. I hope you'll keep it to yourself."

He extended a hand to her. "I want you to stay."

Callie's jacket fell to the floor. "Why?"

"Because we can't part like this," he said, coming toward her. "We're worse off now than when we were strangers."

She frowned. "Why does life have to get so complicated?"

"It must be the length of our relationship," he teased. "We met again yesterday, and here we are talking about love, sex, families, money." He hunched his broad shoulders. "We sound like an old married couple." He held out his arms. "Come here, Callie. Let me hold you for a while."

He didn't know how she got across the room, but as his arms encircled her, she buried her face against his shoulder.

"Are you crying again?" he asked.

She pulled away and looked up at him. "No, no, no, I swear I'm not. I don't know why I'm such a crybaby around you." She touched his cheek. "Now what do we do?"

"I know what I'd like to do, but I'd be taking advantage of you tonight." He guided her into the living room. "Sit down, please." Without another word, he went to the fireplace and built a fire. When he had it burning to his satisfaction, he turned out the overhead light, then the kitchen light. He pulled his sweater over his head and tossed it aside.

"Messy," she scolded. "This man must have maid service."

He grinned and picked up the sweater, folded it neatly and laid it on the arm of a nearby chair. "Better?"

"Much." She patted the sofa cushion beside her, but he shook his head.

"Come over here by me instead," he said. Lounging against one corner of the sofa, he stretched one long leg out across the cushions and kept the other one on the floor. He draped his arm across the back of the sofa, and she came into his arms, settling comfortably against his side and the sofa back. He drew her closer.

They were silent for several minutes, listening to the crackling of the burning logs.

"I feel as if we've known each other forever," she murmured.

"We have," he whispered. He stroked her arm several times. "You have wonderfully soft skin," he murmured.

"How can you tell through this sweatshirt?"

"I have a good imagination," he said. "Tell me, how did you manage to go to Montana? Wasn't it expensive?"

She propped herself up with an elbow on his chest and peered at him.

"Outside," he reminded her, "you mentioned seeing blue heelers there. What took you to Montana?"

She rested her head against his shoulder. "Abbie had a big wedding last year. She insisted she couldn't get married without me. It wasn't true, of course, but I didn't have any money, and she paid my way."

"That seems to be normal."

She slapped at his hand, and it slid to her side. "I promised her I'd repay her and I will. She won't take money, so I'm doing some family research for her." Briefly, she explained her ideas.

"Sounds like a very special way to repay the debt. Tell me about your visit. Did you like it out there?"

She described the flight, the sixty-five-mile drive to the church where the wedding had taken place, then the three days she had spent on the sheep ranch in the mountains. "It's a different world out there. He used to have thirty-six sections of land. Why that's a whole township back here! But he sold off about half of it. Abbie says his sisters and brothers got greedy and wanted out."

She touched the buttons on his shirt, tracing their ridges. "So much land and so few people. We took a ride in his four-wheel-drive truck—everyone out there calls them 'rigs'—and we went over a pass in the mountains to another valley where Dane—that's Abbie's husband—has some friends. On one ranch they had blue heelers. I'd never seen them before, and it was fascinating to watch the dogs work." She sighed. "Abbie had a baby last August. Aunt Min is dying to see them."

"Why don't you call Abbie?"

"I don't make long-distance phone calls. They cost too much, and once you start to talk, time seems to slip away."

"Callie, loosen up. Set your egg timer and keep it brief. Invite her and her family to come and then say good-bye."

"I don't have an egg timer."

"Then watch the clock, for heaven's sake," he said, unable to hide his exasperation.

"But think of the expense. A trip for three people would cost the moon." Callie replied. "I couldn't . . ."

"Is anyone asking you to shoulder the cost?"

"Well, no, but . . ."

"What about a reunion," he suggested. "In the spring."

"They lamb in the spring."

"Summer then, when the weather is good."

"They hay in the summer."

"Then pray for rain," he said. "You can only make hay when the sun shines. Good grief, Callie, surely they get away from the business sometime. Ask them. They might surprise you."

"A reunion?" She unfastened two of the buttons on his ivory shirt and slid her fingers inside. "That's a good idea!" She propped herself up again. "How did you get so smart?"

He grinned. "My momma raised no dumb kids. What about your other cousin? What's her name?"

"Eileen . . . she got married, too, just last spring, but she's about to have a baby—make that babies. She's expecting twins after Christmas. She married a journalist, named Dan Page. Dan and Dane, what confusion there must be when those two get together. I'll bet no one knows who's talking to whom."

"Does Eileen live in Montana, too?" he asked.

"She's a potato farmer in Idaho. She was a widow with three children when she met Dan. He has a son, and now they're going to have two more."

He chuckled. "Sounds like quite an extended family—hers, his and theirs. We could never have that, could we?"

His question startled her, and she lay quietly thinking about it, reluctant to ask for a clarification. Her fingers moved beneath the fabric of his shirt, and she felt his breath catch.

"Invite Eileen and her family, too," he suggested. "They can fly on a quantity discount."

She unfastened another button, knowing she was playing with fire. He laid his hand on hers.

"That tickles," he said.

She refastened two of the buttons and slid her arm around his rib cage. "Don't forget to look for my locket first thing tomorrow. They're very special to all of us."

"I'll set my alarm an hour earlier than usual," he promised.

They were quiet again as the flames burned to embers.

"Are you asleep?" she murmured.

"No, love, just thinking." His hand touched the slope of her torso. "Aren't teddies expensive for a woman watching her dollars and cents?" he asked.

She tensed in his arms. "Abbie and Eileen got this crazy idea last summer that I'd met someone."

"Last summer? When exactly?"

"July or August, I'm not sure."

He grinned. "Then your cousins knew we were going to meet even before we did. It must have been preordained."

She touched his mouth with her finger before he could continue. "Anyway, I couldn't convince them there was no man in my life, and because they had forgotten my birthday they went together and sent me two teddies. One is peach and one is pale blue. I never wore them at first, but now I love them. They're pretty and lacy and—good grief, I do prattle."

His hand slid beneath her sweatshirt again, and he fingered the tricot. "Which color is this one?"

"Just never you mind, mister," she replied.

He started to chuckle and soon was laughing heartily. She began to slide from the sofa and grabbed his shirt. He turned onto his side, and she tumbled to the floor.

"Callie!" He rolled after her, catching her as she came to rest on the rug. "Are you hurt?"

"No, I'm fine," she said, smiling. She stared into his hazel eyes, spellbound by what she saw there. Her voice softened. "What did your sister mean when she called me the A.B.C. woman? She said your brother told her you'd called me that. Why?"

"I was speculating on . . . our futures."

"How? If it involves me, I have a right to know."

He traced her cheekbone from the bridge of her nose to her temple. "I suppose you're right. I told him that someday . . . I expected you to be Mrs. Adrian Coleman. That's all."

Her eyes widened. "That's all?"

"I asked him to be my best man," he said. "But I'm not asking you to marry me."

"Why not? We seem to have covered a lot of territory in the few hours we've been together."

He touched the pulse point in her throat with his lips. "I know, but I don't want to rush into something as serious as matrimony." His mouth inched upward to her cheek.

She laughed. "Adrian Coleman, you're nuts! You're positively crazy, and I—" she grew solemn "—and I think I could fall in love with you without much trouble."

"Would that be so bad?" he asked, his lips working their way toward hers.

"We don't agree on a thing. We live different lifestyles. You have money; I don't."

He kissed her lightly. "You can have some of mine."

"No," she said, shaking her head, but with each turn her lips brushed against his. "I've got to find a way to make my own money. You're talking about retiring, and I'm just starting school. It's crazy. I have two children, and Linda still isn't well. She may never be. I don't even have medical insurance.''

''My dependents are covered under White Glove's group policy.''

''But you're quitting. What then?''

He shrugged. ''We could work it out.''

''I plan to move out of state after I finish college,'' she said. ''It's the only way out for me.''

''I've been looking for some land in eastern Kentucky,'' he said. ''Is that close enough to the state line to qualify? I think I'd like to settle in the Appalachian hills.''

''Oh, my God, no,'' she cried. ''Why there of all places?''

''It's gorgeous country, the people are friendly, there's not many of them and they breed fine mules. I've looked at some property near a town called Shoulderblade.''

''Shoulderblade!'' she exclaimed.

''You make it sound like it's on another planet.''

''I know right where it is,'' she exclaimed. ''My Uncle L.T. lives near Jackson. I've been through Shoulderblade. Don't blink or you might miss it,'' she said sarcastically.

''Then you'd be near relatives,'' he said, grinning. ''It's halfway between Harlan where you lived and Morehead where we first met. Think of the romantic implications.''

''It's beautiful country but there're no jobs, no colleges, no opportunities. It's a terrible idea.''

''A person has to make his own opportunities,'' he said.

''Sometimes a person just can't.''

"I disagree," he replied. "It would be a good place for my mules, my catfish and for Klaus. It would be a great place to raise kids, too."

"Your kids?"

"No, our kids. Conceived in love and passion, Callie, because I can't imagine our lives any other way."

She ignored his innuendo. "No! I just got out of that part of the country. Why would I want to go back?" she asked, trying to pull free of his arms.

"Because I'd be there."

She stopped struggling and stared at him. "You're serious?"

"I haven't made up my mind definitely where I want to go, but I told my father I'll be leaving White Glove by next summer."

"Why so soon?"

"I want to get as far away from coal mining as I can. I know it's all around us, but I don't have to be a part of it. I don't want to be responsible anymore for stripping the land. It's beautiful the way God made it. Callie, I've found another farm for sale near Berea. There's a college at Berea. Also, I have someone checking some land just over the Cumberland Gap in Tennessee." He smiled. "That's out of state."

"Why can't we . . . just stay the way we are?" she pleaded.

"Life doesn't stay constant, Callie. Life sings whether we hear the music or not. I'm hearing the music at last. Listen to it with me. It's as pure as a mountain song, as joyous as a morning sunrise."

"That's enough," she murmured. Her head was pounding with all that he had offered her. "I should go home. Please let me up."

"You're right." But instead of releasing her, he gathered her flowing hair in his hands and let it fall through his fingers. "Someday soon we'll make love. It will be as wonderful as that morning sunrise, as passionate as…as two lovers destined for each other. I promise. Think about it, Callie. I want you more than I've ever wanted a woman."

Her eyes had dilated, her body alive with desire. His mouth hovered above hers. The realization that she wanted him now, tonight, swept over her. She pulled him down, claiming his lips, his tongue. Unable to put into words her need to be part of him, she slid her knee between his legs and pressed her thigh subtly against him. She wound her arms around his neck and pulled him closer.

His tongue explored her mouth, and she arched against him, desperate to be closer, her body reaching new heights of desire.

Suddenly he reached behind his neck and clasped her wrists, pinning them to the rug near her dark mane. He took several deep breaths and peered into her eyes. "God, Callie, another few minutes of this and I'll carry you off to my bed." He sprang to his feet and pulled her up. Grabbing her jacket, he held it for her, looking away as she slipped into it.

As he hustled her out the door, he glanced at his watch. "It's fifteen minutes to midnight, just time to get you home before one of us turns into a pumpkin."

CHAPTER NINE

CALLIE'S CHILDREN STARTED MAKING noise all too early the next morning. She longed to cover her head and stay buried beneath the quilts. Sleep had been slow to come to her after Adrian had dropped her off. With only a brief good-night, he had driven away, leaving her standing in the shadows of the porch.

A glance at the clock on her nightstand convinced her she had no time to waste. She dragged herself from the bed and dressed, forsaking her usual morning shower. The shock of seeing her short hair in the mirror kept Adrian's image alive as she ran her brush through it. By now he would have retrieved her locket. Perhaps he had called.

She went downstairs and into the kitchen.

"Momma!" Linda exclaimed. "What happened to you?"

Callie poured herself a cup of coffee and turned to her family sitting around the table. "I decided to have it cut."

"That's not what Grandpa says," Linda said, giggling behind her hand.

"He said that guy really hacked your hair off," Robbie said, glancing at his grandfather and grinning. "Grandpa says he's a little off his rocker. Eh, Grandpa?"

"I had my doubts about the man's judgment," Finis said between spoons of hot grits and butter. "But I've about decided it's only when he's around your momma here. He's all business at times, I reckon. I'll hold off on making up my mind until after I visit with him about digging out our coal.''

"Are you really gonna sell?" Robbie asked.

"Dunno yet."

"This house, too?" Linda asked. "Where would we live then?"

"We'll see," Ellen said. She glanced at Callie. "Did Mr. Coleman take you to dinner last night, honey? Your daddy went to bed right after he called, but I left a plate of food out for you. You didn't eat a bite."

"We went to his sister's house. She fixed my hair the best she could. Then we drove to his place and . . . just talked."

"His place?" Her father frowned.

"Yes, Daddy, his place. It's between here and Madisonville." She thought of all they had discussed. "It's just a log house," she said, smiling at the understatement. "We talked about . . . lots of things." She took a bite of toast and jam and washed it down with orange juice. "He has some plans about moving, as I do, but we're like two trains on parallel tracks, only we're going in opposite directions—that's for sure." She finished eating and put her cup in the sink. "You kids ready for the bus?" she asked. When they nodded, she hustled them from the room, glad to escape her parents' curious glances.

Upstairs, she signed a permission slip for a field trip for Robbie and reminded Linda not to do too much running around. "I made an appointment for your regular checkup next month," she told Linda. "If you feel lightheaded, honey, you tell the teacher. I talked to the nurse, and she knows all about you, and so does your teacher. Now, don't you be brave and pretend you're fine when you're hurting, understand?"

Linda bobbed her curly head, but still Callie wasn't convinced. "I don't want a call from the school."

"I promise, Momma."

"And where are you going on your field trip?" she asked Robbie, handing him his slip and realizing she hadn't read a word.

He folded it into a lopsided square and shoved it into the watch pocket of his new jeans. "The Tennessee Valley Authority plant at Paradise. The teacher said some of us might get to go up on the catwalks."

"Well, you be careful and do what the TVA men say. They're experts at their jobs. They've had training and everything. You listen to them and listen at school and maybe someday you'll have a job at a place like that. I hear they make good money."

"Ah, Mom, I hate school. You know that." But he grinned as he gathered his nylon tote bag and slung it on his shoulder.

His grades had been excellent since they'd moved to Drakesboro, she thought. And he had stopped asking questions about his father. Over the years, she'd found his questions increasingly hard to answer. At last, torn between telling the truth about his birth and whitewashing the whole dismal affair, she had stalled him with the promise to tell him all about his father on his next birthday.

Once she'd gotten the children ready, Callie gathered up her notebook and the manila envelope that contained her grant and admission applications to Murray State University. Callie smiled. Today, the women from the Second Chance program were going on their own field trip.

As FAR AS CALLIE was concerned, the trip to Murray State University was a bust. The admissions director promised the eighteen women in the Second Chance program that he'd do what he could, but warned them that funds for grants, scholarships and loans had all been cut back and that prospects in the job market were grim.

When Callie returned home, more bad news was waiting for her. Her mother waved a white envelope at her even before Callie had a chance to ask about her locket.

White Glove's corporate name and address was printed on the envelope's upper left corner. "Was Adrian here?" she asked, hopefully.

Ellen nodded. "Stopped by at lunch time. He had a piece of chess pie with me and a glass of milk." She smiled. "He's a nice young man, Callie. You could do worse."

"There's no better or worse to it, Momma. We're just friends," Callie said, but her fingers trembled as she opened the envelope. As she read, her face fell.

The transports were moved before I got there. Still looking, the drivers, too. Problem at a White Glove mine in Floyd County. Will be there the rest of the week. Sorry. Tell your father I've rescheduled him for Monday after Christmas, same time and place. Take care. Miss you.

                                                      A.B.C.

Callie folded the letter and returned it to the envelope. She explained the rescheduling of her father's appointment. "And my locket is probably lost forever," she added. "Once those big transports start rolling, they smash everything in their path. My locket is likely already buried under a ton of dirt."

But even worse news was waiting for Callie. That evening when she had undressed and climbed into bed, a soft knock sounded on her closed door. "Come in," she said. Robbie entered, closed the door and leaned against it. She patted the quilts. "Come sit down, Robbie. Something troubling you?"

He dragged his feet, yanked once on the waistband of his sagging pajama bottom and finally anchored one hip on the mattress. He looked directly at her, his gaze dark and intense. "I seen my pa."

She jerked upright. "What?"

"I seen my pa." Robbie scratched one ear and broke eye contact with her.

"That's impossible! How? Where?" She grabbed his thin shoulders. "What are you talking about? You don't even remember your daddy. You were just two years old when he left us."

"I do remember him, Ma. He was tall, and his hair was reddish. I've always remembered his hair 'cause it wasn't like mine and...and his eyes are blue like Linda's, aren't they?"

"How do you know this man you met is your daddy?"

"We talked."

"My God, Robbie, tell me what this is all about." Her heart pumped violently, and she had to force herself to think rationally.

"We were at the power plant," he said. "Some of us got to go up the elevator to this roof where we could look out and see everything. The water coolers—look just like nuclear towers, Ma. And we saw the conveyor belts that carry the coal and the transformers...."

She touched his arm. "Yes, I know all about those things, but what about this man?"

He frowned. "He was in the elevator when we got on. It was crowded, and we had to squeeze together. I was against the wall and 'cause I'm the tallest in the class I could see over everyone's head. This man...this man had a badge on...and it had his name. Ma, it said, Bob Huff. We all had name tags, too. I stuck mine on my baseball cap, right up front. Well anyway, this guy kept staring at me. At first he gave me the creeps, but then he smiled and nodded, like maybe we was kin 'cause we had the same last name. When we unloaded, he grabbed my jacket and pulled me away from the other kids."

Callie waited, silenced by fear.

"He looked down at me, and honestly, Ma, he said, 'Is your momma's name Callie Ann?' That's what he said, I swear."

Callie sank against the pillows. "What did you say?"

"I said yes, and then he smiled sort've funny like...and I knew right then and there who he was." Robbie scooted onto the bed and pulled his legs up, hugging them and resting his chin on his knees as he peered at his mother. "Are you mad?"

She had hoped this day would never come, but now she knew she had brought it on them herself by moving back to her hometown. What more logical spot for Bobby Joe to return to than where he had been born? "Did you talk about . . . much?"

Robbie shrugged. "After we came back down, we all went to the lunchroom where we had some punch and ate our lunches. He...my pa...came in and sat down in a chair right beside me. He wanted to know where we lived. I told him with my grandpa and grandma Hardesty. He smiled sort've funny again."

"I'll bet he did," Callie murmured, sitting up and crossing her legs beneath the covers. "What else?"

"I asked him if he would come see us."

"Oh, no! Robbie, you shouldn't have. You should have talked to me first." Her shoulders slumped. "What did he say?"

"He said he'd like to see us all again, even you, Ma, and he said . . . I had a sister and . . ."

"Of course. Did you think he would forget all about Linda?"

"No, he didn't mean Linda. He has a little girl named Tracy Lynn. He showed me her picture. She looks just like Linda, only younger. He said she's three years old. Did you know that?"

"No," she whispered. *Has he remarried?* she wondered. *Why not? After all, we've been apart for almost ten years.*

Robbie shook her hand, regaining her attention. "He lives north of Central City. He said he'd try to bring his family to visit us, maybe on Christmas afternoon. Is that okay?"

She didn't answer.

"I liked him, Ma. Not at first, but after we'd talked a little bit, I really liked him. He said he wanted to take me to his place some Saturday . . . if that was okay with you. We'd go fishing and . . . gee, Ma, don't you know how much I've been wishing for this? He's my pa, and he can teach me things, and we can do things together just like I always wanted."

"He left us, Robbie. Don't you understand? He walked out. He left us high and dry."

"But he said he was sorry," Robbie replied. "He said now that he's married again and has another family . . . Well, he said a whole bunch of stuff I can't remember, but anyway, he's coming on Christmas Day. Will you be nice to him?"

How could she possibly make Robbie understand all the heartache and misery Bobby Joe had brought upon her, when Robbie was sitting on her bed, excited about finding his missing father. Had she been at fault in not making Bobby Joe a part of their lives even if he had left them? But how could she, when each time she thought of him the bitter taste of anger filled her stomach?

"I'll be civil."

He grinned. "Thanks, Ma, I knew you'd understand."

"Thank you for warning me," she said, ruffling his chestnut thatch of hair. "Now you get back into bed or you'll never wake up tomorrow in time for school."

He bounced from her bed and loped from the room, a different child from the one who had entered.

ADRIAN PHONED THE NEXT NIGHT. "A pond we made when we reclaimed a site two years ago has turned acid enough to kill the fish that we stocked it with. Now we have to drain the damn thing to find the cause. I'm sorry, Callie. I thought we'd be spending some time together."

"That's okay," she replied. "We were on the verge of being impulsive, and we might have had regrets."

"We have time."

"Did anyone find the locket?" she asked.

"Sorry, hon, not yet. I didn't get there as early as I'd planned. I slept right through the alarm. They had moved most of the equipment when I got there, some of it to a new site up near the Ohio County line. God, Callie, I'm so sorry."

"It's hopeless, isn't it?"

"It could still show up. Don't give up."

"No," Callie agreed. Then they said their goodbyes.

Callie had considered inviting Adrian to spend Christmas with her family, but had decided against it. The fact that her father was doing business with White Glove had strengthened her resolve. She would have felt even more out of place surrounded by Adrian's wealthy relatives. Still, she would have liked him to say something, and when he didn't ask, she hid her disappointment beneath her relief.

The likelihood of Bobby Joe bringing his family to visit, as if they were old family friends, was unsettling enough.

THE HOLIDAY BEGAN long before daybreak, when the children raced down the stairs to open gifts. Callie had slept very little. Lying awake in the dark bedroom, her thoughts had shifted between Bobby Joe Huff and Adrian Coleman, comparing them, charting their strong and weak points, but concern about seeing Bobby Joe again remained paramount as she forced herself to meet the day.

This man had been her first and only lover as a teenager. Had he changed? What would he look like? Why would he want another family when he had resented the one he had created with her? She had been so engrossed in survival during those long lonely years in Harlan that she had given little thought to Bobby Joe's life.

After dinner, with four of her five brothers and their families in attendance, when the dishes had been done and put away, the family story telling began. Her older brothers told tales on each other to the delight of the nieces and nephews. A few stories were told on Callie as well, and Linda and Robbie rolled on the floor in delight.

"That ain't nothin'," her father said, and he told a few on himself that had them all holding their sides.

Callie kept one eye peeled toward the yard, hoping and praying that Bobby Joe had reconsidered the wisdom of reappearing amidst her brothers, who had all expressed their opinions more than once about his dereliction of his marital duties.

Only Ellen Hardesty knew of the meeting between Bobby Joe and Robbie, and she had promised to keep the news to herself and let Callie tell her father when she felt the time was right.

With growing relief, Callie watched the sun edge closer to the western hills. At last her brothers and their families said their goodbyes and left. James invited Finis to go with him to help work on a used car he had bought for his son.

"I dunno," Finis said. "I got chores to do."

"Daddy, you go on now," Callie coaxed him. "Momma and I have cleanup to do. Go help James. We'll get by for a few hours."

"If'n you're sure," Finis said.

Ellen kissed his cheek. "We're sure."

Finis left, promising to return as soon as he could.

"I was afraid he wouldn't go," Callie said, sighing as she leaned against the closed door. "I sure didn't want to see Daddy's face when Bobby Joe knocked on the door."

"Maybe we should've told him," Ellen murmured, collecting the remaining glasses and dessert plates scattered around the room. "He'll have to be told soon. He never did like that Bobby Joe...and we've deceived him."

"Wait until we know what Bobby Joe is up to," Callie said. "I'll tell Daddy tomorrow. There's just no need to upset him on Christmas."

"It sure upset my Christmas," Ellen replied.

A half hour later Callie glanced toward her mother. "I reckon he's not coming," she said, touching her breast. "Thank goodness."

Ellen shook her head. "I'm afraid you're wrong, honey. Unless your Mr. Coleman has a little blue car and another girlfriend besides you, here he comes now."

Callie followed the car's progress up the driveway. The man who got out of the car was a stranger, yet not a stranger at all. She thought back to the last time she had seen Bobby Joe. They had both been nineteen. She peered through the curtains, trying to see him more clearly. What had happened to the lean, lanky young man with the strawberry-blond hair that continually hung over one eye? This man was muscular, his face fuller than she remembered, his hair cut short and receding at his temples. His posture still had a unique touch of arrogance as he took advantage of his six-foot height, a trait that had once thrilled her but now seemed cocky and immature.

When he went to the other side of his car and opened the door for a pregnant blond woman, Callie knew this man was a stranger. Bobby Joe had never opened a door for her, period.

"I'll tell 'em where to come," Robbie said, racing out the door, but as Callie watched through the curtains, Robbie stopped on the second step of the porch.

Then the man motioned to him, and Robbie started forward again, this time his swaggering posture straight and tall, an instant replica of Bobby Joe's. Robbie shook hands with the woman and nodded toward someone still in the vehicle. The little girl, whom Robbie had said was three years old, was twice the size Linda had been at the same age. Yet the girl was normal for her age.

"It's not fair," Callie murmured, taking in the healthiness that radiated from the child now skipping toward the porch, holding Robbie's hand.

Callie heard footsteps behind her and turned as Linda made her way down the stairs.

"Is he here?" Linda asked, her small face pale. "He's not really my daddy. I don't have a daddy. Just you, Momma."

Robbie led them into the living room. "He's here, Momma. Isn't it great? It is him, isn't it? I dreamed last night that you were both just funning with me, but it is him, hey?"

Bobby Joe extended his hand. "Hello, Callie Ann. It's been a while, hasn't it? You're looking pretty good."

She motioned to the sofa. "Sit down, all of you." A numbness settled in, protecting her from the past as she stared at him. The years and his weight gain had added a handsomeness that had only been a promise when she had last seen him. She wondered if he still liked his six-packs. If he didn't watch his beer consumption, he'd have a spare tire around his waist within a few years.

"This is my wife, Mary Lou," Bobby Joe said, "and this is my daughter, Tracy Lynn. We're expecting another in three months." He turned to the blond woman. "Honey, this is Callie Ann, and that's my other daughter, Linda...and that's Callie's mother, Ellen Hardesty." He glanced around the room. "Where's your daddy?"

"He's gone."

"Died?" Bobby Joe said, his face paling.

Robbie laughed and scooted from his chair. He dropped to the floor near Bobby Joe's legs and beamed up at him. "Nah, he's at my uncle James's place," he explained, then went on to describe the car his uncle had bought. "Someday I hope someone buys me a car." His gaze lingered on his father before it shifted to Callie.

Callie stiffened, her anger growing. How could Bobby Joe walk out on her and then come back and have the nerve to sit here with another woman, her belly bloated with his seed, and a healthy little girl who looked enough like Linda to be her twin if it weren't for the age difference?

"Where have you been all these years?" Bobby Joe asked, taking his wife's hand in his.

"Harlan."

He cleared his throat. "Oh. I wondered if you'd been back here long."

"Three months."

He looked startled. "Why did you stay there so long?"

"I was broke."

Ellen rose from her chair. "Would you like something to drink? Water? Tea? Bobby Joe, I have some beer in the fridge. Leander and Farley brung it and forgot to take it with them."

"No thanks, ma'am, I gave up beer drinking when I met Mary Lou. Tea will be fine. Honey?" he asked, smiling at his wife.

The woman nodded, and Callie's attention shifted to her. She was pretty, Callie admitted, and several inches taller than herself, with heavier bones and a fuller bosom. The woman's face was sweet and round, not at all like Callie's, which was almost oval. Callie searched for dark roots near her scalp but found none. The woman's eyes were a clear intelligent blue. She looked Callie's way, and their gazes held for a few seconds.

Six months pregnant, Callie thought again. Apparently, Bobby Joe had had a change of heart regarding babies. "Where did you go when you walked out on us?" she asked.

Bobby Joe flinched. "I . . . bummed around the country for a while."

"How long?"

He shrugged. "A couple of years. Then I came back here. My folks had moved away, but my brother and sister were still here." He grinned and reached over to Robbie, ruffling his hair. "I figured you might have come back, too. Seems our boy here and his cousin paired up in school a few months ago."

Callie's mouth tightened, recalling the comment her son had made about meeting someone with the same last name. "Who?"

Robbie shot to his knees and grinned. "Why, G.W., of course. I told you time and time again, Ma. Didn't you listen? We didn't find out we were cousins until I met my dad again. G.W. was on the field trip, too, and he called him Uncle Bob. Isn't that great? We're real cousins, blood cousins!"

"Yeah, G.W.'s real name is Gideon," Bobby Joe said. "He's my brother Willie's boy. Willie's middle name is Gideon. His son is Gideon William. What a name to tack on a kid." Robbie and Bobby Joe exchanged grins.

"Why'd you stop bumming?" Callie asked, cutting off the interchange between her son and his father.

"I guess I finally grew up, babe. I got tired of not having a woman to come home to, or a hot meal that I didn't have to pay for. And I met Mary Lou. Willie's wife introduced us—at Wednesday-night prayer meeting of all places. Her daddy is a deacon. He works at the power plant, and he got me on, a mighty fine job. It pays a damn sight more than that dog hole I worked in near Harlan. Remember that?"

His face swam before her. "How could I forget?" she replied. She closed her eyes.

He shifted in his seat. "Anyway, now I'm a happily married man and I've got my sh... I've settled down. I even got credit good enough to buy me a new car, brand-new."

She nodded.

"Hey, I noticed you still have that old Chevy truck," he said. "It was a pile of junk when I bought it. How did you manage to keep it running?"

"A little money and a whole lot of luck," she murmured.

"How come you never traded it off for a new car?" he asked.

Nausea churned in her stomach. "My welfare Cadillac is in the garage out back." She met his gaze directly, and to her surprise, she realized he didn't know if she was joking or not.

He coughed. "Well, we bought a car that was economical to drive. Mary Lou was working, too, until last month. We're gonna miss her paycheck, but now she's staying home and being a full-time momma for Tracy."

Ellen Hardesty came from the kitchen with a tray containing glasses of iced tea. The tray shook as she set it down and busied herself with distributing the glasses. For a few minutes conversation stopped.

Bobby Joe set down his empty glass and turned to Mary Lou. "See, honey, I told you she'd be a good sport." He turned to Callie again. "Mary Lou wanted me to get in touch with you when we decided to get married, but I told her it was best to let sleeping dogs lie. I don't mind telling ya' it's a worry off my mind to find out you've forgot and forgiven." He chuckled. "We've been married for five years."

Callie caught the underlying hint he was sending her about their own hasty wedding. She rose from her seat. "I think I'm going to be sick," she said, starting up the stairs. The sound of tires on gravel sounded from outside.

"Maybe Grandpa's come back," Linda said, jumping from her seat. She made a wide berth around the sofa and pulled the curtain back from the window. "No, it's not Grandpa at all." She turned to the group and smiled. "It's Mr. Coleman, Momma, the nice man who took us to Catfish Gap. Remember?"

Callie's knees buckled. She dropped to the steps, gripping her stomach as a pain ricocheted through her midsection.

CHAPTER TEN

ADRIAN COLEMAN parked his truck and drew a deep sigh. After making his excuses, he had left his parents' crowded house and gone home to pace restlessly in his own living room, waiting for Callie's relatives to depart. He hadn't wanted to run the gauntlet of five curious brothers.

Now, as Adrian got out of his truck, he noticed that an unfamiliar automobile was parked in the Hardestys' driveway, a current year's model of a Korean economy sedan. Finis Hardesty's truck was parked next to Callie's old Chevy.

If he could just whisk Callie away for an hour or two, maybe he could manage to keep his mind on the upcoming week. During his trip to eastern Kentucky, concentration had not been one of his strong points.

Linda greeted him at the door and announced his arrival. He entered, searching the room for Callie and found her crouched on the stairway. He frowned, sensing that something was desperately wrong. His piercing gaze took in the other people in the room. The resemblance between the strange man, the little girl and Callie's daughter were striking. Recognition hit Adrian in his gut. *Oh, God, Callie, not that rat of a husband Bobby Joe.*

Ignoring the others, he hurried across the room. "Callie?" he murmured, reaching through the railing and touching her shoulder.

She stood up, and carefully feeling for each step and riser, came back down the stairs, one hand pressed against her stomach, her face a pale mask. Taking Adrian's hand, she approached the others. "Adrian Coleman, meet Bobby Joe Huff. Adrian is a friend," she explained.

Bobby Joe extended his hand but Adrian declined. *So this is the notorious Bobby Joe,* Adrian thought as the other man withdrew his hand. What could have brought him back into Callie's life? His gaze swept over the pregnant woman and little girl who were now standing next to the man. *And exactly who were these two?*

Adrian suppressed his own curiosity and scanned the room again. Ellen Hardesty seemed caught in a situation not of her own making. Robbie had his new-found sister in his arms and was swinging her around in a circle, making her squeal. Each time they faced Bobby Joe, the boy would grin up at his father. Linda remained curled up in a chair, determined to ignore her father, but her gaze flickered again and again to Robbie and the little girl.

Adrian smiled at her. He wanted to go sweep Linda up in his arms, grab Callie's hand and run. *What a hornet's nest I've walked into,* he thought. Never in his life had he seen such a troubled collection of people in one spot. "I...ah...came over to invite Callie...out...for a bowl of beans," Adrian said, grasping for any excuse to rescue her.

"We were leaving anyway," Bobby Joe said, hustling his family out the door. "We'll see you later, Robbie," the man called to the dejected boy lingering in the doorway.

"I don't want to go anywhere," Callie said, her face a sickly gray. She brushed Adrian's hand aside and raced up the stairs.

Ellen gathered the empty tea glasses and went to the kitchen. Adrian followed her. "What's going on here?" he asked.

She set the glasses in the sink. "You'd best ask my daughter."

"She looks sick," he said. "Is she?"

"The best treatment for her condition might be a little drive in the fresh night air. What went on this past hour would make anybody sick. Will you please take her out of here, Mr. Coleman? I'll tend to the children," she said. Then stepping closer to him, she added, "I know my daughter. She hides her pain, but she's a'paining right now. She's probably in her room. It's the third door on the right upstairs. You take her away from here and don't you bring her back until she's starting to heal." She turned back to the sink and yanked the faucet, jumping back when the hot water splattered on her apron.

He took the stairs two at a time, counted the doors and knocked. When no response came, he knocked again. "Callie, I'm coming in." He waited another minute before turning the knob.

The room was spartan, with only a double bed, a dresser and a nightstand holding a small lamp. There was a braided rag rug on the floor to make the room look hospitable and a Shaker-style rocker near the window. Callie stood behind the rocker, holding a wet washcloth to her cheeks and staring out the window.

He crossed the room and peered over her shoulder. The tobacco shed and some farm equipment were the only objects framed by the window. "Callie?" He put his hand on her shoulders and felt her flinch. "Callie, come with me. I've come to take you out of here. Your mother will stay with the children."

He grabbed a jacket lying across the foot of the bed and put it around Callie's shoulders, then led her down the stairs and out the front door.

The headlights of Adrian's truck were lonely twin beams of light in the darkness. The roads were empty of automobiles. *As it should be on Christmas night,* he thought. *Families should be together on a night like this.* But hers was in shambles, and he didn't have a family of his own, yet. He glanced at Callie, who sat stiff and withdrawn against the other door. In spite of the darkness, he knew her mouth was hard and narrow.

His heart went out to her. She needed space to bloom, but for the moment, she needed a sanctuary where she could be assured of unconditional love, tenderness and protection.

Was he being chauvinistic? He didn't think so. Perhaps a little selfish, because he knew his own life would be empty without her.

I love you, Callie. Will you ever need me as much as I need you? Do you want me as much as I want you? Could you love me, Callie?

He returned his attention to the road ahead, giving her time to think and to absorb the anger she had sealed inside. He braked in front of his house, then led her inside.

"Do you really have corn bread and beans?" she asked.

He hadn't expected anyone to believe his menu, least of all Callie. "I just wanted to get you out of there. Would you settle for ham, sweet potatoes and mincemeat pie? My mother, bless her, refuses to let me leave any family dinner without loading me up with leftovers.'' He went to the kitchen, poured two glasses of wine and offered one to her.

She shook her head. "How could he?"

"Bobby Joe?" he asked, bracing himself for what was coming.

She glared across the room at him. "He had the nerve to come to my home and act as if nothing, absolutely nothing had happened!"

He took a sip of wine, knowing she didn't expect a reply.

"He acted like a doting father! Mr. Daddy Goody-two-shoes himself, fawning over Robbie and that fat little girl of his!"

Adrian turned away to hide his smile.

"Did you see what he did to Linda?" she asked.

"What?" He turned back to her.

"He ignored her. She was invisible! Fabulous Father indeed! He...he sat there holding hands with that cow of a wife of his...and completely ignored his own child."

He shrugged. "I thought she was a rather pretty woman."

She frowned. "He bragged about his happy marriage. Why," she sputtered, "he isn't even legally married to her!"

"That could pose a problem," he admitted.

"He's been living with her all those years when I was trapped in Harlan. I thought he was broke, and all the time he was making money, good money. He could have paid child support. I was starving, and he was feasting. My kids were hungry. His kid was warm and cozy." She sneered out the words. "My kids were cold and...and...damn him! Damn him all to hell! I hate the very ground he walks on, the bastard!'' Her eyes sparked with anger. ''Is that fair? Is that justice? Why, Adrian? Why did my kids have to suffer while his had it made? Aren't Robbie and Linda his kids anymore? Should it matter if Linda is sick and Tracy is healthy? Shouldn't he love them both?'' Her mouth twisted. ''If I had had a gun this afternoon I would have shot him right between the eyes....'' She squinted. ''No, I would have aimed a lot lower.''

He chuckled.

She glared at him. ''What's so funny? Robbie thinks he's the greatest father in the world, but he's a fraud!''

Adrian nodded. ''Probably, but that's his problem, not yours. Give him the benefit. People change as they get older. You did the best you could during those years. They're over now.''

''Over?'' She blinked. Her eyes filled with tears, and she blinked again. ''Will they ever be over?'' Her face crumbled, and her body loosened. ''Adrian,'' she moaned, reaching out to him.

He took her in his arms and held her, smoothing her hair as she clung to him.

''Adrian, hold me, hold me and don't ever let me go. I need you...I need you so much,'' she cried, and burrowed tighter into his embrace.

He stroked her dark head. ''It's all right now, Callie, it's going to get better.''

She shook her head against his chest. ''Maybe I waited too long. Maybe I didn't try hard enough...or soon enough.''

''No, love, you're wrong,'' he crooned. ''You'll see. Trust me. I promise you the light is going to get brighter.''

"It never will," she sobbed, looking up at him. "But being here with you helps. I want..." She blinked away the tears. "I want you to...love me."

"I do, sweetheart, I do, very much." He kissed the tears from her cheeks and wiped her lashes with his thumbs. "I do," he groaned, and finally his mouth claimed hers.

She pressed against him, her arms around his neck as she drank from the fountain of love he offered. Hungrily, he kissed her face, her earlobes, her throat, his hands exploring her torso, then sliding down to her tiny waist. He cupped her hips in his hands, lifting her from the floor and pressing her against him.

"Yes, Adrian, love me, love me," she moaned, her hands stroking his body. His clothing became an obstacle to her, and she slid her hands beneath his sweater, her fingers trembling as she fought with the buttons on his shirt. When she finally found his bare skin, she moaned and continued her discovery. "You're so warm, so strong."

He lifted her in his arms, carried her out of the kitchen and down the dark hall into his room and laid her on his bed.

Kneeling on one knee, he removed her shoes and socks. Her hand slid to the snap at the waistband of her jeans. He eased her hand aside and, undoing her jeans, slid them from her shapely legs. Soon the bulky coral sweater she wore joined the growing pile of clothing on the floor. All that remained to cover her body was a pale blue silky undergarment trimmed in ecru lace, its top barely covering her creamy breasts, its bottom a mere wisp of fabric disappearing between her legs.

She was perfection itself, he thought as he gazed down at her. Her breasts were small yet full and in perfect proportion to her exquisite body.

Beneath the blue fabric, the dark shadow at the V of her thighs sent a surge of desire through him. As she inhaled, his gaze shifted to her breasts again. His eyes darkened as her nipples become erect.

As a moan slipped from her lips Callie closed her eyes and touched his cheek. "I need you, Adrian. I want you so much." Her hips shifted on the bed, and her knee rose.

"Callie, look at me," he whispered. "Are you sure?"

Her eyes opened, and the sensual longing he saw in them told him more than mere words.

"I want to make love to you. Now, sweetheart. Now." His hand touched her knee and slid upward across her warm thigh.

She took his hand and pressed it against her womanhood. A tremor shook her, and he understood the depth of her desire.

"Yes," she murmured. "You said this time would come...and you were right."

She sat up in the king-size bed as he removed his clothing. The navy pullover sweater was followed by a pin-striped blue-and-white dress shirt already half-unbuttoned. The well-developed muscles in his arms and chest rippled beneath his bronze skin as he worked the fasteners on his jeans.

His arousal was full when he knelt on the bed again. His finger slid the narrow strap from her shoulder and his mouth took its place. As his lips caressed her skin, he slipped the other strap down, and the lace and tricot settled around her hips.

Her breasts heaved, and he encircled them with his hands, brushing their tips with his thumbs. Never had he felt such intense passion for a woman.

She reached out, touching his skin, caressing it and tracing the scattering of dark hair from his throat downward.

"You're a beautiful woman, Callie, a special woman. Stay here with me. Love me, Callie, love me."

"Yes." She tipped her head back to allow him access to her throat. Her hair drifted across her shoulders as he explored her body. Turning her head from side to side, she moaned softly.

"Lie down," he murmured. He slid the teddy from her hips and dropped it to the floor, then covered her with kisses—moist caresses on her abdomen and ribs. Then he trailed kisses around her breasts until at last he took each crest in turn into his mouth and bathed it with fire.

She touched him, stroked him, guided him to the center of her need and pleaded with him to give her peace from the torment he had fueled in her.

He groaned as he buried himself in her and the timeless rhythmic movements began. He held her tightly as she convulsed beneath him. "Callie," he gasped, "Callie," prolonging the moment as long as he could before finding peace for himself as well.

"YOU SAID THIS WOULD HAPPEN," Callie murmured, her head resting comfortably against his chest. She smoothed her palm up and down his chest. "I thought we should wait . . . until we knew each other . . . better."

He nodded against the pile of pillows behind his head. "I know you better than you think. Are you sorry?"

She thought about the events that had brought her to this moment. "No . . . except it happened too fast."

He chuckled. "The next time will be slower. We were both impatient."

"I was thinking about how long we've known each other," she said. "But actually I have thought about making love with you—if it would happen, what it would be like. When. I've only been with one other man. I wondered if this would be different."

"Was it?"

"Oh yes, very different." She slid her hand around his ribs and sighed deeply. "I'd almost forgotten what it was like."

"And now that you remember?"

"I want more," she admitted.

"Insatiable," he said, tipping her chin up so that he could reach her mouth. When he lifted his lips from hers, he smiled. "We'll have a lifetime to satisfy each other." He tossed some of the pillows to the floor and pulled her into his arms again, tucking a down-filled, cornflower-blue comforter around them.

"This is only the fourth time we've met," she said.

"But we've known each other four months," he replied. "Some day we'll be lying in bed like this, and it'll be four decades. We'll have children, and they'll have children, and we'll still be making love as if it's only been four times. You'll see. They'll have to warn the grandchildren to always call before coming to see Grandpa Adrian and Grandma Callie because you can never tell what those old Colemans might be doing."

She suppressed a giggle against his skin. Her stomach rumbled. "What time is it?"

He glanced at the digital clock. "Seven." He propped himself up on his elbow. "I'm surprised. I thought it was the middle of the night at least. Still, you must be starved."

She nodded.

He untangled himself from her and the rumpled bed linens. "Let's get dressed and eat. I have a Christmas present or two for you. I kept them here. I didn't want anyone else to share the moment when you opened them. I'm selfish, but I want you all to myself for a while."

They dressed. Together they fixed two plates of food. She had never used a microwave, and he gave her a quick lesson.

"Ah, the luxuries of the rich," she said.

He ignored the insinuation.

Later, as they cleared the dishes, he turned to her. "I suppose you're not familiar with an automatic dishwasher, either?"

She blushed. "No."

"I'll give you a quick run-through on all the appliances around this place," he said, giving her a light peck on the cheek.

"Why bother?" she said. "You're going to sell the place."

He arched a brow. "True, but my next house will have even more appliances. I don't see any reason to labor over the maintenance of a home when you can save your time for more enjoyable pursuits." He loaded the dishwasher, put in the detergent and turned it on. "Now, my dear Miz Callie, come with me. I may not have a tree, but none-the-less Santa Claus came a few days ago."

He tried to take her hand but she hid them behind her back. "I don't have anything for you," she confessed. "I . . . I barely squeezed out enough money for the kids and my folks. Adrian, I'm sorry, but I can't accept anything from you."

"You're wrong, sweetheart. Don't deny me the privilege of giving to you." He took her hand and led her to a chair. "Sit."

"Sounds like you're talking to Klaus now," she said.

"And he obeys...sometimes. Follow his example." He went to a closet and brought back three gaily wrapped packages.

She gasped. "Too many."

"There's more." He made another trip, and this time put a long oblong box in front of her. "Open this one first."

She frowned at the package. "It must be expensive."

"That's my business. Open it."

She scooted from the chair and sat on the floor, carefully untying the giant red bow and laying it aside.

"For God's sake, Callie, hurry up!"

She smiled and pulled the box closer, ripping the gift wrap away. The cardboard carton was unmarked. She looked up at him.

"Go on," he coaxed. "I hope you find it to your liking."

Carefully, she opened one end and withdrew a black case from the box. "Oh, Adrian, no."

"Oh, Adrian, yes," he said, grinning. "Your mother told me more about your music. I've never heard you play or sing, but she says you're very good. She also told me you haven't played since moving back."

She removed the instrument case from the box and touched the silver latches, then closed her eyes. "I can't...you shouldn't have. Oh, Adrian, I'm going to cry again." Her eyes shone as she unlatched and opened the case. On the crimson velvet lay a mountain dulcimer made of the finest woods she had ever seen.

"The back is black walnut," Adrian said. "The top is curly poplar. I got it in a shop in Berea. The man who made it said it was one of his best. He played it for me. I'm no expert about such things, but I thought it made beautiful music. I'd been told the man is considered one of the best in the business . . . making the instruments, I mean. Hope you like it."

She lifted the instrument from its case and laid it across her lap. "Thank you, but you . . ."

He held up his hand. "Thank you will be enough."

She looked up, her eyes shimmering. "Thank you."

"I didn't know what you preferred, so there are an assortment of quills and noters and some sheet music and songbooks, too," he added. "They're in the pocket in the case. I bought everything the people in the shop suggested. Maybe they spotted an easy target, but I'm satisfied. I hope you are, too."

"I am." She plucked the strings one at a time and listened, adjusting the pegs occasionally, then strummed them individually again. "Dulcimers are temperamental. They need tuning quite often," she explained. "The humidity, the temperature—they can make a difference."

He sat on the floor, one leg pulled up, the other stretched out near where she sat. "Play me a tune, missy."

She grinned. "This is 'Boil Them Cabbage Down.' It's an old fiddle tune Uncle L.T. taught me when I was nine years old."

By the time she had played the simple melody three times and sang it twice, he was laughing and holding his stomach. "Did I spend money on that exquisite instrument only to hear exactly four notes used to enlighten me about cabbage and hoecakes? That's so simple I could do it myself.''

"Try it," she challenged, handing him the dulcimer.

He plucked several discordant notes and grinned, returning the instrument to her. "It's harder than it looks. How about something a little more . . . demanding?"

She sang and played several folk tunes, and he listened quietly. She grinned. "This one is especially for my friend Adrian, the coal operator who wants to move to the hills."

She sang a song about a man who had dreamed of meeting Saint Peter at the gates of heaven, who promptly invited him in to a dinner of corn bread, buttermilk and good old turnip greens.

"It's traditional," she said, after singing several more verses. "You'll love the last verse." She launched into the song again, telling the story of why mountain girls were so pretty. "For the precious little honeys have been raised on turnip greens."

He joined her on the chorus, his baritone voice blending with her soprano.

She played several more songs, then retuned the drone strings and began to finger the instrument again. She sang a poignant ballad about heartbreak, hope, survival and the human spirit. When she finished and quietly laid the dulcimer back in its case, she turned to him, her eyes glistening.

"That's beautiful, Callie. I could feel the pain, the hope. It was very moving. Who wrote it?"

"I did," she said, wiping a single tear from her cheek. "I can't sing it without crying a little. I call it 'Heart Spirit.' I keep adding more verses. I guess it's mostly autobiographical."

He held out his hand, and she took it. "Your mother was understating the truth when she said you were good," he said. "If this is how you sound when you don't practice, you must be magnificent when you do."

"I love my music," she said, edging closer to him. "If I had my druthers, I'd play and sing and write songs all the time. But who can make a living with music? Just those lucky few who get a break and make it to the big time. I have two kids to support. I've got to go to school and get a job."

He touched her face. "Take heart, my darling."

She pressed his hand against her cheek. "I came close to giving up so many times but something kept me going. My music helped me through the rough times. I love to sing, and I guess I carry a tune okay for a person who has never had voice lessons."

"Have you gone to the music festivals?" he asked.

"Once with my aunt Belle when I was eleven, and once when Robbie was a baby," she replied. "But I didn't play. I'd forgotten they had open sessions, so I didn't bring my dulcimer. Anyway, I've never sung before strangers, just my family and in church—for all I know, I might've been stricken with stage fright. I listened and went home and practiced some of the techniques I saw the professionals use."

"So there are professional dulcimer players?"

"A few."

"You have a gift, Callie. Develop it. Share it."

"But how?"

He frowned. "I don't know, but we'll work on it." He pulled her onto his lap and into his arms. "Now, give me a kiss to show your appreciation. For the life of me, I can't remember the last time I gave a pretty woman a dulcimer."

She slid her arms around his neck and pulled his head down. When her lips touched his, he opened his mouth and the kiss changed from appreciation to passion. His hands began to move on her body, and the kiss deepened.

She pulled away, catching his hands and holding them as she tried to steady her breathing. "You're a terrible distraction."

"Likewise," he replied. "But I promise to keep my hands to myself long enough for you to open the other presents."

The next box contained a cassette recorder and two dozen blank tapes. "To use in your classes or when you sing," he said.

She opened the third box and lifted out a bulky knit sweater in the most delicate shade of pink she had ever seen. A pair of size-five tailored slacks in dusty rose lay beneath the sweater. A glance at the labels confirmed their quality.

"How did you know my size?" she asked.

He grinned. "Your mother told me. She said you'd gained some weight, though you're not exactly chubby yet."

Her cheeks brightened. "I'll try them on." She started to get to her feet, but he pulled her down.

"Not yet. You have one more box to open," he said, gesturing toward a flat package wrapped in gold foil. She opened it and pulled out a shimmery satin chemise-style nightgown with deep slits on the sides. She was sure its hem would hit above her midthigh. The pale blue garment, with shoulder straps little more than threads, was trimmed in navy satin piping. A matching thigh-length robe lay folded in the box. "It's beautiful, but what does it have to do with the sweater and slacks?"

"Nothing," he said. "There's more."

Her shoulders sank. "Adrian, you've spent much too much. These are so personal, and the dulcimer alone must have been several hundred dollars."

He brushed her other excuses aside. "I had no idea women's lingerie had become so complex. I came through Lexington on my way home and stopped at a specialty store my sister recommended. I knew you had a preference for teddies." He shrugged. "I couldn't decide between pink or white . . . so I got both."

She slid her hand beneath the blue robe and slowly extracted a skimpy pink teddy with more lace than material. She held up the garment. "It's positively indecent," she exclaimed.

"I know. Most of these gifts are inappropriate," he said.

"I was thinking the same thing."

"Your mother gave me all your sizes."

"Are you and my mother in collusion?"

"I think she's on my side."

"Well, thank you," she said. "Now I'm going to try some of them on." She grabbed the boxes and ran to his room.

When she returned, Adrian rose to his feet. "They fit perfectly," he said, scrutinizing her and turning her around in the center of the room. "Are you happy?"

A wave of shyness swept over her. "I think I'm falling in love with you, Adrian. I didn't want to. What more can I say?"

"You've said enough," he replied. "I worry about you. I want you to find all the happiness you deserve, just don't exclude me."

"We do have our differences and some unresolved problems."

He nodded. "Starting with Bobby Joe Huff and his pregnant wife, and your marital status."

"I'll have 150 dollars saved after the first of the month," she said. "That's not enough."

"I can loan you some. I'd rather give it to you, though."

She shook her head. "Absolutely not. I'll pay for my own divorce, thank you."

He took her hands in his. "Then let me make the initial contact with an attorney for you. I know one in Madisonville. If I talk to him and explain your predicament, would you go see him?"

"Only if he understands that I can't pay very much," she said. Emotions played over her features as she studied him. "Being here with you has taken the fire and anger out of me. I didn't mean what I said about his wife. She's really very pretty, and I wouldn't want to upset her and cause problems. I'd better get this all straightened out as soon as possible."

"Good. Next is your schooling. How are the GED classes coming?"

"They postponed the tests until after the holidays. I was very disappointed. I wanted to be a high-school graduate before Christmas. I haven't heard about my grant application or my admission request. If they accept me, I'll be moving the kids to Murray. Bobby Joe will be out of our hair for a while."

"Don't count on it," he warned.

"Robbie will be disappointed, but he'll adjust."

"Don't deprive your son of his father, Callie. A boy needs a dad in spite of the parents' problems."

"I hate having Bobby Joe back in our lives. How can I avoid him and still let Robbie see him?"

"It's called parental visitation. The courts know all about it. If you deny Bobby Joe that, he might take you to court."

"I'm going to ask for child support, maybe I'll ask for back payments as well."

"Would that affect your welfare payments?"

Her eyes widened. "Probably. Oh, God," she exclaimed, pressing her hands to her temples. "Do I have to jeopardize what little security I have in order to get ahead? I can't go to college unless I get the grant. I can't afford to go to school and take care of my kids, so maybe I'll have to get a part-time job, but then I'll have to pay for a sitter and I can't afford a sitter on part-time work."

"It's called taking a risk," he said.

"I've been dependent so long I'm afraid to break free."

"Hold Bobby Joe responsible for child support," he suggested. "He's got a job. He should provide for their support."

"Never has in the past," she mumbled. "I don't trust him, Adrian. He gets even when people cross him."

"Don't make problems you don't have," he cautioned her. "Won't you have to let the county know you've found your children's father? Won't they go after him?"

"I don't know. I'll have to find out."

"You'll work it all out. I know you will," he assured her.

"You and I won't see each other if I move away, will we?" she asked, a sadness settling over her.

"We'll work that out, too," he promised. "I know how important this it to you. But how will you keep your promise to your aunt if you move away?"

"I don't know. Aunt Min and Uncle Harry are moving back in mid-January. Everything is so uncertain. I hate that! I haven't finished my research on the Hardesty family, and I haven't finished working on the letters, and I just wrote to Bernice Johnson."

"Who's Bernice Johnson?" he asked.

"She's my cousin Abbie's real mother," Callie explained. She clenched her fists. "Adrian, there are so many loose ends. How can I possibly tie them all up in the weeks ahead?"

"Let's start with your cousins. Have you contacted them?"

She shook her head. "I haven't had time to write to them."

"Call them," he suggested.

"I don't use my mother's phone if I can't pay for the calls."

"Use mine."

"Oh, no."

"Oh, yes," he insisted. "Do you know their numbers?"

"I have them written down in my address book. It's in my purse." Her brow furrowed. "Could I really? I won't talk for long. What time is it?"

He glanced at his watch. "Eight p.m."

"That makes it seven there," she said. "It's not too late."

He smiled and pointed to the phone. "Forget the costs and call them both."

She dialed the number of the Grasten sheep ranch in southwestern Montana. On the fourth ring, a woman answered.

"Hello, is Abbie Grasten there?"

"Sorry, she's gone for a few days," the woman said.

"Is this Wilma?" When the woman acknowledged that she was Wilma, Callie said, "This is Callie Huff, Abbie's cousin. I... I just wanted to wish her a Merry Christmas."

"Of course, I remember you. You're the little cousin from Kentucky. Abbie is down at Eileen's place in Idaho."

"Dane, too?"

"No, ma'am. Dane's here driving Moses and me crazy."

"Is there ... trouble?" Callie asked.

"Eileen went into early labor," Wilma replied. "She was having a few problems, so the doctor put her into the hospital in Idaho Falls. Abbie took the baby and went to stay with Eileen's kids. Call her there, why don't you? She left this morning right after we opened the presents. I'm sure she's there by now."

Callie explained the situation to Adrian, then dialed the number at the Idaho potato farm.

Abbie's voice was calm on the phone line, but Callie sensed the concern. "She started having contractions yesterday and held off telling anyone until this morning. Dan called the doctor. The babies aren't due until early February, actually five weeks from now. Dan called just before you did. He said she's comfortable but worried silly. You know how maternal Eileen is. She thinks she has to mother the world."

They chatted for a while.

"Where are you calling from?" Abbie asked. "It's been thirty minutes already, and you've never mentioned the cost."

Callie cleared her throat. "I'm using a ... friend's phone."

"Well, give me the number so I can call you back if I hear anything."

"I . . . I may not be here. He's . . ."

"He? He who?"

"Ah . . . Mr. Coleman."

"Mr., is it? Is he good-looking?"

"Well . . ." She turned to Adrian.

"Describe him," Abbie insisted. "What's his first name?"

"It's Adrian Bradford Coleman. He's tall, over six feet . . . black hair . . . eyes like Eileen's and he's . . . muscular."

She listened for a moment, then replied, "Yes, very. At least I think so." She smiled at Adrian, who had slipped his arm around Callie.

Adrian ran his fingers up the back of her neck and around her ear, then kissed her earlobe. She giggled.

"What's going on there?" Abbie asked.

Adrian put his mouth near Callie's. "She's about to be kissed . . . again."

Callie slapped playfully at him and turned away. "I've got to go. This is going to cost me a fortune. He says I don't have to pay but I will."

"Don't let pride get in the way of a relationship, Callie," her older cousin advised.

"It's easier to give advice than to take it," Callie replied. "Abbie, let me know how Eileen is doing, please. You can leave a message here or at Momma's place. Goodness, I hope all goes well with them. Eileen deserves some happiness."

"So do you, honey," Abbie said. "It's been great hearing from you."

"Oh, wait! I forgot why I called." She explained her idea for a Hardesty reunion. "In mid-August, before school starts again. Ask Eileen, would you? They can bring the children, and the twins will be old enough to travel. You and Dane can bring Anna. Aunt Minnie wants to see her so much. Aunt Minnie hasn't been feeling very good. It's her heart."

She listened a few minutes. "I didn't know she hadn't told you. She keeps her secrets, too. I'm doing this for all of you. It's my way of settling my debts. Try to understand."

"It's not necessary," Abbie replied, "but it's a wonderful idea, and I'm especially glad about Bernice . . . my mother. I want to get to know her better. There must be some secret Aunt Minnie and Bernice never told me. I'll be in touch." Abbie said her final goodbye, and the dial tone sounded in Callie's ear.

Adrian took the receiver from her hand and replaced it. He put his arm around her shoulders and guided her back to his bedroom. Her heart began to pound, and a burning glow of desire ignited deep inside her as he closed the door.

"Now, I want to make love to you until you beg for mercy," he said, a gleam in his eyes. "I'll show you that for us lovemaking is wonderful no matter how we do it." He removed her new clothing, lingering over each piece, kissing each inch of her skin as he bared it, caressing her body until she thought she would surely die of desire.

She stood before him, naked and warm, feeling loved and willing to give love in return. She helped him undress, and together they fulfilled his prophesy.

CHAPTER ELEVEN

CALLIE WOKE WITH A START and sat up in bed. "I've got to go home." She glanced at the clock. "It's eleven o'clock. This isn't right. I never planned to spend the night with you."

Adrian rolled over and groaned, pressed his face against her naked hip and kissed it, then stretched and yawned. "Callie, lie down and go back to sleep. We can talk about it tomorrow." He rolled onto his back, never opening his eyes once.

"No." She left the bed and began to dress in the clothes she had arrived in. "If I stay, everyone will know what we've done."

"It's acceptable nowadays."

"Not for me...or for my family." She pulled on a shoe and tied the laces. "If you won't take me, I'll walk."

"Callie, you're panicking again." He got out of bed and put on his jeans. "What's got into you? You're a different woman than you were a few hours ago."

She ran her fingers through her hair and swept it away from her face. "I wasn't myself. I was in a fantasy world. Tomorrow will come. That's real. I've got to get home."

He grabbed her arm but she jerked away.

"Don't hurt me," she cried.

"Callie, sweetheart," he said, holding her loosely in his arms. "You're trembling. Are you afraid of me? Is that what he's done to you? I've never hit a woman in my life, and I certainly would never hurt you. Look at me...please." He tilted her chin up. Slowly she opened her eyes. "What happened to all the love we shared a few hours ago? Can you erase it so easily?"

She met his gaze directly. "This is all happening too fast. I feel as if I'm being torn apart. It would be very easy to just say yes to all your offers, but that would be wrong, for both of us. I need time to think."

"Why?" The usual sparkle had left his eyes, and for the first time since she had met him, she realized he was vulnerable, perhaps as much as she was.

She handed him his sweater and shirt. "You overpower me, Adrian. You've turned me into a Cinderella with all those beautiful gifts. You're my Prince Charming. You've ridden up on your white charger, and you're willing to carry me off to your castle. But would we live happily ever after? I don't know. I want to be sure. I need time."

He turned away.

"I'll be in the living room," she said, and before she could weaken, she left the room.

A few minutes later, he joined her, grabbed his keys and motioned her out the door. His silence continued as they drove away from the log house. When he braked in front of her parents' house, he still hadn't said a word.

"Adrian, listen to me." She took his hand, and his fingers clamped around hers like a vice. "We shared something special, but we've let our emotions get out of control too soon. Do you understand?"

A muscle in his jaw twitched. "I know you have priorities."

"Adrian," she said, reaching to kiss him lightly on his cheek. "You are one of my priorities, too, but you've made a mess of all the others. That's exactly why I need

time to work them back into order. Be my friend again.
I need a friend right now. Very much.''

He opened the door, walked around to the other side
of his truck and opened hers. As she slid to the ground,
he trapped her between the vehicle and himself.

"I want more than friendship," he murmured, "much
more."

A sob tore from her throat. "You've awakened a
woman inside of me that I didn't realize was there. She
needs time to settle in." Her arms slid up and around his
neck. "I thought moving away to a new future was the
most important thing in my life, but the thought of
moving away from you tears me apart. Still, I've got to
work this out for myself. Don't you understand? I have
a chance to make something of myself. I can be a worth-
while human being, not just a drain on the welfare system."

"Why the obsession to do it alone when we could be
together, Callie? It doesn't make sense."

"But it does to me," she replied. "You'll be with me
in spirit, wherever I go. I promise."

"Then I'll give you time," he promised. "I'll keep my
distance, but if you need me, I'll come."

"Thank you," she whispered.

"WHY GIRL, WHAT ARE you doing still here?" Ellen
Hardesty asked.

Callie sat at the kitchen table, hunkered over several
sheets of paper. She glanced up. "Did Daddy get off to
Madisonville?" She tried not to think about the man with
whom her father would be spending the morning.

"Yes, he did," Ellen replied. "We've been talking and
talking and we agreed we'll take his offer. The place is
almost clear of debt, so we're gonna take the money and

run...right over to Greenville and buy that property next to Harry and Minnie's new place." She smiled. "Your daddy has spent enough years coaxin' tobacco and soybeans, sorghum and sweet corn from the land. It's awearing him out, and I want to see him and your uncle have time to go fishin' or to drive down to Lake Malone and rent a boat and just loll around in the sun. With those two men out of our hair, Min and I can get down to some serious quiltin'."

"That's great," Callie said absently.

"Don't you have classes today?"

"Not until one," Callie replied. "The instructors have a staff meeting, something to do with funding for next year."

"So what are you doin'? You moped all day yesterday," Ellen said. "Frankly, I was surprised to see you come back Saturday night. Your daddy reconciled himself to your spendin' the night with that nice man."

Callie glanced up. "Daddy called Adrian a 'nice man'?"

"That's my phrasin'."

"And what did Daddy actually say?"

"Something about nature taking its course and the modern generation," Ellen replied.

"What did he say when I came in?"

"Nothin', but he stopped tossin' and turnin' and finally went to sleep once you made your presence known."

Callie smiled. "Sorry I stumbled over the skateboard Robbie left in the hallway. I didn't intend to wake the whole house."

"Just as well. That way we knew you'd changed your mind."

"Changed my mind? Was everyone expecting me to stay with Adrian the entire night? Is that what you all think I'm like?"

Ellen patted Callie's shoulder. "No, honey. Robbie was so engrossed in meeting his real daddy, he didn't care one way or t'other. Linda had her nose buried in a book, but I think her mind was on her real daddy, too. Your own daddy just doesn't want to see you hurtin' again."

"And you, Momma?"

"I think you should follow your heart." She poured two cups of coffee and sat down. "Why did you come back?"

Callie took a sip of coffee and stared out the window for several seconds. "He says he loves me."

Ellen's brown eyes lightened. "It's plain to see he has eyes only for you when you're together. That's why you came home?"

"Partly." Callie described the gifts Adrian had given her. "Momma, he gave me the most beautiful dulcimer I've ever seen. Its notes are clear, its tone perfect."

"That's because of your playing."

"Maybe. I left them all at his house. I didn't know how to take them without making him think everything was fine... and it's not. He talks about when we're old married folks. He insists he's not asking me now, but he keeps talking as if it's already happened, as if we're living in the future. It's romantic when he says it, but then I get to thinking about it, and I resent it. I have living to do. I've just started! I want to go on to college. I want a career."

"He's a reasonable man," Ellen said. "He'll understand."

Callie frowned. "But he doesn't understand. How can he when he's never been where I've been? I don't want to be on relief. I don't ever want to hear people make nasty remarks behind my back when I buy groceries with food stamps. When I get that grant, I'll be moving and taking the kids with me. Someday I'll be able to pay you and Daddy back for letting us live here."

"You're payin' rent and helpin' with the chores," Ellen said. "And we didn't ask for the rent. The rooms were empty anyway."

"But we've used electricity and the grocery bill is bigger and the laundry is . . ."

"You've done all your family's laundry and ours besides. You've got no reason to feel you owe us a thing," Ellen said. "We've loved having you. These few months don't begin to make up for the years you were away when we hardly ever saw you, honey."

Callie leaned back in her chair. "It's hard to figure out the right thing to do. I've been trying to sort all these changes looming ahead, but nothing seems to work, and when I bring Adrian into the picture, it just becomes unsolvable."

"Do you love him?"

"I didn't want to, but I'm slipping. If he had just stayed out of my life for a while, I could have accomplished so much, but when I'm with him, all I think about is how wonderful he is."

"I reckon you've more than slipped," Ellen hinted. "Why can't you love him and go to college, too? He could help you."

"No!" Callie insisted. "I'll do it myself."

"Honey, that sounds downright spiteful," Ellen said. "A woman doesn't have to choose between a man and all the other things she may want in this world. Maybe you can't have them all, but maybe some of them ain't so important as you think."

Callie's shoulders heaved. "I don't want to love him until I've proven to myself I can succeed alone." She shook her head. "If I keep seeing him, I'll weaken. He turns my knees to jelly and sets my heart to thumping." She smiled. "Is that the beginning of true love? Or just lustful desire?"

Ellen cocked a brow and smiled. "Tain't no reason why you can't have both."

Callie turned around. "You mean you and Daddy? Is that the way it is with you two? Even after all these years?"

Ellen smiled as she refilled their cups but didn't reply.

"I hurt his feelings the other night when I insisted on coming home," Callie explained. "But I couldn't give in, even after..." She looked away, embarrassed at her remark.

"Have the two of you...? Have you...been with him? Goodness, Callie, this isn't easy for a momma." Ellen tucked a wayward strand of graying hair into the bun on the back of her head. "Parents expect such things from their sons, but somehow we imagine our daughters stay pure and untouched." She laughed. "Silly, isn't it? How do we think our daughters get those babies? From the stork?"

Callie patted her mother's hand. "Yes, Momma, we made love, and it was wonderful, and I'd love to spend the rest of my life with him...but not yet."

Ellen squeezed Callie's hand. "You've just begun to live, honey. You've been treading water ever since you and that no-good Bobby Joe got married. Your daddy and I were wrong to force the wedding, but we can't undo what's in the past. I know we were wrong to let you shut yourself off. We should have come to see you...seen for ourselves that you were okay. We forsaked you, our only daughter. I can't forgive myself for that. Maybe that's why I'm so glad you're back home for a while. We know you'll leave again, because now you're living again. You're making up for lost time."

"What if Adrian refuses to wait?"

"If he loves you, he'll understand."

HER FATHER WAS STILL GONE when Callie drove into Greenville.

Judith Norwood, the Second Chance instructor, began the class with an announcement. "I have some good news and some bad news," she said, running a hand through her stubby gray hair. "We've been notified of new funding, so we'll be here for another year."

The women, who were sitting in a double semicircle, clapped their approval. "But we're being cut by twenty percent." The women groaned. "We'll adjourn after today and reconvene Monday after New Year's Day. Some of you have children who are out of school for the holidays. If we take a few days off, it will save money on your child-care costs and on our budget. Unfortunately, that means the G.E.D. tests will be postponed as well."

"Doesn't that put them terribly close to the start of the second semester at the colleges?" one woman asked.

Judith nodded. "And that's the bad news. I don't want you to get discouraged, but many of the colleges and universities in the state have lost a large percentage of their grant monies. Some of you will have to wait until the fall...unless you can find alternative funding. Maybe you can find a sugar daddy."

The class booed. Judith smiled. "That's the way. Don't depend on anyone but yourselves. It's the only way."

FINIS HARDESTY CAME HOME in the late afternoon, carrying a fat white envelope in his hand. "We struck a deal. He's taking the place off our hands, and we won't have to move out until next fall. He's gonna merge it with the Dickens operations."

At dinner Finis detailed the transaction, withholding only the price he'd gotten. "He'll be takin' our west section first. After the first of the month, he'll be storin' some of the heavy equipment there and doin' some preliminary clearing." He shook his head. "That's a sharp businessman for a fellow as young as he is. I think he could charm the clothes right off a woman's back."

Callie blanched and took another bite of fried apples.

"No offense intended to you ladies," Finis added, "but he made me feel like I'd come out smelling like a rose. Only I reckon the White Glove Mining Company is the winner in the long run."

"Daddy, did he say anything about . . . finding my necklace?"

"'Nary a thing, Callie. Coal business was all we talked about. He did say he was goin' to be busy these next few months."

OVER THE NEXT WEEK Adrian phoned twice but the conversations were brief and general. After confirming Callie and the children were fine, he would promise to keep in touch and say goodbye.

A week passed without a call, and she grew apprehensive.

Two weeks later a legal notice appeared in the local paper. "Notice of intention to mine, pursuant to Application Number," Callie read. Then she blinked and the print all seemed to run together. In the body of the announcement appeared a concise explanation that the

Dickens mine was being expanded to include land formerly owned by Finis Hardesty and Abigail Grasten.

"Abbie agreed to sell?" she asked her father.

Finis chuckled. "He must have charmed her, too."

"Oh, no," she murmured as she read on. "He's asked for a proposed land use change from 'forest, water impoundment and pasture premining land use to water impoundment and pasture postmining land use.'" She glanced up at her father. "Does that mean he plans to tear the trees down and never replant them?"

Finis nodded. "It'll make good grazing land."

"I was just thinking about our secret glen where Eileen, Abbie and I had our club meetings," she added. "The glen won't exist after he gets through."

"That's progress," her father said. "He's paying me a fair price, so he can do what he damn well wants to do, as far as I'm concerned." He frowned at Callie. "I haven't seen him hanging around here lately. You two have a spat?"

Callie shrugged. "He's busy. After all, he was looking for you when we met again. He got what he wanted, I reckon."

"His picture is on page one of the second section," her father said. "Tain't nothing to do with coal. Seems he got interviewed about mules and huntin' dogs."

She skipped to the next section. Staring back at her was a smiling Adrian Coleman, alongside two other men. She scanned the article. "Adrian B. Coleman, a successful vice president in the family-owned White Glove Mining Corporation, has filled the mantle of his contemporary log home with numerous trophies...."

She laid down the newspaper. "It says here he's a vice president. It's hard to think of him all dressed up."

Finis laughed. "He was wearing a fancy gray suit when I did my business with him. Right good-looking young man, if'n you ask me. Miss him, Callie?"

"A little," she admitted.

Her mother took the paper and snipped out the article and photograph, then handed the clipping to Callie with a smile. "No reason to throw it out," she said, turning away before Callie could respond.

When Callie returned from Greenville the next day, her mother handed her a note. "Abbie called this morning. She's got news about Eileen. I promised you'd call as soon as you got home. Abbie's back at the ranch in Montana. Now, there's the phone, and you know the number."

Robbie and Linda came into the room while she was dialing. By the time Abbie answered, Callie's father had also joined the anxious crowd gathered around her.

Callie tightened her grip on the receiver. "What are they? Boys? Girls? One of each?"

She listened intently then sighed deeply and smiled. "Hold on, Abbie." She pressed the receiver to her breasts and said. "Two healthy boys. Six pounds each—monsters for twins."

"Praise the Lord," Ellen said.

"Amen," Finis added.

Robbie grunted and bounced his basketball, then sidled out the door when his grandmother shook her finger at him.

"That's wonderful," Linda sighed. "What did they name them?"

Callie asked, then listened. "Daniel Andrew to be called Danny and Shelby Anthony to be called Tony. Dan is after the father, of course. Shelby Anthony is after Eileen's father."

Callie listened again. "Now she wants to talk private woman talk."

When she'd waved the others out of the room, Callie said, "I'm alone now. How's Eileen?"

"She had a very rough time of it," Abbie replied.

"When were the babies born?"

"A week ago."

Callie dropped to a kitchen chair. "And you're just now letting us know? What happened?"

"Everything," Abbie said. "She was in labor for two days. One of them was breech. She had a C-section and complications. Now she's recovering from a hysterectomy. Callie, you know how important children are to Eileen, and now there won't be any more. She's been depressed. The babies were fine, home in three days, but Dan just brought Eileen home yesterday."

"Were you there all the time?" Callie asked.

"I got home a little bit ago. Dane's been so understanding about all this. He says it makes him think twice about us having another child."

"Are you?" Callie asked.

"Ask me in a year or so and I'll probably tell you I'm X number of months pregnant. Anna is almost six months. Soon she'll need someone to play with. Say, Callie, I called your Mr. Coleman's number, expecting to find you there," Abbie said.

"When?"

"New Year's Day. Then Eileen had problems again, so I waited. I called again just a bit ago. We chatted."

"You and Adrian? What about?"

"You," Abbie said. "I don't know all the details, but that man is hurting."

"So am I," Callie admitted.

"He seems terribly nice. He's confused. He doesn't understand why you've shunned him."

"Telephones work both ways," Callie said. "He hasn't called for three weeks. When I told him I needed time to think, I didn't mean I never wanted to see him again."

"Why don't you call him?"

"What would I say?"

"Invite him to dinner."

"Where?" Callie asked, thinking of the divorce fund she had stashed beneath her lingerie. "I do have a little money saved up. Abbie, I've never paid for a man's dinner in my life!"

"Then it's high time you did. Swallow your pride and give him a call. I know he's home."

"What if he turns me down?"

"Ah, but what if he says yes?"

CHAPTER TWELVE

WHY NOT? CALLIE THOUGHT as she hung up the receiver. The worst he could say was no. She dialed his number three times without even getting up enough courage to let it ring more than once. But the third time he answered before she could hang up.

"Damn it, who is this?" Adrian asked.

"Just . . . me," Callie replied, her voice unsteady.

"Callie?"

"I . . . I wondered if you have any plans . . . for dinner tonight." The words tumbled over each other. "I'll understand if you're already committed, but if you're free I'd like to invite you out. It's on me, and I'll drive, too, and pick you up."

"Did your cousin put you up to this?" he asked.

"That's irrelevant. Do you want to?"

"Yes, damn it. When?"

She glanced at the clock. "Thirty minutes." She hung up. Wanting no time to think about her impulsive actions, she found her mother in the sewing room. "Can you keep an eye on the kids?"

Her mother nodded. "I'll be starting dinner in a few minutes. Will you be here?"

"I'm taking *the* Mr. Coleman out to dinner."

Her mother spun around. Before the questions could begin, Callie kissed her on the cheek and ran out the door.

In her closet, Callie pulled a mint-green wool knit coat-dress Eileen had sent her for Christmas from its hanger. The shawl collar and easy drape of the full skirt accented her petite figure. It was loose at her waist, confirming her recent loss of appetite, but a fabric belt gave the dress some more shape. She pulled on her only good pair of panty hose and stepped into black pumps. Racing down the stairs, she swung to a stop near her mother.

"If you were a man, would you find me attractive?"

Her mother laughed. "Ask Adrian. I'm partial." She rubbed her chin. "But then, he may be too."

She hugged her mother, kissed Robbie and Linda and ran out the door.

When she squealed to a stop in front of his home, Adrian was lounging against a porch post, looking devastatingly handsome in a gray flannel suit. She motioned him to the passenger side. His features were somber as he strolled toward the truck.

"Where to?" she asked.

He slammed the door and stared straight ahead. "You're in charge. You decide. Make a decision—take a risk." He adjusted the maroon tie around his neck.

Irritated at his flip manner, she shifted into reverse and spun around. "No catfish," she said. "I hate catfish."

He shrugged. "There's a great little restaurant in Madisonville."

She stiffened. "I took fifteen dollars from my divorce fund." She turned to him. "Is that enough?"

"Yes, the restaurant isn't too expensive." He gave her directions.

When they were seated in a booth in the restaurant, he coughed twice, a deep rasping sound that stopped her reading of the menu. She peered over its top. "Are you sick?"

"I had a cold last week. The doctor treated me for a bronchial infection. I missed several days work."

"Why didn't you let me know?"

"I didn't want you to worry," he replied, raising his menu again. "You have enough to be concerned about."

She stared at the top of his head showing above the menu. Did he think she had stopped caring? Her lips tightened as she concentrated on the entrees, scrutinizing their prices. If he ordered first, she could adjust her own selection downward to avoid any embarrassment when the check came.

He ordered a full country-steak dinner. She switched from shrimp to fried chicken.

Adrian pointed to her scribbling on the paper napkin. "I'll take care of the tip, if that will help so that you won't have to keep a running tab on the evening's expenditures."

Callie stopped writing and shoved the pen back into her purse. "You're poking fun at me."

"No, I'm not."

"I know you never have to worry about something as trivial as money, Adrian, but can't you be civil and respect my situation?"

"Of course." When the waitress returned with their bowls of soup, he said, "Add a piece of cherry pie to the bill, with ice cream."

The waitress turned to Callie. "The same for you, ma'am?"

Callie shook her head. "But give me the bill, please."

"Sure?" The waitress shifted her attention to Adrian.

"Do as the pretty lady says," Adrian replied, dipping his spoon into the soup. "She's the boss tonight."

They ate in silence until dessert arrived. With nothing to eat, her attention was drawn to the handsome man enjoying his cherry pie. "Adrian, I need your help."

He laid down his fork and stared directly at her.

She reached into her purse and withdrew an envelope, pushed it across to him and waited.

He slid his index finger beneath the unsealed flap and lifted it enough to see inside.

"It's one hundred fifty-eight dollars," she explained. "I dipped into it at Christmas...and for tonight. Would you give it to that lawyer friend of yours and tell him I'll have more in the months to come? I'll agree to any amount he wants. I can't wait any longer. I want a legal divorce from Bobby Joe."

"Why the rush after all these years?" he asked.

"Robbie's been spending Saturdays with him. I...I don't know what my rights are, my legal rights, I mean. I need help."

He shoved the envelope into his inside jacket pocket. "I'll call him tomorrow and let you know."

She studied his gray suit. "You look...very nice—handsome, I mean. I've never seen you...all gussied up." She smiled, her expression lightening considerably. "I'm sorry I couldn't afford to take you to a fancier place."

"Likewise."

She glanced up. "You mean the restaurant?"

"No, Callie, I mean you. You're lovely in that dress. It's a good color on you. You look very soft and feminine." He took another bite of pie. "What's new with school? Are you a graduate yet? On your way to college?"

She inhaled. "I find out tomorrow. MSU accepted me, but I haven't heard on either the G.E.D. tests or my grant."

"I believe they'll admit you without your G.E.D. if you're over twenty-five," he said.

"But I want to know that I can pass the test."

He shrugged. "You'll be moving soon?"

"Yes."

"Then I wish you the best, and much success in all that you do. I'm sure you have a promising future."

His impersonal congratulations irked her. "Is this your way of saying goodbye?" she asked. "Can't we still be friends?"

"I want to be more than your friend, Callie," he replied, his face a mask. "I'm realistic. With you living in Murray or Bowling Green or wherever the hell you decide to settle, the odds are against our meeting very often, aren't they?"

"Yes," she mumbled.

He finished the pie and pushed the plate back a few inches. "Have your aunt and uncle returned to the area?"

She smiled. "They moved in last Saturday. I'm going to try to teach her to read. She never went to school, can you imagine?"

"Your Aunt Minnie has a lot of company, I'm sad to say," he replied. "As many as one-third of the adults in this state can't read beyond a rudimentary level. I grew up in a home surrounded by books. Both my parents are avid readers. Many children never know what that's like. They grow up and become part of the mass of functional illiterates. I think it's a disgrace."

He reached for his pen, wrote a phone number on the corner of his napkin and tore it off. "If you're serious about your aunt, why don't you talk to Ms Emily Oldham at WKU. Here's her number in Bowling Green. She's involved in a literacy program that's about to go statewide. She can either give you some pointers or suggest someone who can help. It might be best if you pass the task on to someone more impartial."

"Who is this Emily Oldham?" she asked.

"She's Cindy Lou's aunt."

"Cindy Lou?" She put the triangle of linen-weave paper into the coin compartment of her wallet. "Thank you."

"Cindy Lou and Emily spent the weekend at my place recently. They explained the program. Her aunt is very excited."

Callie's mouth tightened. "Are you seeing Cindy Lou again?"

"She's between semesters."

"She's a teacher?" Callie asked, dreading the answer.

"She's an English professor at the University of Tennessee in Knoxville." He glanced up. "She received her Ph.D. two years ago. She did her dissertation on formal English as a second language to regional colloquial vocabulary and speech. She and Emily have received joint grants to develop a literacy program to improve the success rate when working with adult new readers."

"She...she must be very intelligent," Callie murmured, her self-esteem taking a nosedive.

"That she is." He accepted a refill of coffee from the waitress. "When we were kids, she wanted to play school all the time and I'd take it until she got too bossy." He laughed. "Then I'd sneak away and go fishing."

"Playing school is better than playing doctor," she said, but immediately blushed as red as his cherry pie.

"We did that, too, when we were older." He turned his spoon over several times. "We were each other's first sexual partner on a hot summer day when we were seventeen."

"Obviously she didn't get pregnant," she said.

He straightened. "No, she didn't get pregnant, and we were wise enough to stop experimenting."

"And I wasn't?"

"I don't know what you and Bobby Joe did, and I don't care. That's water under the bridge as far as I'm concerned, just as it is with Cindy and me."

"When you move you'll be closer to Knoxville," she said.

"Yes, I will."

A pained expression settled in Callie's eyes. "Are you seeing her again?"

"I told you once that we had an affair." He straightened in his chair. "Actually we had two affairs. The last time was after college. It didn't last, and it won't be resumed. She's met someone from Knoxville, a fellow professor. I met him. They're a perfect match. She's a friend, and I want her to stay a friend."

She reached for the check and opened her wallet, removing two bills. "Thank you for accepting my invitation. It was good to see you. I...I missed you...our talks. Perhaps we can do this again sometime."

"Of course," he said, helping her with her jacket. "The next time will be on me."

On the way back to his place, she told him about Eileen and the twins. "And my kids are fine," she added. "Linda's a little pale, though, and the doctor wants to see her again in a month. She may need another operation. I'll have to make arrangements through Medicaid. I don't know if they'll consider the grant as income or not. It might cause problems in my qualifications."

"If I can help, you know I'm willing," he said.

She shook her head. "I'm sure that won't be necessary." She flicked on her left turn blinker and waited for traffic to clear. "And the permit for the mine? Did it get approved?"

"Yes, we'll be moving some heavy equipment in next week," he said. "We'll put high fencing around it, of course, but I know how curious children can be. Sometimes they climb like monkeys. Warn Robbie and Linda and their friends to stay away. I wouldn't want anyone to get hurt."

"Of course," she murmured.

She parked near his front door and killed the engine. "Well," she said, "we're here."

"Come in for a glass of wine?"

"No, thank you, not when I'm driving."

"You left your gifts here," he said. "Would you like to take them home now? I had a hard time explaining to Aunt Em why a pink sweater and rose slacks were hanging in the guest closet, and of course I didn't try to explain the teddies."

She blushed again. "Yes, I'll take them, and the dulcimer, too, unless you've returned it."

"I gave you the dulcimer without strings...excuse the pun. It was a gift. They're all yours to keep. I hope to hear you play again someday. Come inside and I'll help you take them to the truck. How's it running?"

She smiled. "This old Chevy has been on its last leg for so many years I've lost count." She climbed from the truck and followed him into the log house. The interior was as warm and friendly as she remembered, but memories of their lovemaking sent her heart racing. "Are you still going to sell?"

He nodded. "It's listed already, and I've narrowed my choices to Berea, Kentucky, or Harrogate, Tennessee. I'm taking another trip in a few weeks to make my final choice. Then I'll put this place up for sale. I've already signed a contract and made a hefty down payment to a log-house builder. He's waiting for a place to deliver the logs."

"I'm pleased for you," she said. "I wish I could see my future as clearly as you see yours." She walked into the hallway. "The clothes? Tell me which room and I'll get them."

"In my room. You know the way. I'll get the dulcimer." He turned, leaving her standing alone in the hallway.

Sweet memories assaulted her when she opened the door to his bedroom and entered. Her glance skittered across the bed as she hurried across the room and opened his closet. Amid his shirts and jackets and the aroma of pine cologne, she found the sweater and slacks on a single hanger. The teddies, gown and robe were folded neatly in the gold box, on his dresser alongside a book he had been reading. Despair took her breath away. *So easy,* she thought, *so easy to ask him to love me again.*

The door opened, and she whirled around.

"Did you find everything?" he asked, coming around the bed to where she stood.

Callie was unaware of her tears until he wiped them away. "I love you," he said. "But I won't pressure you again." His lips grazed her cheek. "I'm sure you're anxious to have tomorrow come. Good luck on getting your G.E.D. and the grant. Call me and let me know."

She nodded, but a catch in her throat stopped the words.

"The whole world is about to open up to you, Callie. I wish you the best." He reached for the door as she did, and their hands touched. "Oh God, Callie." He pulled her roughly into his arms, pressing his cheek against hers until she thought she would faint.

He eased his hold, his arms still encircling her waist. "I wanted to give you all my worldly possessions...but you want the stars. I'll wait." His mouth hovered near hers. Slowly his lips parted. She saw the white of his straight teeth, the shadow of his dark beard on his clean-shaven upper lip—a lip she wanted to taste once more.

She wound her arms around his neck and pulled his head down, claiming his kiss, savoring the passion they had shared, wondering if ever again they would share the ecstasy of his promises.

If he loved her, he should be willing to wait, but if she was falling in love with him, could she?

ADRIAN COLEMAN WATCHED her walk away, the mint-green sway of her skirt glowing in the darkness.

He had never seen her look more beautiful nor carry herself with such dignity and determination. Perhaps she was fighting an internal war of wills between her drive for self-sufficiency and her need for love and affection.

Why had he been unable to convince her that her future was as stable and bright as his own? Bright? As the red taillights of Callie's truck faded into the night, his own future seemed dim. His long-awaited change of careers and relocation had a bitterness he had never anticipated.

He resisted the urge to go after her, to try once more to convince her of his sincerity. "No," he murmured into the stillness of the night, "the next move is hers."

He went back inside and found that the quietness of the house had become a tomb. He hung up the tailored gray suit alongside the empty hanger where minutes earlier her sweater and slacks had been. Searching through his dresser drawers, he found a pair of denim overalls he usually reserved for mule-pulling competitions and put them on. He caught a glimpse of himself in the mirror as he buttoned the front of a red-and-black flannel shirt.

Was he trying to delude himself, thinking he could find happiness and fulfillment by leaving White Glove and hiding out in the mountains? Could he escape the unsightly hills of reclaimed land surrounding him, some of which he had had a hand in creating?

At one time, he had thought he could make a difference in an industry whose history was filled with abuse and shame, with corruption, negligence and death. Had he chosen to turn his back on it all because he had finally decided one man couldn't make a difference? Reluctantly, he admitted that might be true. But what law of nature or of man required him to stay and beat himself to death? There had to be a time when a man might shake the dust from his feet and move on.

He grabbed a denim jacket, flipped on the light in the backyard and went outside. Calling softly, he unlocked the gate to the run and stooping, went inside to sit on a ledge. Klaus loped up to him and wagged his tail. "Sit," Adrian said, and the dog settled on his haunches between Adrian's legs.

A surge of emotion swept over Adrian, leaving him aching and empty. He put his arms around the dog's neck, and Klaus nuzzled against him. Seldom had Adrian ever been bothered with depression, but since meeting Callie he had been on a roller coaster of ups and downs and now found himself in a valley of despair.

His eyes filled with tears. He hadn't cried since he had been a teenager and had seen his younger brother waste away and die of bone cancer. Perhaps he was overdue. He rubbed his cheek against Klaus's glossy coat.

He couldn't just walk away from Callie. What if she stumbled and fell? Who would pick her up? But why would she fall? She was on the verge of getting the financial help she needed to continue her schooling. She was an intelligent woman with untapped potential, a delicate bud about to unfurl and have her day of blossoming in the sun.

It all hinged on her getting the financial help she needed. He tried to imagine what life would be like without the security money provided. He had been born into wealth, but it had not been handed to him irresponsibly. His parents had made him a responsible money manager, both in his personal life and in his professional position at White Glove. He had invested wisely. He had bought added shares in White Glove. When he cashed in his shares he would have a nest egg to reinvest, which would carry him for years, possibly for the rest of his life.

Callie had found herself with nothing but forty dollars, a broken-down truck and two babies, one of whom had been in need of serious medical attention—and still was. Could he have carried such burdens, especially at her age? At nineteen, he had completed two years of college with a straight-A average. But every semester, he'd been able to take it for granted that checks for tuition and dormitory fees would arrive and on the first of every month, he'd receive his allowance check.

Other than the summers when he had talked his father into a job at White Glove, he had never worried about part-time employment. He had never had to go job hunting as had so many of his fellow graduates from MSU. His career position had been waiting for him. He had worked his way up the corporate ladder, interrupted that climb with a four-year enlistment in the air force and returned to a vice presidency that he still held.

Callie had managed to get a check each month, too, he thought, a check that had repeatedly filled her with self-loathing, because she'd had to beg for enough to keep her children from starving. And all the time he had been enjoying luxuries that Callie could only imagine.

She had displayed courage and perseverance when she'd been little more than a child herself. A burst of rage toward all those around her filled him. Where were her parents during those years? Her brothers? Her aunts and uncles and even her cousins? Their absence in her time of need was inexcusable and unforgivable. But most of all, he held Bobby Joe Huff responsible for her plight, for abandoning her when what she needed most was the love and support of a husband.

Adrian buried his face against Klaus's neck, and his shoulders shook. Emotionally, he assumed her burden, transporting himself to her cabin in the eastern mountains, seeing her in his mind's eye as she lost her child, wanting to reach into the imaginary scene and rescue her. He sobbed for her and for everyone who needed someone to care for them, to love them.

"Oh, Callie," he cried, weeping against Klaus, who sat patiently by his master, his stub of a tail wagging his devotion.

CALLIE ARRIVED LATE TO CLASS the next morning. Unable to sleep, she had tossed and turned until three in the morning, angry at herself for letting Abbie talk her into such a stupid act. Why had she wasted fifteen precious dollars just to see a man who fascinated her, who professed his love for her, but who forced her to initiate a kiss and who was determined to walk away from all he had accumulated? She questioned his very sanity. Callie was so distracted that, when she arrived at the center, it took her a minute to notice that her classmates were all huddled together in small groups.

"What's the matter?" she asked, approaching the front of the room, where Judith Norwood stood with a handful of white envelopes.

"Would you all take your places, please?" Judith called. "I have your G.E.D. certificates here. I'm very pleased to report that you *all* passed the tests with flying colors."

The room filled with chattering, excited voices as Judith called their names and the women accepted the long-awaited proof of their competency. The room settled down.

"And the grants," Judith continued. "We were warned some time ago that there wouldn't be enough money for all of you."

"How was the determination made?" one woman asked.

"Financial need—"

"We all qualify there," another woman said, and they all laughed.

"Age . . ."

"We're all mature adults," the first woman said, then turned to Callie, "except this pretty little thing. She's still a baby."

"Ability to fulfill the requirements of the program." Judith continued. "Frankly it's a combination of subjective opinion and just plain old luck of the draw." She began calling names and passing out the envelopes.

Callie accepted her envelope.

Marian West, the woman sitting beside Callie, opened her envelope and shrieked, "I got it! Tuition and housing and the whole bit! I can pack my bags and head to Bowling Green." She danced a jig around her chair and dropped back into it. "Ladies, you're lookin' at a future graduate in social sciences from Western Kentucky University, and I'll only be fifty-three when I get my degree. That bastard of a husband who left me holding the bag can— No, that's wrong. If he'd stayed, I probably would have stayed, too, until we both died of atrophy."

The other women chuckled and began opening their envelopes. Some were ecstatic, some wept with pleasure, others in disappointment. Callie's envelope lay on her desk.

"I'll open mine later," she said.

The class resumed. "Next week, we're going to have two microcomputers installed, compliments of a computer store in Louisville," Judith announced. "We'll have sixteen new members joining us. It seems there's no end to the women who want to find new direction in their lives. Now then, let's get down to business."

As Callie drove home, she passed a gate and high chain-link fence that had replaced the long-standing pole-and-barbed-wire fence her brothers had helped her father install years earlier. A sign had been posted, warning of future blasting schedules and stating that the property was now owned by White Glove Mining, Inc., of Madisonville, Kentucky.

At dinner, the conversation centered on the heavy dozers and drag lines that had been moved onto the property.

"They sure do make the place look different," Finis said, a hint of boastfulness in his voice. "But since we'll be here until the fall, I'm still gonna start the tobacco beds in March just like I always do. No need to waste the time and ground even if I will have all the money I need."

After the meal, Robbie sidled up to Callie. "Ma, my pa wants to know if I can go with him and Mary Lou and Tracy Lynn to his folks's place in Paducah next Sunday.

Did you know they was my grandparents, too? Just like Grandpa and Grandma Hardesty? Gee, I can hardly wait to meet 'em. Can I go, huh?''

Her heart tightened. ''Just you?''

He glanced toward his sister, who had curled up in a chair with a book. ''Yeah, is that okay? I told him Linda hadn't been feeling so good, and he said it would be better if she stayed home. He said she could go some other time.''

Callie sighed. ''I suppose so. You're entitled to know that side of your family, too. When did he call?'' she asked.

''Mary Lou called when I got home from school. She's sure nice,'' he said, beaming a boyish smile at her.

Upstairs in her room that night, Callie lay propped up on several pillows, the unopened envelope across her knees. Her future lay inside. No longer could she postpone the results. She had been collecting boxes in case a sudden move was in the works. Now she would know if she had a need for them.

She slid her finger beneath the sealed flap, tearing it in spots as she carefully opened it. Pulling out the sheets of paper, she closed her eyes and counted, trying to calm her pounding heart. She opened her eyes and read, ''We at Murray State University appreciate your application and request for a grant to attend our fine school.''

She stopped, closing her eyes before reading on.

''Unfortunately, this year's funding through grants and scholarships has decreased significantly and we regret to inform you that your request for a grant has been denied....'' The rest of the letter blurred as she blinked back the tears.

"Denied? Why?" she gasped, sitting up and throwing her legs off the edge of the bed as she searched the letter. No other reason was stated other than lack of funds. Someone had stuck a peel-off note to the sheet that read, "Sorry, the well ran dry."

CHAPTER THIRTEEN

SHE STARED ACROSS THE ROOM, seeing nothing, thinking nothing, until the vacuum of shock and disbelief exploded into anger. Her gaze fell on the rejection letter again, and she picked it up, ripping it into quarters and dropping it to the floor.

Rolling over, she buried her face in the pillow, her body stiff and uncompromising. Not a tear fell as she lay unmoving in the bed. The hands of the clock ticked around its face. A hardness settled in her heart, and the night eased into morning.

When the alarm sounded, she got out of bed and walked to the bathroom down the hall, showered and dressed, made breakfast for her children and hustled them off to school.

Surely there had to be a way, if not this route then some other, she thought as she drove back to Greenville. In class, surrounded by the women who had become her support group over the months, her composure crumbled.

"No money," she said between hiccups, wiping the streams of tears from her cheeks. "It's always that way, no money. Why does the whole darn world have to depend on money? Why do I have to be a have-not when so many have it and don't care?"

They consoled her, but their words rang hollow, especially from those who had been successful in their search for funding.

Judith Norwood suggested they find out which women got money and what majors had been shown preference. They found that in-state schools had been less generous than three out-of-state universities. Social work majors had faired better than other applicants.

"That makes sense," Judith commented. "Perhaps it's not fair, but it makes sense. You've all known the stigma of being on public assistance, so hopefully you'll remember those days when you're working with clients. It's a crazy world." She turned to Callie. "What major did you choose?"

"Business administration."

Judith frowned. "Business? Are you interested in working in the business world? You've never mentioned it before."

Callie scanned the faces around her as they waited for her reply. "I thought that would be the most likely way to get a job. Accountants, secretaries, computer operators..." Her voice faded into uncertainty.

Judith touched Callie's shoulder and returned to the front of the room. "Perhaps I've failed to get through to some of you," she said. "Money should be your secondary reason to continue your education. Callie, if you could study anything you wanted to study, without regard to your family responsibilities, the time you have available or your pocketbook, what would it be?"

One by one, Callie met the curious gazes of her classmates. "I never thought of it that way. If by some stroke of genius or good luck...?"

"Or a sugar daddy," an older woman interjected.

Callie smiled, thinking of Adrian Coleman and all that he offered. "If the impossible came curling out of the smoke of a magic lantern—" she looked out the window for several seconds "—I'd get some voice training, learn the more complicated techniques for playing my mountain dulcimer, write music, study folk music and crafts and talk to the people in the mountains about their lives and the songs they've passed down from generation to generation."

She turned to Judith. "This isn't costing me a thing?"

"Strictly blue-sky fantasy," Judith replied.

Callie smiled. "My uncle L.T. used to call this kind of daydreaming 'druthering.' Well, I'd travel up every holler I could find and collect old quilts and musical instruments."

Judith smiled. "And who is this Uncle L.T.?"

"He and Aunt Belle lived near Harlan. I stayed with them for three summers when I was a child. She taught me how to play the dulcimer, and he showed me how to make them. They were the sweetest couple in the whole world. She's gone now, and he moved to Jackson. I haven't seen him in years. Momma knows how to sing and play, but she hasn't played since I was a little girl."

"Haven't you been researching your family?" Judith asked.

"Yes, at least the Hardestys from Muhlenberg County." She ran her hand through her loose black hair and frowned. "I never thought about my mother's family. The Campbells were from the southern Appalachian area and...that's all I know, except for my aunt and uncle."

Judith smiled. "Perhaps you take after the Campbells more than you do the Hardestys. With your love of mu sic, your interest in mountain crafts and history, perhaps your future lies in the arts instead of business."

"Whoever made money from the arts?" Callie asked.

"Are there other artistic members in your family?"

"My brother Riley is a potter in Taos, New Mexico. But that's different. He's building a reputation, and he makes a living. All I can do is write songs and play and sing."

"The world sings, whether you listen or not," Judith replied. "Perhaps you should try singing along with it. You might be able to make it a more melodious place to live, wherever you are."

Hadn't Adrian once said the same thing? she thought.

BOBBY JOE KNOCKED AT THE DOOR early Sunday morning. Callie made him wait on the porch until Robbie came racing down the stairs, taking them two at a time.

"When will you have him back?" she asked, still suspicious of Bobby Joe's new paternalism.

"By eight," Bobby Joe promised, winking at her as he left, his hand draped protectively around his son's shoulders.

EILEEN PAGE PHONED Sunday afternoon. "The babies are fine, growing like crazy. All the other kids are fine, too."

"And you?" Callie asked.

"I'm finally getting my strength back," Eileen said. "We're letting Mrs. Jasper go the end of next month. Dan insists on keeping her till then. It's not necessary. Dan married a wife and mother, not an invalid."

"I'm sure he married the woman he loves," Callie said. "Didn't your vows talk about sickness as well as health?"

"Yes, but I never expected to actually be sick."

"Linda goes for a checkup the middle of next month," Callie said. "She's been so listless, and her color isn't good. Dr. Heltsley wants to do some tests. As for Robbie, he's almost as tall as I am and gets more handsome every day," Callie reported, then explained Bobby Joe's reappearance in their lives. "Robbie is getting too attached to his father," she concluded.

"And what about you?" Eileen asked. "Abbie told me about the grant. I'm sorry. What are you doing now?"

"Still in the program in Greenville," she said. "I've sent off new grant applications. We'll see. I'm learning to use a computer. It's great fun, but I'd hate to have to sit at one for eight hours a day."

Eileen laughed. "Dan writes on a computer, and he was trying to put our business accounts on when I started having problems. He's working on them now. The babies are asleep, the girls are visiting at their friends' house down the road and the older boys rode their bicycles into Idaho Falls to a movie, so I thought it was a perfect time to visit with you. Abbie said something about a man. Addison Coleman, is it?"

"Adrian," Callie said. "Adrian Coleman. Remember the White Glove Mining Company? He's one of those Colemans."

"Those rich Coleman boys from Madisonville! I remember some of them. They all played football, and gracious were they all hunks! At least when I was sixteen I thought so. They were always getting their names in the newspapers for their sports prowess in high school. Which one is he?"

"He's the youngest," Callie murmured, thinking of Adrian's muscular build. "I...he's still...rather well built. He's thirty-four. Maybe you saw him at one of the football games, since you were a cheerleader."

"Umm, I'll have to dig out my old school annuals. We played a game at their homecoming when I was a senior. A Coleman was homecoming king. I remember him because he had these gorgeous eyes. They sort of sparkled."

Callie laughed. "That sounds like Adrian, sparkle and all. He's always finding the silver lining on my dark clouds."

"Maybe I have a photo," Eileen said. "How is this relationship with your friend Adrian?"

"Terrible. Eileen, he actually wants to marry me and rescue me from all my poverty!"

Eileen laughed. "It sounds like Cinderella and her Prince Charming. Take him up on his offer."

"I can't. Besides, we've only known each other since September." She explained how they met. "And the last time we went out I had to invite him or we never would have spoken again."

"How do you feel about him?"

"I tried not to, but I've fallen in love with him so much I actually hurt inside."

Eileen was silent. "Callie, I denied my true feelings for Dan for months, and because of my pride, I almost lost him completely. Self-sufficiency is fine to a point, but having someone to share life with is just as important. Dan and I have our differences, because we're different people with separate pasts, but when the night comes and we crawl into bed together, it's...it's...well, it's personal and private, but it's the most wonderful thing I've ever experienced. Leave it at that."

"Adrian and I have our compatible side," Callie murmured, thinking aloud about the brief night they had shared. "But it takes more than that to keep a relationship alive. Let's change the subject. Are you going to come back here for a visit this summer? Did Abbie tell you about my idea?"

"Yes, she did, and of course we are," Eileen replied. "We're going to fly. Just set the date as soon as possible so we can get in on discount fares. I think a reunion sounds great. I don't think the Hardestys have ever had one. I put a check in the mail yesterday to help with the expenses—postage and paper and stuff like that." She laughed lightheartedly. "Abbie and I plan to wear our lockets, too, so the Secret Society of Sisters and Friends can have its own reunion."

"I lost mine," Callie said, and explained what had happened. "But thanks for the money. It'll help."

"Send me a photo. I'll bet you look different with short hair. Hey, listen, I hear Danny. If I don't get him out of the nursery right away, Tony will wake up, and I'll have two screaming babies on my hands. Take care, Callie, and we all send our love."

"How can you tell them apart just from their cries?"

"Trust me on this," Eileen said, laughing. "I'm a pro."

CALLIE THREW HER ENERGY into the reunion plans. Her mother made some calls and presented her with names and addresses of relatives, some Callie had never heard of. They chose a date, and she wrote a form letter on the computer at Second Chance, revising it over and over again.

At first Callie had planned to keep the reunion a surprise from her aunt, but the secret plans were spilled by Linda at a Sunday dinner, and Minnie offered her house as the gathering place for the families.

"If they want to camp out, we have ten acres of woods they can hide in. If not, they can get a motel in town."

"I thought you bought five acres," Finis said to his brother.

"Min didn't want the neighbors abutting up against us, so I bought another five to keep 'em at bay."

The invitations were mailed. Callie continued her research. Her mother dug out an old trunk from a corner of the attic, and together Callie and Ellen went through each letter and document. Some long-forgotten relative had written the names of people on the bottoms of photographs in a velvet-covered album, and Callie began to put faces with the names she'd been researching. She expanded her search to the eastern part of the state.

Each afternoon as she drove home from the Second Chance program or the library, she steeled herself for the possibility of seeing Adrian Coleman, but he had apparently done his part in negotiating the acquisition of her parents' land and was now busy with other affairs for White Glove. She tucked her newly acknowledged love for him into a corner of her heart and pretended he didn't matter. The days and weeks passed.

Her father had burned and plowed his tobacco bed the previous fall. As the days began to lengthen and the sun's rays began to warm the earth, Callie helped him finish preparing the one-hundred-by-nine-foot bed. In early March, they planted the tobacco, seeding the bed by hand three times. They sprayed for weeds, fertilized the bed, applied a thin mulch of clean straw, then covered it with cheesecloth and pegged it down on all sides.

"Hope to God it don't freeze," Finis said at dinner in mid-March. "Them seedlings are coming up like crazy. With a little luck, and the good Lord watching over us, we'll have a fine bed of transplants by the middle of May."

Because of her father's small quota, he usually depended on his family to help him weed, sucker and top the plants at the appropriate times during the summer growing months. Callie didn't relish doing stoop labor in her father's tobacco patch, but in the end, she knew she would volunteer again.

"Daddy, why don't you just skip it this year? If we don't smoke it, why grow it?" Callie asked, and immediately regretted it. They had been over that discussion many times before, and she was in no mood to hear it again. "I know, I know, you need the quick cash at tax time. But this year you won't be responsible for the taxes."

He grinned. "Then it makes even more sense to grow it for one more season, don't it? I can line my own pocket this year. Why, that nice Mr. Coleman hand-delivered the first payment from White Glove this morning and..."

Callie dropped her fork. "He was here? Here at our house? What did he want?"

"I told you, honey, he gave me the first payment," her father replied, a satisfied grin on his weathered face. "He asked about you, but didn't say if he'd be back. Didn't leave no message, neither. Seemed a little preoccupied."

CALLIE SAT IN FRONT of the microfilm viewer at the public library in Greenville, engrossed in scanning the reel of film for other members of the Campbell family, her adrenaline pumping, because she'd just discovered the whereabouts of her great-great-grandfather Campbell and his family.

Something touched her shoulder. She pulled away. "Excuse me," she mumbled, glancing up. "Oh," she gasped, staring at the large brown hand resting comfortably on the pink knit of her sweater.

Adrian Coleman pulled a chair from a nearby table and dropped into it, then tried to find space beneath the table for his long legs. He draped his arm along the back of her chair and peered at the screen.

She stared at his profile, from his intelligent forehead down to his stubborn chin with the tiny dimple that only appeared when he frowned. His cheek was inches from hers, close enough for her to see the pores of his skin and the darkening shadow of his beard. She scanned his features, taking in his furrowed brow as he studied the film, the long dark lashes that shielded his hazel eyes, the slope of his nose, which held only a hint of a bump. Her heart began to thud as her gaze dropped to his mouth—the mouth she longed to have against hers, to kiss her just once more.

She jerked away. "What are you doing here?" Only the upward pull of one corner of his mouth indicated he had heard her question as he continued studying the screen. "How did you find me?" she asked, collapsing against the chair back.

"I called your house," he said, curling a thick strand of her hair around his finger and letting it slide free. "I had a chat with Linda. She said her mother had become a grouch."

She ducked her head. "She wouldn't have said such a thing."

He trailed a finger across her shoulder. "She was also kind enough to tell me you were here...and that you wouldn't be home until nine at least."

She let out the breath of air she had been holding. "The library stays open until nine tonight. I ordered some reels of microfilm from...from..."

His hand settled on the pink knit again. "You're wearing my sweater. It looks good. I compliment you,

Adrian, for knowing what color Miz Callie would look great in. Why, thank you, sah, and she must like it, too, becuz' she's a'wearing it this very day."

"Are you talking to a fool?" she asked, as she jotted down the statistics onto her form, and tried to suppress her own smile.

"Could be," he said, straightening in his chair, "but a persistent one who's dedicated to the cause."

She wasn't about to ask him to identify his cause. She found her place on the screen again, then hastily copied down a name on her yellow work pad.

He pointed to the screen. "It's Sivilla, not Cevilla," he said, then pointed to her misspelling. He glanced at the large clock on the wall above the librarian's head. When he smiled at the gray-haired woman behind the desk, she smiled back.

"I'm terribly busy, Adrian. Couldn't you come back later?"

"No, I have a meeting at my father's house at eight. It's five-thirty. Are you going to eat?"

"I'm not hungry."

"Your momma said you'd lost some weight. Stand up so I can see." He unfolded himself from the seat.

She jumped from her chair in exasperation. "Adrian, now..."

He tilted his head from side to side, his gaze caressing her body as he stroked his chin thoughtfully. "Can't say that I can see it. You've still got enough curves for me." He motioned to the woman behind the desk, who came scurrying to him. "Is anyone going to need this machine?"

The woman shook her head. "I don't believe so, sir, and if they do, I can mark down where the counter is and remount the reel when you get back. You go right ahead and have supper now. She's been working real hard and deserves a little break. You take her to dinner. I'll keep an eye on her papers.''

Callie felt as if she were invisible as Adrian and the librarian continued to chat over her head. "Okay, I give up, I'll go with you, but I want to be back here by seven at the latest.''

"Fair enough, ma'am.'' He grabbed Callie's arm with one hand and her purse with the other, hustling her through the tables and out the door, nodding and smiling at all the curious library patrons.

CALLIE LAID DOWN HER FORK and wiped her lips. "Thank you for dinner. The chef's salad was delicious, and I was hungrier than I realized. How was your steak?''

He nodded. "Fine. Callie, I need to talk to you, and the phone seemed so impersonal.''

"What about?'' she asked, her curiosity aroused.

"First, I'm sorry you didn't get the grant.''

Her eyes widened. "How did you know about that?''

"Abbie told me.''

"You've been talking to Abbie? Why would you still be talking to Abbie?''

He shrugged. "We've established this long-distance relationship. Don't worry, I've become friends with her husband, as well. Anyway, I'm truly sorry. What are you going to do now?''

"I'm still at Second Chance, in a program that involves career counseling. I told my caseworker about finding Bobby Joe, and she's investigating the situation. I'm sure it's going to cost me some benefits...and I'm looking for a job.''

Her posture stiffened. "I can't do very much, and I have no experience except three days of waitressing in Harlan." She smiled confidently. "I took typing in high school, and I'm learning to use a word processor. Who knows what might happen now? Got any openings at White Glove? I can't reach the brake pedals on the transports but I could type a letter or two."

He grinned. "I'll check with personnel. The corporate offices are in Madisonville. Can that Chevy truck make it that far twice a day?"

"Doubtful." She tracked a piece of lettuce around the side of her salad bowl. "I'll let someone else have that job. Anyway, when I'm not busy with all that, I'm working on genealogy, and coordinating the first-ever Hardesty family reunion. It's scheduled for the first weekend in August. And I try to spend time with my children," she said, and went on to tell him about Linda's health and Robbie's growing fascination with his father.

"That brings me to the other reason I needed to see you," Adrian said, reaching into his wallet and extracting a white business card. "Call this man when you can. I went to school with him. I explained the situation with Bobby Joe, and he's agreed to take the case for 175 dollars. I paid him the seventeen dollars you were short."

She took the card. "I don't have any money right now."

"I've put it on your account."

"My account?"

"Let's see," he said, pulling another card from his shirt pocket and studying it as he cupped it in his hand. "I've extended you an open line of credit for say... five hundred dollars, so if you need a withdrawal, just let me know. I'll deduct it from the balance."

"Adrian!"

"Pay me back when you can," he said, tucking the card back into his pocket. "It should make you feel a little more secure, just knowing it's there in case you need it. No interest, no strings." He motioned to the card still in her hand. "His name is Matthew Daws. He's a good guy. He says if you can get to him early next week so he can talk to you and have you sign the papers, he can make you a divorced woman by May first."

"So soon? How can he do it so fast?"

"His uncle is the judge."

She looked at him, her features very solemn. "I thought perhaps you'd forgotten all about it. I was thinking of asking you for my money back. Thank you."

"My pleasure," he said, giving her a mock salute. "If you need someone to hold your hand, I'll be glad to go to court with you."

"Thank you, Adrian, but you don't have to."

"I know, but you've told me things you may not want your parents to know. So if you do want a little moral support..." He reached for his wallet again and withdrew a twenty-dollar bill and several ones. "Now then, about your daughter. Have you considered taking her to the hospital in Louisville? I know two physicians on staff in the cardiac wing there. They're good."

"Is there anyone you don't know?"

He shrugged. "I've been around."

"We'll stay under the Medicaid umbrella for now. Thanks, anyway." She put the card in her purse.

"Did you call Emily Oldham?"

"Yes, and we both owe you a big debt of gratitude for that one," she said. "Aunt Min is going to be part of a pilot program for senior citizens who want to learn to read. Ms Oldham came to Aunt Min's house two weeks ago to personally explain the program. Aunt Min is very excited. I'm sure you were right about me trying to teach her to read. I wouldn't know how to begin.''

"You could be trained as a volunteer," he suggested.

"That would be very interesting," she said, nodding her head, "but for now I'm finding myself overloaded.''

"Have you found Abbie's natural mother?" he asked.

"Yes, she lives in Evansville, Indiana," Callie said. "Adrian, it's almost as if she's working her way home. I tracked her through Paducah to Louisville and Lexington, to Newark, New Jersey, back to Cincinnati and now to Evansville. Why, Evansville isn't more than an hour's drive on a good day. I couldn't believe it! I've been typing up a batch of letters from her," Callie said, explaining briefly how the letters had come into being. "They're the saddest bunch of letters I've ever read—No, that's not right, either. They're a mixture of hope, regret and sadness.''

"The story is getting more interesting," Adrian remarked, taking a sip of coffee.

"Aunt Min and Bernice are half sisters," she continued. "But they had some sort of falling out.''

"Over what?" Adrian asked.

"That's what I don't know. Aunt Min won't talk about it, and Bernice didn't say in the letter she sent me last month, but my mother hinted it had to do with Abbie's daddy. Anyway, Mother broke the ice the other day. She called Bernice on the phone and invited her to a visit at our house a week from Saturday. Abbie is flying in to Evansville and driving down with Bernice. It's a little scary to think of a reconciliation after all this time. What if it doesn't go right?''

"You could let sleeping dogs lie," he hinted.

She pursed her lips. "I really don't know what I've gotten myself into. Something happened a long time ago, and no one wants to talk about it, but for Abbie's sake I'm keeping my nose in it." She smiled. "Want to come and be the sergeant at arms?"

"Not on your life," he replied, grinning. "But let me know how it comes out." He glanced at his watch. "It's almost seven, and I promised you I'd have you back by then." He laid a tip on the table, grabbed the bill and headed toward the cashier, leaving Callie to trail after him.

He accompanied her back to the library. "It's good seeing you again, Callie," he said, then turned and walked away.

"Adrian?" Only a deeper hunching of his shoulders indicated he had heard her. He jammed his fists deep into his jacket pockets and never looked back.

CHAPTER FOURTEEN

"BERNICE AND ABBIE said they would be here at ten," Callie said. She laughed nervously. "I suppose I should start calling her Aunt Bernice."

Minnie took a sip of coffee and settled into her chair. "Callie, honey, before they get here, I want you to know I don't hold no hard feeling. You started all this out of love for Abbie, and I admit that I need it, too."

Callie sighed. "Thank you. Abbie loves you, and she says finding out you're her flesh and blood just adds icing to the cake. She might call you Aunt but she thinks of you as Momma."

Minnie dabbed at her eyes.

A car drove up and parked. Callie, Minnie and Ellen waited expectantly inside. Voices and laughter sounded on the porch, and Callie opened the door before anyone could knock.

Abbie Grasten entered, tall and slender in a belted form-fitting navy blue jumpsuit, carrying a babbling seven-month-old baby girl in her arms. The baby's hair was blond. Abbie went directly to her aunt and kissed her, then promptly deposited Anna on her lap. When the chattering slowed, Ellen took the baby and put her in a nearby playpen.

"Bernice?" Callie asked, turning toward the door again.

A tall woman, slender as a willow, stood at the open door, her auburn hair softened by white but her eyes as green as Abbie's.

Callie extended her hand. "I'm Callie. Please come in. You know everyone else."

Bernice entered. She shed her jacket and gave it to Callie. Tension mounted as Callie hung the garment on a peg near the door. No one moved or spoke. *Oh, God,* Callie thought, *what do I do now? Call the whole thing off?* She took a deep breath. "Come, *Aunt* Bernice," she said, taking the woman's hand and leading her toward Minnie's chair.

Minnie pushed herself from the chair. Callie's attention jerked from Bernice to Minnie and back. She held her breath. Out of the corner of her eye, she noticed a hand waving, and she turned to look. Ellen motioned her to step back and leave the two older women alone.

To Callie's surprise, Minnie Hardesty held out her arms to Bernice.

"Welcome home, sister," she said, her voice breaking with a sob. "I've held a grudge for too many years. I love you, Bernice. I ain't got many years left, and I want to patch it all up." She hiccuped and wiped her wet cheeks. "For Abbie's sake and for Anna's sake, but most of all for our sakes, will you forgive me?"

"Oh, Minnie," Bernice cried. "Of course, but there's nothing to forgive. I did it, not you." She touched her sister, and they embraced.

Minutes passed as they stood in the middle of the room, hugging each other. Ellen left the room and returned with a tray of sandwiches and snacks and fresh coffee. She cleared her throat. "Enough of this sobbing, you two. Let's eat and talk about it. My daughter here is crying as much as you two, and she doesn't even know what she's a'crying about.''

Callie wiped her eyes and smiled. "Why don't you two sit together on the sofa?"

Bernice and Minnie sat down, and for a few minutes they enjoyed the food and talked about Anna, who was content exploring the new playpen.

"I reckon it's time to get down to business," Minnie said. She reached into her purse and withdrew a manila envelope, tipped it upside down, and out poured old photographs.

Callie smiled at Minnie. "Why don't you tell us about them."

Bernice patted Minnie's hand. "Go ahead, Minnie. It seems like only yesterday, doesn't it, until we look in a mirror?"

Minnie spread the photographs out, pointing at various pictures as her story unfolded.

"Bernice is five years younger than I am. We were always rivals, now that I think about it. She always wanted to do what I did, have what I had, and usually she managed it. We both knew how to get what we wanted from our daddy. Tyson Smith was one of the nicest fathers two girls could want, but he was a pushover.

"It was the middle of the Great Depression. I was fortunate enough to have a job cleaning a rich woman's house. Bernice waited tables in a greasy spoon in town. Drakesboro was a bit livelier in those days. One Saturday night at a dance I met this really great-looking man. His name was Phillip Andrew Hardesty. Everyone called him P.A. He and his family had just moved from Mortons Gap. For me, it was love at first sight. We started going together, and I heard wedding bells. I'd considered myself well on the way to being an old maid. I was twenty-three years old, you see.

"Everything went fine for about three months," she continued. "He was a'pushing me for you can imagine what."

The tension broke, and all the women laughed. Cups were refilled and a platter of cookies made the rounds while Abbie made a quick diaper change on Anna.

"Go on, Aunt Min," Abbie said, slipping out of her shoes and tucking her feet beneath her. "It sounds so contemporary."

"Well, I didn't want to take no chances on getting pregnant like some of my friends had, so I held off. I brought him to a picnic one Saturday after a big tobacco auction had finished, and that was my mistake, because he spotted Bernice and began to make a play for her. Of course, it takes two to tango," she said, sending her sister a knowing glance.

"Now, now," Ellen said, "none of that."

"You're right," Minnie said, sighing deeply. "Well, to make a long story shorter, Bernice and P.A. disappeared, leaving me stranded. P.A. had come with his cousin, Harry, who lived around here. He was even better looking than his cousin, but I had eyes only for P.A. Harry took me home, and I thanked him with a kiss on the cheek. One thing led to another with my sister and P.A. until she cried 'pregnant,' and they were married."

"Was that me?" Abbie asked.

"No, you came twenty years later," Bernice said.

Callie frowned at Bernice. "Were you really pregnant?"

"Yes, but I had a miscarriage three months later."

Minnie nodded her head. "Harry had asked me to marry him, but when I heard Bernice had lost the baby,

I held off, hoping and praying that they'd split up and P.A. would come back to me. Oh, what a lovesick fool I was—that jewel of a man Harry right under my nose and me a'mooning over what I couldn't have.''

"But we didn't split up," Bernice said. "We moved away and had a good life. We really loved each other, Min. Didn't you know that?"

Minnie shrugged. "A year later Harry and I got married, and we went on to have three boys. We'll be celebrating our fiftieth anniversary next year. I love Harry Hardesty with all my heart, but it took a while, let me tell you. Maybe it's true a woman never forgets her first love."

"Yuck," Callie exclaimed. "I certainly hope I'm an exception to that rule."

"What happened next?" Abbie asked. "Where do I come in?"

"One day, out of nowhere, P.A. and Bernice came visiting. They had this beautiful little redheaded baby with them. You see, my own children were all robust and lanky black-haired boys. The youngest was already ten years old, and they were all filled with vim and vinegar. 'Course I loved each and every one of my boys, but here was this little girl who I knew was part of P.A. Well, those old feelings started to rise again."

"We had been married for almost twenty years," Bernice explained. "I'd never taken precautions because we really wanted more children, and then out of nowhere I got pregnant and Abbie was born. We wanted to show her off. I thought by now my sister would have forgiven me for stealing her man."

Minnie picked up the story. "They kept a'coming back to visit. I got so envious of Bernice with that baby. Why, little Abbie got prettier and prettier as she grew older. Her hair was just like mine, and her eyes were green. I plumb ignored the fact that Bernice has the same coloring. I wanted that little girl so much I actually prayed for the Lord to give her to me."

She buried her face in her hands and wiped her eyes again. "I got her, too, but what a sacrifice. P.A. never glanced once toward me. Bernice, you know that. He had eyes only for you and Abbie. But one morning when he was forty-nine and Abbie was about five or six, he was killed in a mine explosion. I grieved, and Harry let me be. If it's possible to love two men, I guess I did. Bernice remarried about a year later to a man named Johnson. I don't even remember his first name."

"Curly Johnson," Bernice said, laughing softly. "Samuel 'Curly' Johnson."

Abbie straightened in her chair. "I remember him! He used to spank me, and he kept hiding my dolls. I hated him."

"He was as worthless as P.A. was good," Bernice said. "I was seeing my fiftieth birthday coming 'round the mountain, and I didn't want to spend my life alone, so I married him. Only he didn't want Abbie tagging along in our lives. He couldn't hold a job, and we were broke most of the time. Traveling around was no life for a little girl in school, so I brought Abbie home to my sister and asked her to take care of her for a while."

"So you see," Minnie said, "I got P.A.'s little girl after all. Harry and me, we talked it over, and I suspect he could see through my motives, but at the same time, Abbie needed love and a stable home. What could Harry say, exceptin' yes? Two years later I convinced Bernice to let us adopt her legally. She didn't want to let her go. I threatened her with neglect charges if she didn't. That's where I went wrong."

"I tried to stay in touch," Bernice said. "I'd write from wherever we happened to light. I fell into a good job in Newark, New Jersey, and when Curly wanted to move on, I said no. We divorced, and I stayed there." She smiled. "I stayed there long enough to retire and get a pension. I kept writing to Abbie, but I never heard from her except for a few times. I came back for a visit several years ago and learned that my own sister had been withholding the letters. We had some cruel words that day, and every angry feeling we ever had against each other came out. I vowed I'd never again set foot in her door."

Callie turned to Minnie. "Why did you save the letters?"

"I tried to read some of them, but the words didn't mean a thing, so for a while I just made up what it said. That worked until Abbie asked one day to read one herself. I wouldn't let her. I finally just added each new letter to the shoe box where I was a'saving 'em, and the lie began to grow. To make it believable, I started giving Abbie a five-dollar bill on her birthday. I stopped that when she laughed one time."

"I was fifteen," Abbie said. "Fifteen-year-olds can be very insensitive. I was angry and hurt. I was sure that in her eyes, I was worth just five dollars a year."

Minnie studied her swollen fingers. "Once I tried to write to Bernice. Abbie was in school, and I got out those letters and I studied them postmarks and the return addresses on some of them, but no matter what I tried to come up with, the letters just wouldn't jell into words or places I'd ever heard of." She smiled weakly at Callie. "That's why most of them were still unopened."

"That explains why my checks never cleared my checking account," Bernice said, dryly.

"What checks?" Abbie asked.

"The ones I found when I opened all the envelopes," Callie explained. "I showed them to Momma. There's close to a thousand dollars in uncashed checks. I didn't know what to do with them. Some of them say 'Happy Birthday,' some say 'Merry Christmas.' I got all choked up when I found them."

Abbie shook her head and wiped her eyes. "Oh, Minnie and Bernice, why didn't you involve me in all this? All these years I could have had two wonderful mothers."

"I finally decided my daughter didn't want to hear from me," Bernice said, blowing her nose. "I never wanted to lose contact with Abbie. It just happened over the years. Callie," she said, "without your interference I'd never have hoped to see Abbie again, and when you told me about her having a baby, I got down on my knees and prayed for another chance."

"Your wish has been granted," Callie said. She touched the photographs and told them about the book she was making for Anna. "It was going to be a secret but if I can use some of these photos, I can give equal space to both families."

"Bernice is flying out to Montana in July," Abbie said. "We're going to teach her how to herd sheep. She'll come back with us when we come for the reunion in August. Dane's coming, too, and we'll stay for two weeks. We'll make up for lost time."

Callie's hand went to her throat. "What about the lockets? Why did you make them for us, Aunt Min?"

Minnie nibbled on a cookie and stared into space for a moment. "I reckon it was so you three girls would learn the lesson I'd flunked with my own sister. I wanted you to be sisters and friends because I'd spent so many years hating my own sister, and I knew deep down in my heart of hearts that I was just as guilty as she was. I seen them lockets in a store window in Greenville one day.''

"They didn't quite match but that didn't matter. They weren't trinkets for little girls, but real gold lockets, and I had the jeweler engrave them for me. I hustled home and told Harry. He thought it was a great idea, and when we sold our tobacco that fall I got them out of layaway and began working on the little picture inside.''

Minnie looked at Callie. "Pride can make a person do a lot of foolish things, honey. I'm indebted to you mightily because I'm so thankful Bernice came today.''

Minnie turned to the other woman. "What do you say I call Harry and have him come and get us?''

Bernice smiled and patted her sister's hand. "That won't be necessary. I have my own car, and Abbie's been driving me about. We'll drive you home. It'll be great seeing Harry again . . . and you're right, sister, Harry always was the best-looking Hardesty of them all.''

She turned to Ellen. "But that Finis was great looking too, and so is Shelby. Now, before we go, tell me all about the other families. I've got a lot of catching up to do.''

MATTHEW DAWS PHONED. "Good news, Callie. The judge has put your case on his docket for April 14.''

"So soon?'' she asked.

"Might as well get it over with,'' Daws said. "Having that wayward husband of yours resurface speeded it up considerably. We had an address for the process server. I'll see you next week.''

FOR THE THIRD CONSECUTIVE Thursday evening, Adrian Coleman showed up at the library promptly at five-thirty.

"I wasn't sure if you would come," Callie said, her brown eyes troubled. "I didn't want to start taking you for granted."

He dropped into a chair beside her. "I couldn't wait to hear about your aunts' reunion."

She stopped her work. "I tried calling you. Abbie wanted to invite you to dinner." She smiled. "She was dying to meet you."

"I was out of state for four days," he said, trailing his index finger across her shoulder. "I've been busy. As a matter of fact this country boy has too many irons in the fire. I long to settle down." He looked at the ceiling. "And the reunion?"

She looked directly at him. "It was the most beautiful sight I've ever seen. After all my worrying and fretting, they fell into each other's arms and made up."

"Then hurry and let's get out of here," he said, pacing impatiently as she straightened her work papers. "You can fill me in on the details."

She told him more about the sisters' reunion as they walked to the restaurant. "Adrian, it was so wonderful to see them all at peace. Now Abbie has two mothers, and I'm giving them equal space in the book I'm preparing for Anna."

He put his arm around her shoulders and gave her a squeeze. "That's great, honey, and you can take credit for bringing them all together."

She leaned against him for a moment before pulling free. "Abbie is weaving two small tapestries, one for each of them."

"Small as in inches?" he asked.

She laughed. "No, silly, small as in three feet by three feet. For Abbie, that's small. She has several wall hangings she did on commission that are huge. They hang in the corporate offices of an electronics company in Salt Lake City. She sent me pictures years ago. Anyway, she's going to bring the little tapestries she's making to the reunion, and we'll get to see them.''

"Sorry I'll miss it."

"Why?" She turned to him.

"I've moved my quitting time at White Glove up a month," he explained. "I want to be settled in before winter. No reason to move in a snowstorm, is there?"

"No...I suppose not. Which place did you decide on?"

"The spot in Tennessee," he said. "We both have exciting changes to look forward to, don't we?"

"Yes," she murmured, but her lack of enthusiasm said more than her reply.

"You should see the house, Callie. I decided to have it built nestled in this little meadow, on a hillside, actually. There will be trees behind it and a huge oak tree in front that will provide shade in the summer. I bought two hundred acres. I'll be going down there every weekend to work on the cross fencing for the stock and to check on the progress of the house. Damn, I'm looking forward to moving. Once I make up my mind, there's no turning back, I reckon."

His smile tore at her heart, and her own plans to complete her education and then to work in some humdrum job while raising two children alone paled. "I'm pleased for you, Adrian. I wish you the best."

"Thank you, Callie," he replied, burying his hand in her cloud of dark hair and letting it come to rest against the nape of her neck. "I'm just sorry I haven't been able to find your locket. I issued an all-points bulletin at White Glove for all the field workers to be on the lookout for it. Take heart." They passed an alley, dark shadows of dust. He stepped in and pulled her with him. "I love you, Callie," he whispered, seconds before his mouth settled on hers. His arms tightened around her, drawing her hard against his body.

A soft moan escaped her as she responded to him, her lips opening and her tongue playing with his.

He eased away, his breathing ragged as he released her.

She stepped away and ran a hand through her hair. "Gracious, Adrian, that was a surprise, and in such a public place, too." She smiled. "You should do that more often."

"Give me a little encouragement and I might," he replied, grabbing her hand. "Now let's eat."

Inside the restaurant, they found a booth near the window where they could watch the people strolling by and ordered sandwiches.

As they finished Callie said, "Mr. Daws called yesterday. The hearing will be at the courthouse here in Greenville at two in the afternoon on Tuesday. Are you... still willing to be there with me?"

"Of course," he replied, placing his hand over hers.

ADRIAN MET CALLIE AND Matthew Daws, her attorney, in front of the courthouse. He shook hands with Daws and followed them inside. The judge nodded to Adrian. Adrian had known the judge since he was ten, when Matthew and he had played on a baseball team and the judge and Matthew's father had been the coaches. But Adrian had never liked the judge.

The proceedings moved quickly as Callie answered questions from her attorney. The judge questioned her extensively about her plans for the future, her present financial condition and her current lack of employment.

"Mrs. Huff, why didn't you obtain a divorce years ago?" the judge asked. When Callie tried to explain her situation, the judge's face flushed. "Young woman, I find your attitudes typical of many who live off welfare. It's high time you took charge of your life. Your actions affect many others, don't you see that?" He scanned the room. "We'll take a short recess and resume in twenty minutes. This case was described to me as straightforward, but this morning Mr. Huff's attorney came to me with his client's request to appear on behalf of his son's interests. He and his attorney are here. I've asked them to wait in my chambers." The judge rose and quickly disappeared through the door behind his bench.

Adrian joined Callie and Daws at the petitioner's table.

Callie turned to Daws. "What's happening? I thought you were the judge's nephew."

"I am, but that merely got me an early date on the calendar. Damned if I know what's going on. Give me a few minutes to find out." He left.

Callie looked up at Adrian. "Could he be contesting the divorce? He was served papers, but I never expected him to come here. He never called me, and Robbie hasn't said a word."

Adrian's arm went around her, and he pulled her close. She buried her face against his chest as he massaged her back through the blue-and-white striped material of her shirtwaist dress. "It'll be okay. What could possibly go wrong? His wife is pregnant. Surely he wants to be free to marry her . . . again, if that's what one does in a bigamist situation."

The judge returned, followed by Callie's attorney, Bobby Joe Huff dressed in a dark blue suit, his attorney and a black woman with close-cropped graying hair who had not been present earlier.

The proceedings resumed.

"This court is very troubled by this case, so I'm taking the liberty to interpret the law broadly," the judge said. "Taking two wives at once is a serious matter, and Mr. Huff admits he neglected to check if he was still married, because at the time, he wasn't ready to fulfil his financial responsibilities. However, in Mr. Huff's shoes, I would have assumed that after nine years, my wife would have taken the necessary legal action to dissolve the marriage. Mrs. Huff never got around to it. Her negligence has inflicted needless pain and suffering on the other Mrs. Huff, who happens to be in the family way and needs to be protected from such stressful matters."

The judge leaned back in his chair and studied each person in the courtroom. "Mr. Huff has filed a petition with the court asking for an amendment of the child support section of the decree. He acknowledges that he was negligent in his early years in carrying out his parental responsibilities. Now he's a different person, as he's proved by his steady employment, his good credit rating, his church membership. He's submitted several fine character references from men who know him well."

The judge glanced up from his notes. "In addition to teaching a Bible study class, he's just been elected deacon at my church and still he finds time to serve on the building committee. He's a fine upstanding member of the Central City community. Regarding his delinquency in making child support payments, Mr. Huff is contrite. Further proving his new maturity he has handsomely volunteered to make restitution by paying a lump-sum amount to settle those years of back support."

The judge coughed, and for a moment his heavy gaze touched on Callie before returning to the papers before him. "In recognition of his reformed character, Mr. Huff is asking this court to appoint him the custodial parent of his son, one Robert Joseph Huff, age eleven, with the boy's natural mother having visitation rights twice monthly and for one full month during the summer."

CHAPTER FIFTEEN

CALLIE SHOT TO HER FEET. "No!" Her attorney pulled her back into her chair.

Adrian's heart stopped. For a moment he couldn't comprehend the judge's words, but when he looked at Callie, he knew he had heard correctly. She sat immobile until she lifted her hand to touch her cheek, and he saw it tremble.

"No," she shouted. "He has no right to take Robbie away. He never said a word...about..." Her voice faded in hopelessness.

"Mr. Daws, caution your client, please," the judge warned, "before I find you both in contempt of this court. Such hysterics will not be tolerated."

Matthew Daws put his arm around Callie's shoulder and whispered in her ear. She stiffened, but remained silent.

"Because this petition was filed only this morning, and the court has not had time to process and serve it," the judge continued, his drawl deepening and slowing, "and because this hearing had been scheduled as a special case to be given expeditious treatment due to its implied simplicity, as stated by the plaintiff's counsel—" he sent his nephew a scathing glare "—I'm granting a postponement for one week while the court talks to the child. The child is—" he glanced at the papers again "—almost twelve, and his father describes him as mature for his age.

Therefore, I'm asking Mrs. Louise Haslam, a child psychologist whose opinion I hold in great esteem to talk with the boy."

He nodded toward the black woman sitting to one side of the courtroom. "Until the court reconvenes on April 23, the boy will remain with his custodial mother. She's not to take him out of state without this court's permission." The judge pounded his gavel. "Mr. Daws," he added, glaring at his nephew, "I want to see you again in my chambers." The judge left with Louise Haslam close behind.

Adrian's attention shifted from Callie to Bobby Joe Huff.

Bobby Joe sauntered to the table where Callie sat. He gripped the table ledge with his hands and leaned toward Callie. "Hey!" He snapped his fingers, and Callie's head jerked up. Their faces were less than a foot apart.

"You hurt Mary Lou real bad, Callie Ann," he said. "She's a pregnant woman and needs protection from the likes of you. We both thought our marriage was legal and proper. It's my fault for trusting you. You tricked me, back when you got pregnant, and now you've done this, but you'll be sorry. Robbie wants to live with me. I asked him, and he said sure." His mouth twisted into a sardonic smile. "This evens the score, sugah."

His attorney took his arm and shoved him through the gate and up the aisle to the exit.

Adrian clenched his fists. His first inclination had been to go after Bobby Joe and settle a few scores for Callie himself, but he couldn't help Callie by assaulting Bobby Joe. Callie needed him beside her.

He pushed the swinging gate aside and went to her. Kneeling before her chair, he gripped her arms. "Callie, are you okay?" He shook her gently. "Callie?"

She gazed down at him. "How could this happen?" she asked, her voice barely audible. "I would have been better off leaving well enough alone. What did it matter if everyone thought we were divorced? Look what I've done. I've gained child-support money but paid for it with my son," she said, as the color drained from her face.

She crumpled against Adrian, who held her in his arms as she began to cry softly.

Matthew Daws reappeared. "This way," Daws said, motioning them into the judge's chambers.

Inside the room, Adrian eased into the nearest chair, still holding Callie.

"There's a back exit," Daws said. "I'll bring your truck to the alley and you can go out that way. The judge has gone home for the day. Stay here as long as you need to."

Adrian shifted Callie and retrieved his keys, tossing them to Daws before returning his attention to Callie.

Daws touched Callie's shaking shoulder. "Damn it, Callie, I'm as stunned by this move as you are."

Daws left, and they were alone, with only the soft sound of Callie's weeping disturbing the silence and tearing at Adrian's heart.

"Sweetheart, oh, sweetheart, cry," he crooned, holding her closely against his chest. "Cry your heart out. Wash it clean of all the hurt and the pain and the anger. It's the only way to heal yourself." He rocked her as she cried heart-wrenching sobs, his arms sheltering her against the pain and failures and despair that had been so much a part of her life.

Daws returned with Adrian's keys and dropped them onto the table. He motioned toward Callie.

"She'll be fine," Adrian said. "I'll take care of her."

Daws left and again the chamber room was quiet.

When the bell in the courthouse steeple chimed the hour of four, Callie was asleep.

Adrian carried her to the judge's sofa and laid her down, then wiped the tears from her cheeks with his handkerchief. Her black lashes lay in spikes against her pale skin. He brushed the damp hair from her forehead, smoothing it away from her face, then continued his vigil while she slept.

The steeple bell chiming five roused her.

"What happened?" She touched her face. "I don't know what happened to me. Did I fall asleep?"

Adrian pulled his chair closer to the sofa and took her hand. "The shock," he said. "You couldn't accept it."

She slid her legs to the floor and sat up. "I need to get home. My truck is in front of the Second Chance office and..."

He helped her to her feet. "I'll take you home. We'll worry about your truck later." He put his arm around her and steadied her as he led her through the rear exit.

ROBBIE HAD LITTLE TO SAY when Callie tried to talk to him. She suspected Bobby Joe had coached him into silence. How could she have overlooked her son's withdrawal from her, from his family?

Louise Haslam phoned, and two days later the court-appointed psychologist came and talked to Robbie, to both of them, and finally to Callie alone. "Boys his age often want to live with their fathers," Mrs. Haslam said. "It's normal."

"But he's my son. I raised him," Callie exclaimed. "I diapered him and toilet-trained him and saw that he had his shots and that he got to school on time. I stayed up with him at night when he was sick, I listened to him when he asked questions."

"And were some of those questions about his father?"

"Yes," Callie acknowledged.

"And how did you answer those questions?"

"I . . . I told him to wait . . . I'd planned to tell him all about his father and me . . . on his next birthday."

"Perhaps he needed to know bits and pieces all along," Mrs. Haslam said. "Robbie was in an emotional vacuum in his quest to find his father. Well-intended though you were, you kept the solution from him. Meeting his real father again has been like stumbling onto an oasis in a desert. He has yet to drink his fill, Callie."

"But it's not fair! Bobby Joe never had time for him when he was little. Now he comes sashaying back and takes him away."

"No, Callie, it's not fair," the woman agreed. "You did a fine job raising him. His grades in school are excellent. He has friends. He plays sports and has many other interests. He's quite a boy."

"Then why does he want to live with Bobby Joe?"

The woman nodded in empathy. "Boys want their mothers when they're young and need their fathers as they get older. We don't own our children, Callie. We must let them go when the time comes. Robbie still loves you, but he wants a turn with his father now. Don't retaliate by withholding your love for him or by making him feel guilty about his choice. That would be as cruel as what his father has done to you."

"I wouldn't do that," Callie assured the psychologist.

"I know Mr. Huff's motives are suspect, my dear, but I feel that Robbie belongs with his father now. If he changes his mind, he can always come back. Can't he?"

CALLIE SAT UP IN HER BED staring at the certified check balanced on her knees. The court had accepted Bobby Joe Huff's request to gain custody of Robbie. The judge had given an eloquent speech on the needs of a prepubescent male, reminded Callie that she was to have Robbie ready to leave the following Saturday morning and handed Matthew Daws the check.

Seemingly as an afterthought, the judge reminded Bobby Joe that he was still responsible for making monthly support payments for Linda. Bobby Joe had scowled.

Only the hope that the change in custody could be temporary had given Callie the courage to endure the session. Adrian had stayed by her side, always being supportive when she needed someone to talk to, willing to listen when she shared her innermost feelings and never judging her past actions. He had become a very special friend in her time of need.

"Call me," he had said when he'd driven her home earlier in the day. "I'm always available."

She picked up the check and brought it closer, analyzing the red numerals, touching the perforations in the paper. "Eleven thousand, eight hundred eighty dollars and no cents," she murmured. "Ninety dollars a month for eleven years." She rested her head against the headboard. She speculated on how far she could have stretched ninety dollars each month in order to feed, clothe and shelter two children.

She straightened out in the bed and rolled to one side, laid the check on her nightstand and turned out the lamp. As she lay in the darkness, alone with only her thoughts to keep her company, a single word exploded in her mind, "Victim." She rolled the word around in her mind, analyzing it in all its ramifications. Too many times she had set herself up for becoming a victim, accepting the consequences as unavoidable, coping with the aftereffects as if she'd had no choice.

"No more," she vowed aloud. She couldn't stop the wind, but in the months to come she could certainly control her own sails and change the direction of her ship's course.

ADRIAN SAT STARING out the window of his second-floor office, thinking about Callie. He hadn't seen her since the final divorce decree had been given. He had called twice, but both times she had declined to have dinner, saying that she needed time to get her life in order. Twice he had spoken to her mother, just to keep in touch.

He had been marking time for three weeks. Now half his worldly possessions had been moved to his new home. The other half was still waiting to move. Three weeks and more was too long to be betwixt and between. A confrontation with Callie was the only way to clear the air. Perhaps he was playing the fool. She had never expressed her feeling for him in so many words, though her actions had led him to believe she cared deeply. He had to lay his plans for their future in front of her and convince her she could have all her goals and him as well.

He grabbed his jacket, unwilling to stay cooped up inside another minute. "Take messages, Jessie," he said, waving to his brown-haired secretary.

Jessie paused, her fingers hovering over the calculator she had been operating. "Do I need to know where you'll be?"

He stopped, scratching his head for a few seconds. "I'm going to the shop to see if they've finished the work on my truck. Then I'm going to check on the two transports in for repairs. We need to get them over to the new section of the Dickens property. After that I'll be at the Dickens site for a few hours. If you need to get in touch, call me on the radio phone in my truck."

Callie's face materialized before his mind's eye, and he smiled, his hazel eyes regaining their customary twinkle. "When that's all done, I'm going looking for love."

Jessie laughed as he strolled away. "Let me know if you find it," she called after him.

"I already have, Jessie. But now I'm going to give her a sales pitch she can't refuse, and she'd better listen."

He met his brother, Nate, at the building's entrance and caught a lift to the shop.

When they arrived he went into the office, and asked about his truck.

"It's all ready, Mr. Coleman," a young clerk told him. "Zack said it was nothing more serious than a leaky gasket on the intake manifold, whatever that is."

Adrian signed the release line on the work order. He retrieved his key ring and dropped it into his slacks pocket, then strolled out the rear door into the repair area of the shop.

The facility was huge. It ran a hundred feet in width and more than twice that in length. Movable side panels opened to provide ventilation in fine weather. Building such a huge shop had been his own idea. The savings the company had realized over the years because the employees were able to work on the huge pieces of equipment regardless of the elements had more than offset the initial capital outlay.

At the far end of the building two yellow coal transports were parked for maintenance. A rotund man stuck his balding head out of the door of one of the cabs. "Hey, Adrian, get over here—on the double."

Adrian waved but as he walked across the open shop two men who were busy at grinders detained him for a moment.

"Hey, Adrian, get a move on," the bald-headed man shouted, then followed up his words with a string of profanity. "You may be the boss's son, but I get paid by the hour and if'n I keep standing around here holding this pretty doodad in my hand, someone is gonna accuse me of being lazy." The man dangled a small oval object from a tiny loop held between his stubby thumb and forefinger. He pressed it against his chest and danced a jig on the flat nose of the engine compartment, his belly shaking in time to his steps.

Adrian stopped. "What is it, Abe?" he asked, knowing before the answer came what had been found.

"I think it used to belong to that pretty little gal who lives next to the Dickens site, but I don't think she'll want it a'looking like this."

Adrian climbed up the ladder. "Oh, God," he groaned as Abe dropped the dirty piece of jewelry into his palm.

The chain was gone. Grease and coal dust had soiled the metal. With his finger Adrian rubbed a spot on one side. "Give me a grease rag."

Abe promptly slapped one against Adrian's outstretched hand. Adrian rubbed the surface, and the letter *C* appeared, scarred by a deep dent running from one side of the locket to the other.

He turned the locket over and rubbed the back side. Gradually the words "Sisters and Friends" became readable, in spite of the grime.

Abe peered over Adrian's arm. "I'll be damned. There's some degreaser over on the counter." He followed Adrian down the ladder and across to the open can of cleaning compound.

Adrian laid the locket on a fresh cloth, cleaned his hands, then began to rub the tiny grooves and etchings. After several minutes of labor, he straightened.

"Man, that's a gorgeous piece of jewelry," Abe said. "No wonder she wanted it back. Is it an antique?"

Adrian glanced at the ruddy-nosed employee. "No, but it has great sentimental value, Abe. Where did you find it?"

Abe beamed. "Casey Fowler came in complaining about finding hair in his cab. He cut as much of it away as he could, but without taking the floor panel out, he couldn't get it all, and there was a pile of it down out of sight," Abe explained, laughing as he slapped his thigh.

"Didn't he read the posters I put out?" Adrian asked.

"The posters talked about a locket," Abe reminded him. "They didn't say a word about gorgeous black hair. 'Sides, Casey can't read much beyond stop and go or on and off. The rest of the guys have been covering for him as long as I can remember."

Adrian chided himself for being out of touch with his company's employees.

"Casey said every time he turned on the heater, the perfume from that gal's hair drifted up to his nostrils and made him think of his old woman at home. Then he'd get hotter than the devil." Abe guffawed and blew his nose on a red kerchief. "Casey said he finally just stopped using the heater 'cause his old lady started rationing him to twice a week."

Adrian contained his smile. "So how did *you* find it?"

"Casey brought his rig in for maintenance and asked me to clean out all that perfume, or else his happy home life was gonna go down the drain. I took the seat off and the floor out and bingo! The locket fell down into that pile of hair below like an egg dropping into its nest. Near as I can figure it, the locket was wedged between the panel and the sidewall, and with all that hair it just got buried.'' He shrugged. "Well, I'd best be gettin' back to my work," he said, and hurried away, still shaking his head over his discovery.

Carefully, Adrian pressed the clasp. To his surprise, the photos inside the locket were intact. His gaze fell on a pretty seven-year-old Callie smiling back at him. He had to blink to clear his vision. "Oh, Callie," he murmured, "what are we going to do about us?" He examined the counted-cross-stitch design of the rainbow and hills. "Damn." A spot of grease had soiled the scene. He put the locket into his shirt pocket and ran to his truck.

When he reached Madisonville, he parked in front of a jewelry shop specializing in custom design and repair. Inside, he showed the locket to the elderly man behind the counter. "Can you take out the dents, Mr. Langley?"

The man examined the damage through the magnifying lens attached to his glasses. "Might take a while."

"How long?" Adrian asked, leaning over the counter.

"A few hours."

"I'll wait."

"Today?" The man peered at Adrian. "You young guys are always rushing through life. What's the hurry, Adrian?"

Adrian smiled. "It's a matter of love, sir."

Mr. Langley frowned. "Oh? I expected you to say life and death. If it's just love..."

"Ah, but this is of far greater importance, sir, because without love, what is life? What consequence, death?"

Mr. Langley broke into laughter. "Well, when you put it like that, what can I say? I'll start on it right away, but without your help. Come back in two hours, not a minute before. If I let you hang around here, you'll drive me crazy."

Adrian left the shop, his nerves on edge. He debated driving into Greenville to see if Callie might be at the Second Chance classrooms. If she wasn't there, he could try the library or call her home. No, he decided. He'd wait until the locket was repaired, the needlework cleaned and a new gold chain added. Then he'd present her with the locket, and all would be well. She'd throw her arms around his neck and kiss him. Then he'd carry her away to his castle, where they would live together forever.

He climbed into the cab of his truck and stared through the windshield. How the hell could he convince her to come with him instead of moving to the opposite side of the state in search of her dreams?

Two hours later to the minute, Adrian returned to the jewelry shop. "How did it come out?" he asked.

The elderly man smiled. "Except for a hairline scratch on the back, I don't think anyone could tell it was ever damaged."

Adrian examined the locket, turning it over and over in his hand. "How did you do it? If I hadn't brought it in myself, I'd never know. It's almost perfect."

"I've been in the business for a decade or two more than you've been living, young man. I have my trade secrets, and I consider them quite valuable, as you'll discover when I present you with the bill. Do you think the lady will be satisfied?"

"Yes, the lady will be satisfied. And to heck with the cost. It's worth every penny." He glanced along the glass counter. "I need a chain to match this locket."

The man draped several gold chains across his hand. Adrian pursed his lips and mumbled under his breath.

"May I suggest," Mr. Langley murmured, "one for the locket and one for the lady to wear at other times?"

Adrian laughed. "Great idea."

He selected two, and the man attached the longer chain to the locket.

"Anything else, Adrian?" the jeweler asked.

"Yes," Adrian replied, throwing all caution aside. "Rings. Something practical but elegant."

"Engagement, wedding... or just friendship?"

"All three," Adrian asked.

"This way." They worked their way to another counter.

"She's sensitive... about wealth," Adrian explained, "but I want her to know that she's special to me." He looked up at the older man. "Do I make sense?"

"Of course," he replied. He pulled three sets from the case and set them on the counter.

Adrian shook his head. "She's a very small woman, about this high," and he marked a spot on his chest.

"Does the lady have a favorite color?"

"Lavender."

"And what month was she born?"

"May... I think. Oh, my God, I've probably missed her birthday. I don't even know what day in May!"

"Perhaps one of the chains corrects that oversight," the man suggested, smiling. He reached into the case and withdrew a pair of rings. The engagement ring was adorned by a full carat diamond surrounded by alternating amethyst and emerald stones, the emeralds in a muted green that harmonized with the amethyst. The wedding band had one chip each of amethyst, diamond and emerald embedded in a gold band.

"And the groom?" Adrian asked, glancing up at the man. "Would he be so fortunate as to have a matching band?"

"Of course." He pulled the groom's ring box from the case and laid it alongside the bride's. "Would you like to try it on for size?"

Adrian slipped it over his knuckle, and it settled into place. He removed the ring. "I'll take them all."

"Would you like me to put them on your account?" Mr. Langley asked. "We haven't seen much of you for several months. Has it been the coal business or your mules?"

"Both, with this love problem tossed in, too. Put them on my account, and I'll settle with you before the end of the month."

"If there's a problem with the size of the bride's rings, just bring them back," the jeweler said as he rang up the sale. "Actually they're quite small. That's why I haven't been able to sell them before this. They're lovely rings."

"For a lovely woman," Adrian added, heading toward the exit. At the door he turned. "Thanks," he said.

The man waved. "Send me a wedding invitation."

Adrian drove away, elated over the locket and rings but still troubled by the soiled spot on the inside of the locket. Perhaps his sister Emma could help. Within minutes he was at her door.

Over coffee and a cinnamon roll, he showed her the locket. "Can you fix it?"

"I think I can get it out," Emma said, washing her hands and going into a large sewing room. "I use this cleaning solution on my own handwork," she said, and as she went to work on the spot with a cleaning solvent, he brought her up to date on his relationship with Callie.

"Oh, Adrian, she must be devastated with losing her son!" she said, stopping her work and turning to him. "If I lost custody of one of my children, I'd just die!"

He sighed. "A mother has to pick up the pieces and go on with her life, doesn't she? Remember when LaMar died?"

She nodded. "Perhaps Callie feels the same way Mom did. I remember how depressed Mom stayed for over a year."

"LaMar was just a few months older than Robbie is. Robbie is really a great kid, but I think Callie feels he rejected her by choosing to live with his father."

Emma put her arm around his shoulder and gave him a hug. "She should count her blessing, honey. At least her son can come back for a visit. Momma wasn't so fortunate."

He nodded. "Is it ready?" he asked.

"Almost," she said, turning away and reaching for a needle and thread. "There's just this little spot where it needs something . . . to complete the design."

He peered over her shoulder. "What the heck are you doing?"

Using a single strand of black embroidery floss, she began to stitch along one side of the smallest tree in the design.

Adrian watched as the black thread evolved into a tall shadowy tree behind the front tree.

She took a long stitch beneath the Aida cloth, clipped it close and rubbed the end out of sight with her finger-tip. "That's you." She snapped the locket shut and handed it to him. "Good luck, Adrian."

CHAPTER SIXTEEN

ADRIAN DROVE AWAY feeling lighthearted. He still had to put in a token appearance at the Dickens mine, but then he'd stop at the Hardesty house in case Callie was home. If she wasn't, he'd say hello to her parents, find out where she was and go get her.

He glanced at his watch as he turned into the mine gate. Three in the afternoon. Good, he thought. Plenty of hours left in the day to spend with Callie.

Taking the new road cut across the fields where Finis Hardesty had grown soybeans the previous year, he saw the house in the distance. He parked not far from a small tobacco field. The green plants were already a foot tall. He was surprised to see that Callie's father had decided to grow one more year's crop. He smiled, guessing that old habits died hard.

He bounded up the steps, making no secret of his arrival, and knocked on the door. No one came. He knocked again and tipped his head, listening. He thought he heard a sound but couldn't identify it. He waited a while and knocked again. The door was opened, but less than an inch.

"Hello, Mr. Coleman," Linda whispered, her voice so faint that he had to lean closer to hear her.

"Linda? Can I come in?"

"Sure," the faint voice replied, but the door didn't open.

He opened the screen door and eased the heavier wood door inward. He found the child squatting against the wall just inside. "Linda? Are you okay?"

She straightened but continued to lean against the wall. "I don't feel so good."

He knelt on one knee and took her hands in his. They were limp, almost clammy to his touch. *Perhaps she's ill,* he thought. Her fair complexion was paler than he'd ever seen it. "Do you have a cold, honey? Upset stomach?"

She pressed her hand against her chest and moved her head slowly from side to side.

"Where's Grandma?"

"She went into town to the store."

"Why didn't she take you with her?"

"I was taking a nap," she said. She took a deep breath, but when she exhaled her blue eyes were filled with pain. "We had a substitute teacher, and she made *everybody* run 'cause Shawn Morton was bad." She stopped to catch her breath. "I'm not supposed to run. Momma says so, and now she'll be mad 'cause she told me not to run...and it hurts when I breath...and...and...I don't...feel so good."

He picked her up in his arms. She was no heavier than his four-year-old niece, Cathy, Nate's youngest child. She rested her strawberry-blond head on his shoulder, and he felt her faint breath tickle the side of his neck.

He carried her into the kitchen and drew a glass of water. "Want a drink?" he asked, feeling helpless because he knew so little about a child's likes and needs.

"No," she whispered.

"Want to sit down?"

"No."

"Well, I do," he said, easing himself into a hard kitchen chair. Sitting her on his lap, he smoothed her plaid skirt over her bony little knees. Her head lay against his chest. "Linda, look at me," he said. She moved her head only a few inches, still resting it against him. "Where's Grandpa?"

"He went fishing with Uncle Harry."

"And where's Callie...your momma?"

"Workin'."

"You mean at school?"

"No, sir, she's workin'."

"You mean she's at the library doing her genealogy?"

"No, sir, she's workin'. She said since we quit welfare, she had to get a job...to earn us some money, don't you see?" She raised her head, her pretty blue eyes meeting his. Her rosebud mouth opened as she smiled. "So she's workin'." Her head fell against his chest again. "Can I go back to bed?"

He slid her to one side and leaned her back in the crook of his arm. "What kind of a job, Linda? Where's she working?" His inquisition stopped abruptly when he noticed the bluish cast to the skin around her mouth. "My God," he murmured. He rose from the chair and swung her legs over his other arm, hugging her to him as he returned to the living room. The front door opened and Ellen Hardesty entered, a paper sack of groceries in each arm.

"Thank God," Adrian exclaimed. "Linda is sick!"

The sacks crashed to the floor, the cans and plastic packages clattering and rolling in all directions. Adrian read the panic in Ellen's face. "Just call her doctor. We'll meet him at the hospital. Hurry," he said, trying to keep a confidence in his voice that he didn't feel. Linda stirred in his arms.

"Can I lay down now?" she asked weakly.

"No, honey, we're going to take you to the hospital so you can get well," he murmured, kissing the top of her curly hair.

Linda touched his cheek with her hand for a few seconds before it fell to her lap. "I love you, Mr. Coleman, 'cause you're a very nice man." She tilted her head back to see him.

"And I love you, too, sweetheart," he whispered.

She closed her eyes again. "I want my momma."

"We'll find her, sweetheart. We'll find her."

Ellen raced from the kitchen. "He'll meet us there. Take her to the hospital in Greenville. Maybe we should call an ambulance," she cried, her eyes filled with alarm.

"In the time it would take them to get here, I can have her there. Let's go," he said. She ran ahead of him and opened the door to the truck. "Get in," he insisted. "You can hold her."

They were on the road in minutes. "Do you think she'll be all right?" Ellen asked several times.

"I pray to God she will," he replied. They drove to the emergency entrance. There the medical personnel took over. Adrian explained how he had found her at the house and what had happened at school.

"We've been trying to stall for time until school was out," Dr. Helstley said. "I've told Callie to take her to Louisville, but she says she can't afford it and the welfare office has fouled up the Medicaid papers, and— Oh, hell! I wrote a statement to the school requesting that Linda be excused from all physical activity."

"What will you do now?" Ellen asked.

"We'll examine her, put her on some IV drugs to stabilize her and give her some relief from the pain, but this child needs more than we can offer here. She's a sweet little girl, and I'd sure like to see her healthy for a change." He glanced around. "Where's Callie?"

"She's at the library," Ellen said.

"But Linda said she was working somewhere," Adrian said.

"Linda was right," she replied. "Callie got a job three days a week at the library. We've got to let her know about Linda."

"Good God," Adrian said. "I'll go tell her and bring her back."

He was out the door before the others could say a word.

CALLIE FINISHED RESHELVING the returned books and worked her way back to the checkout desk. She stopped to chat with a seven-year-old boy, answered some questions from three teenage girls and took a drink from the water fountain. She had been working for two weeks and had just received her first paycheck earlier in the day.

Filled with pride, she had gone to the bank during her break and deposited the check into the passbook savings account she had opened with part of her settlement from Bobby Joe. The rest of it had gone into a short-term certificate of deposit.

Callie smiled as she remembered telling her caseworker she had received the money and that Bobby Joe had been ordered to pay monthly support.

"Well, honey," the woman had said, "this may be the end of our relationship for a while, but if Bobby Joe's promises turn out to be as empty as most wayward daddies', y'all come on back. Meanwhile, if you can find a job somewhere, I'd take it if I were you."

Callie had done just that. One evening, several days after she had packed Robbie's belongings, kissed him goodbye and watched through tear-filled eyes as he rode away with Bobby Joe, Callie had gone to the library wanting to get away from the house. Without her son, the house was just too quiet and depressing.

"Callie, we've been looking for you," Mrs. Menderson, the librarian, said as Callie walked through the door. "Since you've never checked out books, we didn't know your last name or where you lived, so we couldn't get hold of you. Our request for a part-time employee was approved."

Callie nodded dumbly.

The librarian squeezed Callie's hands. "My dear, we'd like to offer the job to you. We've all been impressed with your skills, not only with your work, but your willingness to help others. We can only pay you five dollars an hour, and it would just be twenty-four hours a week to start, but are you interested?"

Callie had accepted on the spot, cut her time at Second Chance down to one day a week and started work at the library the next morning. Now her only concern was lack of time to spend with Linda.

Finding time to think about Adrian Coleman, though, was no problem. He stayed in her thoughts most of her waking hours, regardless of what she was doing, and at night he haunted her dreams.

Today's paycheck would prove to him and to herself that she could earn her own way, that she no longer had to take handouts. Callie shook her head. Her list of things to buy was much too long for the small paycheck. Still it was hers and she had earned every cent.

She planned to call Adrian from the pay phone outside the library after she got off work this evening and invite him somewhere—anywhere—just to tell him her good news. Perhaps she would even try her hand at a little seduction.

She hoped he hadn't given up on her. Certainly she had been unresponsive to him, but did he expect her to jump into bed with him every spare moment? She sighed, thinking of how few spare moments she had in her busy schedule. Their emotional lives had become intertwined, but their physical relationship had been put on hold.

Of course there had been the subtle touches she had grown to expect: the caress of his hand against her neck when he buried his hand in her hair and rubbed the tension away, the tentative touch of his fingers when he dropped into the empty seat beside her at the library and draped his arm across the back of her chair....

These were touches she longed to reciprocate, but she hesitated, unsure about the wisdom of letting her emotions sway her from her chosen course. Now with proof of her self-sufficiency, small though her check might seem, she could take the risk and tell him of her love.

Oh, for one night with him. They had never spent an entire night together. The thought of waking up to a new morning, pressed against him, with his arms around her, filled her with both joy and despair. She had her own needs and wants. She would tell him so.

Maybe he had found someone else who knew how to treat a man with more love and attention. He had his own needs and desires, hopes and dreams. Maybe with her neglect and her self-centered attitude, she had let him slip away. *Oh, Adrian,* she thought. *It's time I told you of my love. Will you still want it? Have I waited too long?*

The main door opened, and she glanced up. As if to fulfill her wish, Adrian walked in, his tall handsome presence easily overshadowing any other man in the library. She smiled and gave him a discreet wave of her hand. Her smile disappeared as he approached. *He hasn't smiled,* she thought. *Adrian always smiles.*

He reached the desk. ''Callie?''

''Hi, I was going to phone you when I got off work. You must—''

''Callie, something's happened,'' he said, squeezing her hand.

A cold chill traveled down her spine. ''What's wrong?''

''It's Linda.'' She paled and he tightened his grip. ''She's okay, but she's at the hospital here in Greenville. Your mother is with her.''

''I'll get my things,'' Callie said, her voice trembling as badly as her knees. She notified the other woman on duty, grabbed her purse and hurried to the door. When she spotted his truck a half block away, she broke into a run.

''How bad is she?'' she asked, as he pulled away from the curb.

He explained the condition he'd found her in. ''We'd better not speculate. The doctor did say he wanted her transferred to a place that can give her the care she needs.''

She wiped her cheeks dry. ''Poor darlin'.''

In the hospital a nurse directed them to the small cardiac care unit. They found Ellen sitting in a chair near a closed door. She jumped up and ran to Callie.

''I would never have left her alone if I'd known she was sick,'' Ellen sobbed. ''I thought she was just tired, a dose of spring fever maybe.'' She shook her head. ''It's all my fault.''

''No, Momma, it's my fault for not being home,'' Callie replied, and the two women hugged each other.

"No one's at fault," Adrian said. "I'm just thankful I found her." He put his arms around both of them. "Say a prayer for that little girl. We'll find a way to help her."

Dr. Helstley came out, nodding to Callie. "I'm glad they found you. It happened, just what we were trying to avoid. There's an opening between the chambers. Her little heart sounds like a slush pump when I listen to it. She can't get enough oxygen into her blood supply. We've got to get her to Louisville. If we don't . . . she may not— God, I'm sorry, Callie."

"How will we get her there?" Callie asked, her heart pounding as she choked down the lump in her throat.

"I'll call the Life Flight service," he said. "They'll send a helicopter. I'll be right back." He turned. "They'll want to know about insurance . . . payment responsibility. They'll come anyway, but you might be thinking about it."

"How much?"

He gave her an estimate.

She nodded. "I have Bobby Joe's money in a savings account. It'll cover it."

"Fine. I'll call the hospital in Louisville, too," he added. "Do you have any preference in a physician? They're all good."

Adrian touched Callie's arm. "Try Dr. Leonard Sandifer or Dr. Adam Stevens. Tell them Adrian Coleman recommended them. They're old friends," he explained. "I went to MSU with them."

The physician left.

"Momma, you'd better call my brothers and Aunt Minnie," Callie said. "They don't need to come, but they would want to know. You don't want Daddy coming home to an empty house and starting to worry, do you?"

She dropped several coins into her mother's hand and pointed her toward a pay phone down the hall.

Dr. Helstley returned.

"May I see her, please?" Callie asked.

"Not yet," he said. "The medication I gave her for the pain has made her drowsy. She's sleeping now." He turned to Adrian. "I spoke directly with Dr. Sandifer, and he says to give you his greetings. He's accepted the case and is on call for her arrival. But we have a new problem. All the Life Flight helicopters are out on trips. They checked a two-hundred-mile radius, and it seems the state is filled with emergencies."

"Must the helicopter be a special type?" Adrian asked.

The physician shook his head. "Just so its interior is big enough for a portable gurney, two medical attendants and Callie…and you, too, if you want to go. I was about to call the Greenville Flight Service to see what they could find. The sooner we get Linda on her way, the better her chances of making it."

Adrian reached for Callie's hand. "I'm with White Glove Mining. We've used a medium-size helicopter that's based in Madisonville and belongs to Clarence Hainline."

"The man who owns all those horse farms around Lexington?" the physician asked.

Adrian nodded. "I'll call the pilot and see if he'll fly down here and get her. If he can come, where should he land?"

"We don't have a landing pad, but we have permission to use the field behind us. We have portable spotlights. I'll call the police chief, and he'll keep curiosity seekers away. Tell your pilot we'll use a circle of red lights as markers."

"I'll pass on the information...and I'll take care of the arrangements, the money, too," he added.

"Use our phone," Dr. Helstley said, then turned to Callie. "We'll worry about the Medicaid mix-up later."

In a moment Adrian had completed his call. "He's on his way, sir," he said. "What do you estimate all this might cost, just so we know?"

The physician hunched his shoulders. "You should be prepared for the worst. It might run as high as fifty...sixty thousand or more before she's home."

Callie paled at the amount. She mentally calculated how much she had in her account. "I...I have eleven thousand, four hundred fifty dollars...and I got paid today. That's another one hundred eighty-five...." She glanced at the two men. "And I have fifty dollars in my wallet. They can have it all. I've been wondering how to spend it.... Now I know."

Adrian put his arm around her and buried his hand in her hair. "I'm good for the rest."

She hiccuped. "I tried to get medical insurance for the two of us when I knew Medicaid was going to be a problem, but no one would cover her. A 'preexisting condition,' the agents all said. They'd be glad to issue a policy but they wouldn't pay any claims for two years." She looked up, wiping the tears away again. "Linda needs it now. She may not be here in two years to collect their darned coverage."

Adrian turned her back into his arms. "Easy, honey. Getting more upset won't help. Look now," he said, motioning to the door as it opened and the edge of a gurney appeared. "Here she comes. I think I hear the 'copter overhead. You stay with her. I'll go lock the truck and be right with you."

"You'll come with us?" she asked.

"The devil himself couldn't keep me away."

THE TRIP TO LOUISVILLE would have taken at least two hours by highway, but it seemed to Callie they had barely left the ground when the pilot began talking to the personnel at the landing pad on the top of the large medical institution.

Adrian had spent most of the flight in the front talking to the pilot. They seemed to be old friends. Callie had stayed out of the way of the two nurses who monitored all the apparatuses attached to Linda. Linda was unaware of her presence.

Someone on the pad helped Callie down and motioned her aside. Feeling forlorn, she watched as her daughter disappeared into the cavernous building. She followed. A clipboard was shoved into her hands, and she signed form after form wherever an X had been made. Someone motioned her to wait in a small, dimly lit room. She obeyed. A cup of coffee was extended. She took it, sipping the bitter black brew until suddenly it brought a wave of nausea to her stomach. She waited.

Someone shook her shoulder. She raised her head and tried to open her eyes.

Adrian knelt before her. "Honey, I want you to meet two old friends of mine. The tall one is Dr. Sandifer and the other is Dr. Stevens."

Instantly, she was awake and standing, brushing at her wrinkled clothing. "Where's my daughter now? What can you do for her?" She reached for Adrian's hand and held on as though he were her lifeline.

"The heart catheterization shows the repair of the large ventricular septal defect that was done several years ago had a section that never completely closed. We don't know why. Your physician in Greenville told us she's been feeling progressively more fatigued in this past year. We have new procedures not available eight years ago. The surgery is lengthy, and she'll be on a heart-lung bypass machine. There are potential problems and complications, so I don't want to underestimate the seriousness of it, but if all goes well, you'll have a healthy little girl by summer's end."

"I understand, Dr. Sandifer," Callie said. "Please just take good care of her. She's the only child I have now." She turned to Adrian and sensed the strength, confidence and love he offered.

"It's going to be a long six to eight hours, folks," Dr. Sandifer said gently. "Adrian, why don't you take Callie out for a meal. There are restaurants all around here. Go for a walk. Time will pass faster if you keep busy. I'll put in a request for blankets and pillows, and when you come back you can bed down right here if you like."

The two surgeons left, their heads close as they discussed the case. Adrian took Callie's hand and led her to the bank of elevators. "Let's take his advice."

At dinner she picked at her food. "Isn't it ironic that Bobby Joe's money is going to be spent on the daughter he didn't want? She was born with a cleft palate, you see, and her lip wasn't right. He said she was the ugliest thing he had ever seen. Did you know that cleft palates often go with congenital heart defects? The repair to her mouth was done when she was just a tiny baby, and unless you look really close and see the tiny line, you'd never notice it, would you?"

He smiled. "She's a beautiful child. Her coloring may be from her father, but the rest of her is definitely you, Callie."

"I called Bobby Joe's sister after the divorce was final," Callie said. "I asked her where the money had come from. He was never much of a saver."

"And what did you find out?"

"He borrowed a third of it from his folks. They'd been saving for their retirement. Some came from Mary Lou's father. The rest was from an insurance settlement he got from a car accident. That's how he got that new car. Someone ran into them, and he cried whiplash and back injury. His attorney suggested the payment to me to tip the scales of justice in his favor when he got the idea to ask for custody of Robbie. Seems the judge is very chauvinistic in his view of who should head families."

She smiled. "It's crazy but I feel better knowing Bobby Joe isn't the noble reformed man he makes himself out to be. I hope Robbie will understand I did the best I could."

"I'm glad to hear you talk that way," Adrian replied. "Now you can get on with your own life." He wiped his mouth and laid the napkin on the table. "Let's take Dr. Sandifer's advice and walk. There's a park a few blocks away. I spotted it as we came in to land. We can talk. We haven't seen much of each other lately. I've missed you, Callie."

She nodded. "And I've missed you, so very much."

They strolled through the park. She sat down on a bench beneath a tall black locust tree heavy with white blossoms that filled the evening air with their fragrance. Adrian stood on the walkway, his legs apart, his hands in the pockets of his red windbreaker.

"I'm back where I started, Adrian," she said, glancing up at him. "I'm broke again. I'll probably lose my job because of excessive absenteeism, and I won't be able to go to school." She felt as though she had been thoroughly beaten, both physically and mentally. "It's selfish to even think about it right now, with Linda in that operating room, with her heart stopped and her life depending on that bypass machine...." She closed her eyes and squeezed them to suppress the moisture she felt building. "I hurt, Adrian. I hurt...and I don't want to hurt anymore.

"When I was living in Harlan, I wanted so much to be able to take my kids and go shopping in a big fancy mall like you find here in Louisville. I wanted to go into a nice department store and buy something new and pretty, without having to worry about the price. I actually did my shopping in the Baptist Women's Home Missions Thrift Store. The church women in the county worked there as volunteers, and they'd make up little grab bags. They'd put the toys their husbands had repaired into these paper sacks, tie the sacks with pretty red ribbon left over from Christmas and sell them for twenty-five cents."

She pursed her lips. "Once we were there to find Robbie a pair of jeans and some shirts so he'd have something to start the second grade in. He wanted a grab bag, too, but I didn't have any money to spare. I couldn't take a chance on running low because it was still two weeks before my check was due." She smiled weakly. "The woman felt sorry for us. Because I didn't have two quarters to spare for my kids, the woman gave both Linda and Robbie a grab bag."

He sat down beside her.

"So you see, finding myself without a few quarters is nothing new," she said. "That's why I felt so good with that money in the bank, even if it did come from Bobby Joe. Now, I'm just thankful I have it for Linda."

"Linda's life is about to turn around, and so is yours," Adrian replied as he reached into his pocket and pulled out a small red plastic sack. "How about a grab bag for yourself?"

She frowned. "What's in it?"

"Open it and see. Did Robbie or Linda just sit on a park bench and stare at their grab bags? Or did they rip into them?"

"Where did it come from?"

"I've been carrying it around since this afternoon," he explained. "That's why I found Linda. I was looking for you. Now are you going to open it, or shall I just pitch it into that trash barrel over there?" He grabbed the sack from her hands and feigned a throw toward the green can a few yards away.

"No!" She grabbed his arm and pulled it toward her, working her hands down his arm to his wrist. "Is it really for me?"

"I reckon I wouldn't have wasted my money on any other woman," he said, his eyes sparkling.

She opened the sack and peered inside. "Oh, there're two little boxes. Which one shall I open first?"

"Try the smallest one."

She withdrew it and carefully pushed the lid off. The lid fell to her lap. On a cushion of cotton lay a gold chain of exquisite workmanship, the links so fine and delicate that she brought the box closer in order to examine the design. "Adrian, it's beautiful. But why?"

He leaned closer. "I think I missed your birthday."

"It was May 11. I was so anxious about going to court it just slipped by," she confessed.

"May I put it on?" he asked.

"Yes." She turned her back to him and lifted her shoulder-length hair. His fingers brushed her skin as he worked the tiny clasp. When he finished, he kissed her nape, and a quiver shot through her. She dropped her hair, and he smoothed it.

"Your hair hasn't grown much since Emma cut it," he said, combing it with his fingers.

"That's because she cut it a second time," she replied, turning around to face him. "She phoned one Saturday and asked how I was doing. She was on her way to Bowling Green, and I asked if it wasn't out of her way to stop by Momma's place. So she and her girls stopped for coffee and... she just happened to have her trusty scissors with her. She's very nice, Adrian, and she and Momma got along so fine. Her girls played with Linda, and for a moment, it was like... like we were all just one happy family."

"That's my Emma. She's always been my favorite sister."

She laughed. "She and Momma got to comparing birth dates of all the Hardesty and Coleman children, and do you know that Momma saw you when you were less than three days old?"

"That's impossible," he said, laughing.

She explained about her brother Riley's birth.

He laughed again. "Small world." They sat quietly for a few minutes. "Why don't you open the other box?"

When she opened it, she gasped. "No, it's impossible," she murmured, lifting the treasured locket from its bed of cotton.

He explained how the mechanic had found it.

"Was it damaged?" she asked.

He arched a dark brow. "Does it look damaged to you?"

She turned it over in her hand. "Just this tiny scratch on the back. Adrian, it's a miracle." She turned to him.

"This is the best present you could ever give me. Thank you."

"Not the best, but it will do for now," he replied. He put his hand on her cheek and turned her face to him, then lifted her chin. His lips settled gently on hers as his hand slid to her neck and his fingers stroked her warm satin skin.

He eased away. "Someday, love, I'm going to ask you to marry me. I want you as my wife. I love you, and with time... Well, this isn't the time. But I wanted you to know the locket had been found. That's another reason I was looking for you."

He stood up and pulled her to her feet. "Now, let's go back to the hospital and wait for Linda to come out of surgery. She asked for you, and I promised I'd bring you to her. I keep my promises, all of them. I don't make promises lightly. Take heart in that, Callie, my love."

CHAPTER SEVENTEEN

ADRIAN'S VOW TO KEEP his promises haunted Callie as she stared out the window of her bedroom.

Six weeks had passed since the flight to Louisville. She had stayed in support housing. Her parents had arrived the morning after the surgery, and Adrian had ridden back to Greenville with them two days later.

Linda's recovery from the cardiac surgery had been a miracle. Even Dr. Stevens and Dr. Sandifer had expressed their surprise and pleasure in the child's resiliency.

"Perhaps now she can truly taste the joy of good health," Dr. Sandifer had said, when he had made his final examination before signing the discharge papers. "She's anxious to get on with her life. You should get on with life, too, Callie."

Adrian had called several times from his corporate office in Madisonville to ask about Linda's progress, he'd come for brief visits after she was moved from the cardiac care unit to a regular room in the pediatric wing, and he'd driven them home three weeks later when Linda had been released.

A week after that an invoice from the hospital arrived with a balance due of exactly eleven thousand four hundred fifty dollars. The invoice, with its detailed listing of charges, showed a single credit for customer payment and the amount was staggering. How could she ever repay such a debt to Adrian?

Callie had called White Glove Mining in Madisonville. A woman who identified herself as Jessie answered. "I'm sorry, ma'am," she said. "Mr. Coleman is no longer at White Glove, but he does occasionally call in. May I take a message?"

"No, thank you," Callie replied and quietly hung up.

She fretted for two days before calling his home. Her heart stopped when the recorded message informed her that the number had been disconnected. As a last resort she drove to his house. She parked near a rental truck being unloaded by several men.

A woman walked over to Callie's truck. "Can I help you, ma'am?"

Callie tore her eyes from the workers. "Yes, can you tell me where Mr. Coleman is?"

The woman had shrugged. "We took possession here on July 1. Maybe if you check with the Realtor, he can tell you." She'd pointed to a Realtor's sign propped against one of the porch posts, an offensive red Sold sticker plastered across its face.

The phone rang, jolting Callie out of her reverie. But she resisted the impulse to race down the stairs. If Adrian was on the line, her mother would let her know soon enough. Her mother didn't call for her, and dejected, she returned to her study of the landscape.

A half hour later, her mother came to the door with the oversize Hardesty family Bible in her hand.

"Who called?" Callie asked.

Ellen shrugged. "Just some man. Callie, could you let me see your divorce decree? I've been updating this Bible, and if you also have the children's birth certificates handy, it would be such a help—and can you give me your own, too? I want to make sure I have it all correct, spellin' and everythin'. I'll give them back in a bit. Hurry now, 'cause I want to have this finished before I start fixin' dinner.''

Absently, Callie went to the drawer where she kept her legal papers and gave them to her mother. "Is Linda still outside?" she asked. "She sure has been doing a lot of running around these last two weeks."

"Yes, she's outside, honey, and you've got to stop a'worrying about her. Between planning the reunion, taking care of Linda and working three days a week at the library, you haven't had a free minute to call your own."

Callie shook her head. "I'm fine." She turned again to the window, glaring at the tobacco plants in her father's patch. The thick green leaves waving gently in the summer breeze were growing larger and heavier by the day. Some of the plants were blooming, and she had volunteered just that morning to top them. It had turned out to be a very disagreeable morning.

As the sun beat down on her kerchiefed head, the insects had begun to bite and tobacco juice found its way into the tiny cuts on her hands.

At one point her father actually ordered her out of the field. "Now, Callie, what did them plants ever do to you to deserve that kind of treatment?"

She pressed her hand to the small of her back and glared at him, wiping the sweat from her forehead with her shirttail. "Am I doing something wrong?"

"You sure as heck are," he said. "The way you're whacking them poor tobacco plants, you're doing more harm than good. 'Sides, the bugs have taken a liking to you, and you've got scratches all over your arms and legs. What's that nice Coleman feller goin' to think when he comes a'calling?"

"He's not coming, Daddy. He's moved away."

"Is that why you're so hard to live with lately?" He tossed his head back and laughed. "Well just in case he does come a'looking for you, you get out of here and go clean up. I can manage alone for a bit. You need to get away from this place."

She'd frowned. Everyone kept telling her to get away, that she'd been under a strain since Linda's surgery. Were her parents hinting that the time had come for her to move out? she'd wondered.

Now she heard footsteps on the stairs and turned away from the window. Her mother appeared at the door to Callie's room with the documents in her hand. "Just put them on the dresser," Callie said.

"Dinner will be ready in a half hour," Ellen replied. "James and his family and some other people are comin'. James is bringing a watermelon he growed himself."

"That's nice," Callie said, giving in to her depression. "Call me when they get here."

"If you're gonna put your feet under my table, you'd best get yourself fixed up. You're a sight." Her mother left.

Several minutes later Callie heard a vehicle arrive. With company coming, she'd better attend to her appearance, she thought, unless she wanted a barrage of questions. She grabbed the white teddy Adrian had given her, the one she had never worn before, reached for a fresh cotton-knit top and a wraparound skirt her mother had sewn for her, and hurried to the bathroom down the hall, suddenly anxious to make a good impression on her brother and his family.

Fifteen minutes later she was back in her room. She buckled the straps of new flat-heeled white sandals, adjusted her skirt and reached for the blow dryer, feeling refreshed and eager to meet the rest of the day. The hum of the dryer drowned the music coming from her radio, but she sang to herself, moving easily from one folk song to another as the tunes drifted in and out of her thoughts. A knock sounded.

"Come on in," she called over the noise of the blow dryer. "I'm almost finished." The door opened. She turned off the blower and laid it on the dresser, fluffing her hair and frowning at her image in the mirror.

A man's lime-green knit shirt appeared directly behind her in the mirror. "You look beautiful," a voice said.

"Adrian!" Her heart stopped as two large brown hands slid around her waist and a dark head dipped to kiss her cheek.

"Where did you come from?" Her hand touched the locket at her throat. "Is this a magic locket, after all? I've...been thinking of you all morning, only they weren't all good thoughts." She turned in his arms. "Adrian, where have you been? I thought you had moved away...forever."

He smiled, gave her a light kiss on her mouth and winked. "I did move away, but some Kentucky birds told me you'd been working too hard and that you've been as crabby as all get out. I got the distinct impression they'd like to have you out of their hair for a few days. Your daughter says you've been hovering. I had a long chat with her downstairs while you showered."

"It was you, not my brother, who drove in a bit ago?"

"We arrived at the same time," he explained, smiling. "I've come to their rescue. Pack your bag, woman, grab that expensive dulcimer I bought you, and let's go."

"I can't." She started to turn away.

"Callie," he said, taking her shoulders firmly in his hands and holding her in place. "I got up in the middle of the night to get here. I didn't talk to you on the phone because, damn it, I'm sick and tired of your hedging. But I've talked to your parents several times and your cousins—even your daughter. We all agree that you can't see the forest for the trees. Every little problem becomes a mountain for you to climb. Honey, it's not necessary to go it alone. We all love you. Now pack a bag and let's go. It's your last chance."

"My last chance?" Confusion flashed over her features as she considered his ultimatum.

"Last chance," he assured her. "Coming or not?"

"Where are we going?" she asked, finding herself caught up in the excitement.

"To attend the Great American Dulcimer Festival," he exclaimed, pulling a flyer from his hip pocket and shaking it out. "It starts this very evening, and Pine Mountain is a long way from here. Where's the dulcimer?"

She pointed to the closet, trying not to think about the proposition he had presented.

"Good. I'll take it to the truck and meet you downstairs. They have amateur night. You can play for them, and I can listen to you, and we'll— Well, who knows what we may do. Now get a move on, Callie. The world is singing, and it's time you joined in."

She threw two changes of clothes into her battered blue suitcase and closed it, opened it again to add the nightgown and robe he had given her and slammed it shut.

Downstairs, she stopped. "I have no money for a trip."

"You don't need any," he insisted. "This one is on me. Now kiss your daughter goodbye."

Linda giggled. "We have a secret, but I promised not to tell, especially not you." She threw her arms around

Callie's neck and kissed her, then bestowed an equally enthusiastic embrace on Adrian.

"You do what Adrian says," Finis said, kissing Callie's cheek.

"We'll take care of Linda," Ellen insisted. "You have a good time and . . . congratulations."

"For what?" Callie asked.

Her mother made a face. "For whatever good fortune might come your way."

Callie hugged her parents and followed Adrian out the door to his truck. As they drove away, she turned to him. "I have to be back to work on Monday."

He shook his head. "I called Mrs. Menderson and explained everything. She says to take a week at least."

Callie settled into the cushioned seat. "Why do I feel like I'm being kidnapped?"

THE AMATEURS' CONCERT was in progress when Adrian and Callie arrived. A man pointed to some vacant seats in the second row, and Adrian and Callie worked their way carefully down the steps in the darkness.

The rows of seats were made of stone embedded in the hillside, forming a natural outdoor amphitheater. The stage was small, but with lights and a sound system that allowed even the guests at the lodge many yards away to enjoy the performers. Many of the performers were quite good. Soon, Callie was so engrossed in watching the finger technique used by a white-haired man playing a medley of bluegrass songs that she had little time to develop stage fright. The man finished and left the stage.

"Are you ready?" Adrian asked.

"I've never sung in public before except in church," she replied. "What if I forget the words?"

"Hum a few bars and play a little louder. It's now or never," he said, motioning toward the stage.

The festival coordinator stepped to the microphone. "We're running a little behind schedule. We have more talent here than ever before. Is there anyone else out there a'dying to perform?"

Callie stayed in her seat. Adrian waved his hand and pointed a finger down at Callie's black head. The man on stage stepped closer to the edge. "Come on, miss, if you sing as pretty as you look, you'll be pleasin' to the ear as well as the eye."

"Go," Adrian whispered. "You'll be fine."

He knew she was frightened. He had spent most of the drive convincing her that she would do fine, that he would be there with her. She would be among fellow musicians. If she felt uneasy, she should search him out, and he'd give her a telepathic transfusion of confidence.

Callie grabbed the dulcimer case and ran up the stairs. She was wearing her pale blue T-shirt, navy wraparound skirt with tiny red sailboats scattered across the fabric and white sandals. Her hair shone beneath the overhead lights, bringing out the blue-black highlights.

As he sat in the darkness of the seats Adrian thought she was the most beautiful woman he had ever seen. Her skin was tan, her dark eyes large and filled with emotion.

Yet it wasn't Callie's beauty that made Adrian's heart pound, but the depth of her love and commitment to her family and to him—and it was the memories of the passion they had shared and of her laughter. Passion and laughter had been missing too much of the time since they had met. Now he had a week to convince her that life could change, that together their futures could be filled with brightness.

On the stage, she waited while the host adjusted the stool to her height. Then she sat down. She laid the instrument across her lap, extending the peg end out beyond her left knee and pulling the other end closer to her body. Her right foot disappeared beneath the folds of her skirt as she tucked it beneath the spindles between the stool's legs.

The audience quieted as they watched her graceful movements. She reached into a patch pocket in her skirt and withdrew the noter, a finger-length bamboo bar. She glanced up, and for an instant Adrian saw her confidence waiver until she located him in the second row and smiled. He nodded. Reaching into her other pocket, she pulled out a lightweight guitar pick.

She put the pick between her lips, and finger-plucked the instrument, checking its tuning. She removed the pick from her mouth and smiled, murmuring, "Perfect." The microphone picked up her voice, and she glanced up as the audience laughed.

She began to play, starting with simple folk songs familiar to everyone, adding her voice as her fingering became more confident. Soon her techniques grew more complex and her voice more sure. "Since I was born near Drakesboro, I reckon I might as well take you back to Muhlenberg County and sing 'Paradise,'" she said, launching into the song that had made the county famous a few decades earlier.

After several songs, she paused. "Do I have time for one more?" she asked the host. He nodded, and she began to strum the melody she had played for Adrian on Christmas night. Her voice was clear, her tone in perfect pitch, but the words were sad, reflecting not only the hard times he knew she had experienced herself but also the hard times of the land and the people of the area. She lost herself in the song.

Adrian glanced around in the dim amphitheater, trying to read the audience's reaction.

After several verses, she stopped singing and simply strummed the melody as she chatted with the audience. "I've been writing this song for over ten years. It's called 'Heart Spirit.' It's like a tale that has no end. As my life changes, I keep writing new verses and this song gets longer and longer. Anyone can do it. You just turn your own feelings and experiences into a song. Try it," she urged.

Then one man from the audience stood and sang an impromptu verse as she accompanied him. The audience applauded.

"See how easy it is?" She made a face. "The hard part is the livin' it." They chuckled with her.

"I want to dedicate these last few verses to a special man," she said. "He dragged me here. I didn't want to come, but now I'm so glad he insisted. Thank you, Adrian."

She began to sing again, the new verses, a poetic depiction of mankind's need to dream, to share joy and sorrow and love.

She finished the song and laid her hands on the strings of the dulcimer to quiet them, sitting quietly until she wiped away a tear that trickled down her cheek.

Not a sound came from the audience. Adrian sat stunned. Could they have not liked her? he wondered. Anger filled him, and he wanted to run to the stage and shield her. She had taken a risk and opened her soul to them. Had they missed the entire message of the song?

Suddenly the audience exploded. A wave of humanity worked its way from the front to the back of the amphitheater as the audience honored her with a standing ovation.

Slowly, Callie stood with them, her features alive with excitement as she accepted their applause. She curtsied and smiled, and the applause built to a crescendo that held for several minutes.

Adrian could tell she was overwhelmed by what was happening, and when she sought him out in the crowd, he nodded and smiled.

The man who had announced her joined her at the microphone. "Please, everyone, be seated. Perhaps, if we're really nice to this little lady from Muhlenberg County, she'll grace us with another song or two."

She nodded. "But this time, you sing along with me," she said to the audience.

For the next twenty minutes, the audience joined in on folk songs that had been sung in the area for generations. Finally she stopped, took a deep breath, and smiled. "I don't know about you folks, but I'm all sung out." She stood up and the audience stood with her, applauding her again. The host took the dulcimer from her and offered to put it away.

"Thank you," she said. "I'll be right back." She flew down the steps of the stage and into Adrian's arms.

He grabbed her around the waist and lifted her off the ground, his biceps bulging beneath his shirt.

"Was I okay?" she asked, her eyes shining.

"You were magnificent."

A FULL MOON SHONE INTO THE CAB of the truck as Adrian and Callie drove away from the festival, heading south on the old U.S. highway.

"Where are we spending the night?" she asked.

"I tried to get us rooms at Pine Mountain Resort in the park, but they were booked full," he said as they approached the outskirts of the last town before the Cumberland Gap.

"Maybe we can get a motel in Middleboro," she said.

But Adrian drove past several motels with vacancy signs still lit.

"We'll be in Tennessee if you don't stop now," she remarked a while later.

"That's right," he murmured, and concentrated on his driving.

A few miles beyond the state line the lights of another small town appeared. "This is Harrogate, Tennessee," he said.

"Where you live?" She looked out the window with renewed interest. "It's not a very big place, is it?" she asked.

"About thirteen hundred people...but the town has a small university. That's it up ahead," he said, pointing at some buildings through the darkness. "It was founded in 1897."

She peered through the side window, trying to get a better view of the facility. When she spotted the name on the entrance, she gasped. "It's Lincoln Memorial University. We had a speaker at Second Chance from here. I didn't make the connection between you...and where you had moved to...and the school...or anything."

"The enrollment is just a few hundred more than the population of the town." He motioned to the glove compartment. "There's a brochure in there. They have a music program. It's an innovative blend of classical and folk."

She opened the glove compartment and located the brochure. Excitement began to build as she read the description of the unique music program. "It sounds fantastic."

"Would you like to enroll this fall?" he asked.

"I ... I'll give it serious consideration." She glanced into the darkness when he turned off on a narrow paved road. "Are we going to your place?" He nodded. She shoved the brochure into her purse and smiled. "Another little log cabin?"

"The square footage is a little bigger," he said, grinning. "The first one was a trial run. This time I knew what I wanted."

A half mile down the narrow winding road, he turned again, onto a gravel driveway that circled through a thick grove of oak and hickory trees.

"Do I see tulip and beech trees, too?" she asked, rolling down her window. "I used to walk the forest near Harlan. I got to know the trees and shrubs. I love them all. This is so lush," she exclaimed. "I can see why you chose it."

The vegetation opened into a meadow, and in the distance, and nestled in a grove of stately eastern hemlock on a slight incline, she spotted the yellow glow of lights coming from the second floor windows of a two-story log house. She strained to see its outline. The house seemed to angle off in several directions.

"Adrian, it's beautiful, but it's huge. And you forgot to turn off the lights," she teased. "Wasteful man. You need someone to manage your personal affairs. You may be great in a corporate setting, but you need some training around the house."

"Want to apply for the job?" he asked. Before she could reply, the truck rolled to a stop near the shaded porch.

He parked and got out, retrieved her suitcase and the dulcimer from the back of the truck and headed for the house, motioning her to follow.

She caught up with him at the door. As he ushered her inside, she tried to get a look at the darkened living room. "Show me the house," she said.

"Later." He headed up the stairs, and she trotted along behind him, running to keep up with him.

"You can sleep in here," he said, opening a door to a modest-sized room with twin beds. "Or you can join me in the master bedroom next door. The choice is yours." He set her suitcase down inside the room, then turned and left her there.

She stood just inside the room, confused by his manner. He had been so supportive since they had left Drakesboro. Without his encouragement, she would never have been confident enough to perform. After the concert, when the organizers had come to her and asked her to play the following night at the professional concert, he had become her spokesman, accepting the offer but asking if the performers were compensated.

"Yes, and we reserve a portion of the budget for new talent," the festival organizer had explained. "We know it takes money to be a serious musician, and Miss Hardesty has more than proven her ability tonight."

She had been flabbergasted by the whole series of events and could hardly think straight, but Adrian had taken it in stride and answered all the organizer's questions about her background and experience.

But now she stood alone again. She loved him with all her heart and all her soul. When she had sung "Heart Spirit" earlier in the evening, she had been singing to him alone. Hadn't he realized that? Didn't he know how much she wanted his love?

She undressed, slipped into the blue gown, and reached for the robe. A knock sounded, and she jumped. "Yes?"

The door swung open a few inches. Adrian leaned against the doorjamb, a pair of red pajama bottoms hanging precariously on his trim hips. The scattering of dark curls covering his chest and abdomen caught her attention.

She jerked her gaze from his body. "Couldn't we go downstairs and . . . do something? I don't feel sleepy."

"You're keyed up from the concert. You have a rare talent, Callie, and you've blessed many people with your singing. You should be very pleased. You're a professional now. Isn't that one of the dreams you've always wanted?"

She nodded.

"You were complaining about being broke again. Maybe they'll pay you in cash, and you'll have your own money to spend on this trip. If that doesn't help you relax, think about something different, something else that can give you great pleasure."

"I have." She smiled. "You." Taking a deep breath she plunged ahead. "Adrian, is there something wrong with me?"

His gaze roamed down her body. "Not that I can see."

"Then . . . why haven't you . . . tried . . . to make love to me?"

"I've come to you enough," he replied. "You've taken and taken from me, Callie. Now it's turnabout. You've got to give before you receive any more from me."

"But . . ."

"Good night, Callie." He turned toward the hallway.

"Adrian," Callie murmured, sliding one hand around his bare waist and pressing her cheek against his back. "Please . . . make love to me."

He turned. Her hands slid up his chest, lingering to make circles on his nipples. They hardened, and he exhaled a ragged breath. "Don't do that unless—" he inhaled again "—unless you— Oh, hell, Callie." He pulled her roughly into his arms.

Her eyes darkened with desire as her tongue moistened her lip. "I want to give you my love, Adrian, all my love. I want to give you the one thing you can't buy for yourself. It's all I have, my darling. I want to give you myself," she said, her voice as soft as the breeze that floated through the open window.

He glanced over her head, but her hand touched his cheek. "I've been selfish, self-centered, so caught up in my own problems that I ignored your feelings, but Adrian, I could never have made it through all this without you."

"You're a strong woman, Callie, you would have survived," he replied. "You've proven that again and again. I wasn't there to hold you up, but because I wanted to be. I care about you."

"And I want to be here," she replied. "I want to love you, and I want you to love me."

"There would be strings," he warned. "I would never be satisfied with having an affair with you. I'd expect a commitment. Callie, where's your locket?"

She pulled away. "In my suitcase."

"Would you get it? Bring it into my bedroom."

She found the locket and followed him into his room, the gold chain dangling from her fingers.

He sat on the edge of the king-size bed, reaching to snap on a lamp. He motioned for her to come closer. She sat down beside him. "Open it, please," he coaxed.

She popped the cover open and peered down at the counted-cross-stitch design. "Who changed it?"

"My sister Emma," he replied.

Her heartbeat quickened as the symbolic shadow on the fabric took form and substance. "It's you and me, isn't it? The way we should be. It's like the little wreath you gave me, all the branches intertwined together...inseparable."

He took her hand. "I'm asking you to marry me, Callie. I told you months ago that I would when the time was right. Is the time right now?"

"Oh, yes, Adrian, the time is right. I can go to school anywhere. My children can live anywhere. I can work anywhere. I can sing and play music anywhere, but the very thought of living away from you brings me so much pain I can't bear it. A part of me would die. I've been so miserable these last few weeks. Adrian, I love you so very much."

He smiled. "And I love you. I loved you from the first second I saw you coming toward me at Morehead. I was even willing to invest the price of a bowl of beans and a slice of corn bread. I was so desperate to find an excuse to talk to you I was willing to make the sacrifice."

"Beans and corn bread! Some investment! Seventy-five cents is hardly a sacrifice!" She studied his face, then glanced away. "I do love you, Adrian. That's what this is all about—unconditional love, and money can't buy love, can it?"

He grinned boyishly, tucked his legs behind her and rolled to the other side of the bed. "No, but money can buy rings." He came back to her side of the bed and lay propped up on an elbow. "I bought these the same day I had the locket repaired, the same day I found Linda.

They're another reason I was looking for you. I wanted to ask you then." He opened the ring box with his thumb.

"Callie, I know this ring is a little pretentious, but will you accept it as a token of my undying love?" He removed the diamond engagement ring with its clusters of amethysts and emeralds and slipped it onto her finger. "Does it fit?"

"Perfectly," she replied, her voice choked with emotion. She leaned forward and touched his lips lightly with hers.

He tossed the case aside and dropped onto the bed, pulling her down on top of him. His hand found the bare flesh of her thigh and stroked it before sliding beneath the gown to her hip. "Oh, God, Callie, do you know how hard it's been for me to keep my hands off you? I've become a sexual hypocrite."

"What do you mean?" she asked, kissing his cheeks and nibbling at his ear.

"I've had so many trial runs, thinking about you, dreaming about us, knowing what we could have, but knowing that you needed time. I had about reached my limit." His hand slid across her abdomen and between her thighs.

She gasped. "The wait is over, my darling," she vowed, her body writhing as his hand grew bolder. She caressed him, exploring his body as he was exploring hers. She tugged his pajamas down and playfully pulled them from his long legs. She tossed them aside, and he laughed when they landed on the lamp shade, casting the room into a warm reddish glow.

His arousal grew, and she watched in fascination, filling her imagination with erotic images of what lay ahead. Gingerly, she touched him, and he groaned aloud. "I want to pleasure you," she murmured, and her hands and mouth grew bold and sure.

Suddenly he stopped her and sat up. "The gown hides your body," he said.

She lifted her arms. He removed the skimpy garment and dropped it to the floor. The red of the lamp cast her skin in bronze, her hair in midnight black.

"I could look at you for an eternity," he whispered.

Her passion leaped as the touch of his fingers stoked the embers of desire to a white-hot flame. His hands slid to her waist, and he lifted her, pulling her astride his hips. She settled against him and felt the hot brush of his manhood against the most intimate part of her body. "Adrian, I want you...so much...don't make me wait!"

"Not yet, love, not yet," he whispered. "We have all night." He eased her body closer, and his mouth touched the base of her throat. He tasted the pulse pounding there, inhaling the sweet fragrance of her body. He cupped her breast. "It's exquisite, perfect." His tongue touched the tip and she moaned.

Her nipple grew hard against his hot moist touch, and when he took it into his mouth she knew she would surely die with ecstasy. She clutched his dark head, guiding him to her other breast, and he bathed its crest with his tongue. His arousal throbbed against her, but still he refused to increase the tempo of the seduction. Filled with desperation, she pulled free and dropped to the bed, taking him down with her.

"I'm going to explode," she panted. "I know it. Kiss me, Adrian, kiss me. Come to me now." Hungrily, she gripped his hips and received him, pulling him deeper and deeper until she had no more to offer.

He buried his hands in her dark mane as he covered her mouth, his tongue plunging into her again and again as he took her with him to the secret primal world of fulfillment.

CHAPTER EIGHTEEN

THEY LAY SPENT, the sheets torn from the bed, the pillows in disarray around them.

She shivered as a gust of cool air swept in from the window.

"Somewhere around this mess is a spread," he said, reaching over the side of the bed and blindly searching the carpet with his fingers. "Found it," he mumbled, pulling the fabric over them. "The nights get chilly here even when the afternoons are scorchers. I like that. It makes for better loving." He settled back on the bed and pulled her close again. He glanced down at her face and found her eyes closed.

"Have you nothing to say, woman?" he asked.

She grunted, her mouth forming a sensual smile of satisfaction. She opened her eyes just enough to look at him. "I don't have enough energy left to think, much less speak. Just hold me and don't make any demands for a few minutes."

He chuckled. "You said the same thing an hour ago. Have you no shame?"

She rolled away, smiling as he moved with her and planted several kisses on her back. "Hmm, that feels delightful," she murmured.

He gathered her in his arms again, and they lay quietly.

"Remember when you told me that someday our grandchildren will come to see us and that they would be trained to call first . . . just in case we were doing something?" she asked.

"Hmm," he agreed, nuzzling her shoulder.

"Is this typical of what we would be doing?"

He buried his face in her hair and laughed. "Might be, with variations on the theme." He ran his fingers down her spine, then followed the trail with his lips. "Now turn over here, so we can talk business."

Her mouth formed a soft pout, but her eyes were filled with love. "I don't want to talk business, not now."

"But this is love-and-marriage business," he said. He left the bed and gathered the pillows, tossing them to her one by one. Then he went about the room, picking up his pajamas and her gown and dropped them on a nearby chair. When the housekeeping was done, he ambled over to a long triple dresser and rummaged through a stack of papers. She admired the way his muscles rippled across his tanned back as he leaned over the dresser. The flesh of his hips was several shades paler. Her gaze roamed downward and settled on his firm derriere.

"You have a beautiful behind," she remarked. Forgetting his search, he turned toward her, his body as smooth and well-muscled as a fine Roman statue. "Front view isn't bad, either," she added.

He strolled toward her, and she knew he was flaunting his maleness. She sat up, and the spread fell to her hips. His body began to react to the sight of hers.

"What are you doing?" she asked innocently.

"Trying to ignore the obvious," he mumbled. He came to the bed and carefully drew the cover up to her chin, then slid beneath it himself. "Now pay attention, Callie." He slapped at her hand as it traveled beneath the spread. "Why, you little vixen!"

He pinned her wrists to the mattress and covered her face and throat with kisses. She arched against him, and he released her hands. With words and movements, she enticed him to love her again, caressing him and discovering new places that excited him.

This time their lovemaking was more passionate than before, leaving them both breathless and exhausted...until passion once again revived them. As the horizon in the east began to lighten, they fell asleep, wrapped in each others arms.

CALLIE EYED THE BLUEBERRY PANCAKES browning on the griddle. "We never got around to discussing the business of love and marriage."

He plopped two cakes on each plate. "Somewhere upstairs in our bedroom is your divorce decree and our birth certificates." He leaned across the breakfast bar and kissed her mouth. "So, my darlin' wife-to-be, if you'll stay here with me, we can drive down to Knoxville tomorrow and get blood tests and the license. The state requires a three-day waiting period before we can make it official. We can kill some time right here, if you don't mind the isolation, or we can drive into Knoxville again, or we can explore the area or whatever."

She laughed. "Let's not forget tonight. I suppose I should practice a little."

"You practiced enough last night," he replied, "but if you're talking about your dulcimer, there are some workshops this afternoon at the festival. Also, some craftsmen have booths there. I'll introduce you to the man who made your dulcimer. I saw him last night and said hello. He was very proud of the way you played his instrument." He glanced at his watch. "We have a few hours."

She tipped her head to one side. "How many people knew about the real purpose of this trip?"

"Promise you won't hold it against me?"

She smiled. "I promise."

"First I told Linda because she had a stake in the outcome," he admitted as he came around the counter. "She endorsed it wholeheartedly. And I dropped a note in the mail to Robbie so he would know he's about to have a stepfather. Besides, I wanted Bobby Joe to know you'd found love and happiness. I needed your divorce decree and birth certificate, and your mother helped, bless her, so of course I had to tell her. I spoke to Mrs. Menderson on my way to your place and told her why you needed a week off and to warn her that she might be losing her newest assistant. She said to keep her posted and wished us a long married life."

"Why didn't you put an announcement in the paper, too?"

"We'll do that when we get back," he replied. "Of course I told Emma and Jarrett, and they're telling my parents and the rest of the Colemans. Your mother is calling your aunt and your cousins out west and all your brothers."

"You're downright impulsive at times, Adrian, and a tad overconfident, too. Are you sure you've got all your bases covered?" she asked, giggling. "What about my daddy?"

He grinned. "Ah, yes, your father. He was so fed up with you destroying his tobacco patch that he donated a twenty-dollar bill for gas and said if that didn't get us far enough to call him and he'd wire us some more."

"Adrian, that had better not be true."

Laughing, he pulled a crumpled twenty from his pants pocket. "I haven't stopped for gas yet."

She shook her fist at him. "And I haven't married you yet, so don't push your luck."

Still chuckling, he began to gather the dishes.

"Can I help wash?" she asked.

"No, ma'am. The maid will do them."

She whirled around. "Was someone else here last night?"

Opening the door of an automatic dishwasher, he dropped the plates and silverware into their appropriate compartments. "Meet the maid. Until Linda comes to live with us, we're all alone. We can do anything we want, anywhere we want. It's the perfect arrangement when the honeymoon comes before the wedding." He grew solemn. "Any more questions?"

"Sure," she said, sashaying around the corner. "What are you going to give me for a wedding present? You're so generous with necklaces and rings, what else do I get?"

"Getting greedy?" he asked. "How about half this house?"

"You're joking," she replied, but gradually her smile faded. "You can't be serious, Adrian, you have to be more careful with your money. You don't have a steady income anymore. You don't know if this catfish business will pay a living wage or if the mule-breeding program will be successful. The money I make tonight may be the only money I'll have coming in for some time."

"No nagging about finances until you're my wife," he said, wagging his finger at her. "For your information, I'll be coming into some money within the month, and so will you."

She put her fists on her hips. "You're crazy."

"Not at all," he replied. "Bobby Joe's medical insurance at work covers his dependents and legally Linda is still his dependent. So," he said, gloating gleefully, "Matt Daws filed a claim for reimbursement through Bobby Joe's employer for all of Linda's recent medical expenses. I suspected Bobby Joe was the primary responsible parent all along, but I didn't want a hassle when Linda was in a life-and-death struggle. You were willing to spend your last dollar on her. So was I. We both took risks and won."

"Then . . . I'll have enough money to attend Lincoln Memorial?"

"Of course," he replied. "But why don't you put Bobby Joe's money away for Linda's education? We'll manage your tuition out of the family budget."

She blinked. "I've never had a household budget before. Will you help me? I'd hate to waste any of it."

"Callie, we won't be broke. Those days are behind you now. We can share the responsibility of watching out for Linda, too. I'll be working at home most of the time. Besides, I think you'll be surprised at how well Linda will be doing. And maybe we can get Robbie down for a week before the summer ends. We'll go to your parent's place for the reunion. After that we're back here for good. Then for a special treat, I just might teach you how to feed the catfish . . . if you promise to do it right."

"Oh, will you?"

"Oh, yes, I will," he said, grinning, and grabbing her hand, he waltzed her around the living room and into an empty room overlooking the meadow. "This is for your music," he said. "And there's another room for your sewing and crafts. There's a library for my books, a room near the back of the house for whatever we decide to get interested in and outside there's an office. I'm building a barn and a big tack room for all the gear, and Jarrett's coming down next month with a new pair of mules he bought. I've sketched out the plans for a separate building for processing the catfish—" He grinned. "But don't worry, that will be far away from the house."

He danced her back into the hallway and stopped at the foot of the stairs. "Upstairs there're enough bedrooms for visiting relatives, but there are rooms for children, too... if you're willing to take that risk with me."

"What if they're sickly like Linda?"

"I talked to Dr. Sandifer," he replied, brushing the hair from her temple. "He's offered to do some genetic counseling if you'd feel better. He said the type of congenital heart defect that Linda was born with seldom runs in a family. I'd never pressure you, Callie, but I hope you'll have a family with me. I want to be a father, but only the father of your children."

Her eyes shone. "In a few years, I think that would be a wonderful idea. Adrian, I feel as if the whole world is singing to me, and I want to sing back."

"I don't know about the whole world, sweetheart, but down the road a piece, they're singing and playing. If we hurry, we can listen, and in a few hours you can make your professional debut as the queen of the mountain dulcimer."

"Adrian, I love you so much," she murmured.

"And I love you," he replied. "That's more than a promise, that's a fact."

REUNION EPILOGUE

THE THREE WOMEN WORKED their way along the creek bank, carrying their sandals in their hands and occasionally stopping to cool their feet in the creek.

Eileen Page, followed closely by her husband, Dan, was in the lead, her shoulder-length wavy brown hair blowing in the breeze.

Abigail Grasten paused and took a deep sigh. "Isn't this the most beautiful place you've ever seen?"

Abbie's husband, Dane, ruffled her curly auburn hair, then grabbed her by her waist and moved her along. "It's almost as pretty as Sweetwater County," he said.

Bringing up the rear was Callie Ann Coleman, clutching the hand of her husband, Adrian.

"Are you ladies sure there's a glen up here?" Adrian asked. "When was the last time you were here?"

"At least twenty years ago," Eileen called over her shoulder.

"I came the last time I was here visiting Aunt Minnie," Abbie said, "but that was eight years ago."

"I don't remember when I last came back," Callie said.

"There it is," Eileen cried, pointing to a spot several hundred yards ahead.

When they arrived at their destination, they stopped.

"It's changed," Eileen murmured.

"It's so small," Abbie added.

"But it's still our secret place," Callie reminded them. "I'll crawl through first. Maybe it's not as bad as it looks from here. It's just a few years overgrowth." She dropped to her knees and worked her way through the resistant vines. "Ouch!"

Adrian reached into his pocket, took out his jackknife and cut the stem of wild rose that had snagged Callie's blouse. She scooted inside and stood up.

"Come on in, everyone," she called. "It's just the way I remembered it."

The others crawled through the briars and into the tiny wooded glen.

Eileen looked around. "It's changed."

"It couldn't have been this small when we came here," Abbie insisted.

Callie turned around once. "It looks the same to me."

Abbie laughed. "That's because you're not much bigger than you were then, pip-squeak." The women broke into laughter.

Callie tugged at Adrian's hand. "Everyone, sit down, just like we used to when we had our secret meetings."

Adrian sat cross-legged and pulled Callie down onto his lap. Dane dropped to the ground, and Abbie settled behind him, her arms draped around his shoulders. Dan and Eileen Page sat close together, holding hands.

"Callie, thanks so much for organizing all this," Eileen said. "You put so much work into the reunion, and we all had a great time, but it must have been a relief to you to see everyone leave yesterday."

Callie shrugged and smiled. "Who knows when you'll come back. People always seem to have reasons to stay at home."

"Agreed," Dane said, "and right now most of our reasons go 'baaa,' but soon we'll have another baby. Tell them, sweetheart."

Abbie kissed the side of his neck. "I'm pregnant. We found out just before we flew back here. Anna is a year old already and there are absolutely no children within fifteen miles. What else could we do?"

Eileen glanced down at her husband's hand. "Our boys completed our family. I'm thankful we had them two at a time."

Dan kissed her cheek. "Why don't we come back here in two years for another reunion, just our three families. We can visit the glen again. Our children represent the next generation. We need to stay in touch for their sakes."

Adrian cleared his throat. "There won't be a glen in two years. It's scheduled for blasting next summer."

The couples were quiet for several minutes.

"I'm sorry," Adrian said, "I feel so responsible for destroying your special place."

Callie patted his arm. "It's not your fault. Perhaps this glen has served its purposes. We're still sisters and friends, and we'll stay that way. Adrian, you suggested I organize the reunion. Without your nudging, we might all still be separated." She sighed deeply. "I owe him a lot," she confided to her cousins. "And just look at all three of us. We're married to wonderful men...."

Dane, Adrian and Dan nodded their agreement.

"A modest and humble bunch, aren't they?" Abbie said. "It's ironic that we're all involved in agriculture. We're sheep ranchers, and Eileen and Dan are potato farmers. Of course, we're involved in other things, too—there's my weaving and Dan's writing and Callie's music.... But Adrian, you're still a puzzle. What are you going to produce?"

Adrian grinned. "Mules...and I have five thousand fingerling catfish coming next April. Consider us the aquatic farmers in the family."

Callie leaned against his chest. "Did you ever see so many tall, thin, black-haired men in one place?" she asked, recalling the reunion. "The Hardesty genes are clearly stamped on most of the men who came."

"I felt a little out of place," Dane said, running his hand through his blond hair.

"Not me," Adrian said. "Callie's uncle L.T. insisted I was a distant cousin."

Dan Page chuckled. "I managed to get some business done. Callie's brother Riley invited us to stop by on our way home, so we're flying to Albuquerque and driving to his studio in Taos. I've always wanted to learn more about pottery making. I plan to write an article. He's a really neat guy, Callie. Thank you for introducing us."

"The second best part of all was having Robbie back for the reunion," Callie said, smiling up at Adrian.

Adrian smiled back. "The best part is that Robbie's coming back home permanently," he announced.

"Callie, that's wonderful," Eileen said. "What happened?"

"Callie still gets choked up when she talks about it," Adrian said, "so I'll explain. It seems that when Mary Lou had a baby boy, Bobby Joe started doting on his new son to the exclusion of Robbie. All those promised fishing and camping trips were postponed. Bobby Joe got sharp with the boy several times. I reckon Bobby Joe got tired of carrying his halo when he found out being a parent to a young boy wasn't as easy as he thought. Mary

Lou resented having Robbie around. She had her hands full with a colicky baby."

"Robbie started to call us," Callie said, wiping the corners of her eyes. "He cried and said he was sorry for ever leaving. We talked to Bobby Joe. Robbie is going home with us from here. He and Linda will go to the same school, and we'll see how it's working at Christmas. I made it plain to Robbie that he can't work one parent against the other. Bobby Joe hinted that he could sure use the money he's paying me for child support, now that his family has grown."

Adrian chuckled. "I go fishing at least once a week. Robbie can help with the catfish business, and I told him I'd pay him part of the profits. I promised to teach him how to work the mules and that he can go with Jarrett and me next summer. The local Little League All-Star team won the state championship, and I told him I'd consider coaching if he wanted to play. Those factors may have had a bearing on his decision to come home." He held up his hand. "But I swear his learning that I was the quarterback on both my high-school and college varsity football teams and that a scout from the Miami Dolphins once came to see me had no influence on the boy."

They all laughed.

"In a year or two, Adrian wants to adopt both children," Callie said. "By then, we may have a baby of our own."

Adrian gave her a squeeze. "But we're not going to tell Bobby Joe about the possibility of adoption yet. We'll make him sweat out several more months of support payments. Then we'll all be Colemans, and we'll have him out of our hair for good."

Callie nodded. "We all have new lives now, new families, new careers. Isn't life wonderful?"

They all nodded.

"Then let's go home to our families," Callie said. "We've got dreams to weave, visions to fulfill and promises to keep."

"Amen to that," Abbie said. "But first let's all hold hands and make our vows."

The couples rearranged themselves into a lopsided circle in the crowded glen.

"The husbands and wives of the Rainbow Hills Secret Society of Sisters and Friends—" Callie studied the faces of the men and women around her "—and Lovers will never forget each other. Even now that we're grown up with families of our own, we'll stay in touch—" her voice cracked "—and we'll stop being too proud to ask for help."

"Amen to that," Adrian said. "And in two years you're all invited to our place in Tennessee for another reunion. We can admire all the children...and we husbands can check up on these Rainbow Hills women to see who was too proud to do what."

Callie pulled her hand free and frowned at him, but he ignored her miffed expression, sweeping her into his arms, and silencing her with a kiss. The other couples followed suit, then crawled out of the glen.

Adrian and Callie lingered behind, savoring the privacy of the secluded spot. He kissed her again, leaving her burning with desire. "I'd like to make love to you here for old time's sake, my sweet Callie, but let's go home. I have promises to keep."

"And I expect to collect on each and every one of them, over and over again. I plan to have a very poor memory." Callie stood on her tiptoes and pulled his head down again.

"I hadn't intended to keep count," he said, smiling as he covered her lips with his. He wrapped his arms around her, molding her to him. "My love," he whispered, "forever."

Harlequin
Superromance

COMING NEXT MONTH

HARLEQUIN SIGNATURE EDITION

CAROLE MORTIMER

JUST ONE NIGHT

Hawk Sinclair—Texas millionaire and owner of the exclusive
Sinclair hotels, determined to protect his son's inheritance.
Leonie Spencer—desperate to protect her sister's happiness.

They were together for just one night.
The night their daughter was conceived.

Blackmail, kidnapping and attempted murder add suspense
to passion in this exciting bestseller.

The success story of Carole Mortimer continues with *Just
One Night*, a captivating romance from the author of the
bestselling novels, *Gypsy* and *Merlyn's Magic*.

★

**Available in March
wherever paperbacks are sold.**

WTCH-1

◈ HARLEQUIN SIGNATURE EDITION

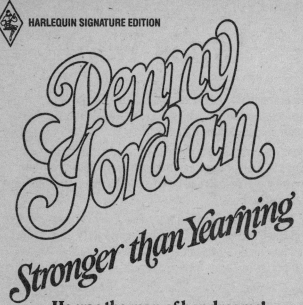

Penny Jordan

Stronger than Yearning

He was the man of her dreams!

The same dark hair, the same mocking eyes; it was as if the Regency rake of the portrait, the seducer of Jenna's dream, had come to life. Jenna, believing the last of the Deverils dead, was determined to buy the great old Yorkshire Hall—to claim it for her daughter, Lucy, and put to rest some of the painful memories of Lucy's birth. She had no way of knowing that a direct descendant of the black sheep Deveril even existed—or that James Allingham and his own powerful yearnings would disrupt her plan entirely.

Penny Jordan's first Harlequin Signature Edition *Love's Choices* was an outstanding success. Penny Jordan has written more than 40 best-selling titles—more than 4 million copies sold.

Now, be sure to buy her latest bestseller, *Stronger Than Yearning*. Available wherever paperbacks are sold—in June.

STRONG-1R

HARLEQUIN SUPERROMANCE BRINGS YOU...

Lynda Ward

Superromance readers already know that Lynda Ward possesses a unique ability to weave words into heartfelt emotions and exciting drama.

Now, Superromance is proud to bring you Lynda's tour de force: an ambitious saga of three sisters whose lives are torn apart by the conflicts and power struggles that come with being born into a dynasty.

In *Race the Sun, Leap the Moon* and *Touch the Stars*, readers will laugh and cry with the Welles sisters as they learn to live and love on their own terms, all the while struggling for the acceptance of Burton Welles, the stern patriarch of the clan.

Race the Sun, Leap the Moon and *Touch the Stars* ... a dramatic trilogy you won't want to miss. Coming to you in July, August and September.

The Welles Family Trilogy

LYNDA-1A